On the underside of the fallen tree, small worms, little grubs and pill bugs flopped and twisted, falling onto the dirt below where panicked insects burrowed back into the ground. Cora grabbed Basajaun and placed him in the concave dirt hollow. She pulled up some dirt, leaves and twigs, and used them to cover him up. Then she raked her hands all over the forest floor until she'd amassed a small pile of debris. Cora made her body as narrow as possible as she lay down in the slim trench, and dragged the dirt, leaves and sticks on top of her. Basajaun, who lay at her head, moved smoothly beneath the leaves as he crawled down her cheek, past her neck, to stretch out at her chest.

The footsteps were loud now, and Cora felt the little 'thumps' in the ground as they approached. She was trying to hold her breath when she gasped.

"Oh no." Cora poked her index finger out of her covering and pushed a single leaf aside. There, lying on its side in plain sight, was the pail.

The thumps reverberated through the tightly packed earth, into Cora's ear. The footsteps were almost upon them…

BASAJAUN

Rosemary Van Deuren

WOODEN
SMITH
BOOKS

First Wooden Smith Books edition 2009

Copyright © 2009 by Rosemary Van Deuren

ISBN-13: 978-0-615-26958-0
ISBN-10: 0-615-26958-3

Cover design by the author

www.rosemaryvandeuren.com

Published in the United States by Wooden Smith Books

Printed in the United States of America

For Guy

and
for Hazel

"Yet each man kills the thing he loves
By each let this be heard,
Some do it with a bitter look,
Some with a flattering word,
The coward does it with a kiss,
The brave man with a sword!

Some kill their love when they are young,
And some when they are old;
Some strangle with the hands of Lust,
Some with the hands of Gold:
The kindest use a knife, because
The dead so soon grow cold.

Some love too little, some too long,
Some sell, and others buy;
Some do the deed with many tears,
And some without a sigh:
For each man kills the thing he loves,
Yet each man does not die."

—Oscar Wilde, *The Ballad Of Reading Gaol*

BASAJAUN

PROLOGUE

"He's insane."

"He has strange tastes, you know. Everyone's been saying it."

"Well, I wouldn't have sent for him if I'd known he was a religious zealot. Nobody told me that!"

"He's not a religious zealot, he's a witch!"

"No, he's both!"

"How could he be a religious zealot, *and* a witch? We made a mistake. The sooner we get him out of here, the sooner he'll stop harassing all the civilians."

"But he won't go. I've asked him. He's dedicated to— to—to whatever it is he thinks is going on. It's an embarrassment to the real officials. People are losing faith in what our experts are doing, because of him. It's making us all look bad."

"Can't we lock him up?"

"Lots of luck to you, getting a holy man locked up. No, there is another way. I've received a letter from a small town near Caldsparrow. They heard about our rabbit problem, and wanted advice."

"Oh, you're not going to send him there? That's terrible."

"He'll make a complete mess of everything!"

"Their rabbit problem is nothing, not even fifty-thousand. All they need is a little guidance."

"You think *he* can give guidance?"

"Someone to make them feel as though they're making progress. It's just a few thousand rabbits! He can handle that. He does have experience."

"So now you think he's qualified?"

"For a *farm town*! These are a bunch of rubes; they don't know a rabbit from a radish. He gets them organized, and we forget about him for good."

"What about the crazy talk?"

"Don't worry, I'll tell him to let up on that."

"What makes you think you can possibly hold any sway over him once he's gone? You've had none since he's been here."

"He wasn't like that when he first came. You remember. I don't know if something happened to him here, or if the sheer volume of the task was too much for him. We just need him out, and he needs to get out."

"What about the girl? The pregnant orphan? He's more or less adopted her, you know."

"Yes, so he can hold her up as a sign of the depravation and impurity ransacking the town. Some reason to adopt."

"Let him take her. She has nothing here, and she's better off with him than alone."

CHAPTER ONE

1906 ~ THE AUTUMN OF THE RABBIT MAN

Cora stared at the rabbit, and the rabbit stared at her. "Here, I brought you a root," she said, and edged the sweet vegetable toward the cluster of bushes. The rabbit blinked. She wanted to grab the rabbit up in her arms, squeeze it and hold it tight. It took enormous self-control to keep her knees pressed into the dirt. "It's good. I know you like these," the girl laid a palm against the earth and leaned forward until the prickly branches almost touched her face.

"What are you *doing*?"

A kick sent the root flying out of Cora's hand. The rabbit zipped into the brush and disappeared. Cora turned and looked up at the boy from the grain farm across the street. He was one of many who tended the largest farm in town, but only two years older than she was.

"This is *my* rabbit," she said. "I'm giving him a root from *my* garden. It's mine to give."

"You don't *give* food to the vermin! Are you crazy?"

the boy slapped Cora's empty hand. Cora scowled at him and scrambled into the grass. "And it's not your rabbit, anyway," the boy stood over her. "They're all the same!"

Cora put her cheek against the ground, peering into the knotted vines below the foliage. "Well, then they're all mine! And this one, especially!"

"I'll tell your father! I will! I'll tell him you tried to feed the rabbits!"

"Go ahead, I don't care."

"The Pennebrows are hungry!" the boy pointed to his right, up the dirt road. "How can you offer food to the vermin? They take it all as it is!"

"No they don't!" Cora stood and clenched her fists at her sides. "They don't do it for spite, they are hungry! And they never get in the fences—hardly ever!"

"People are hungry," the boy said. "People all around you."

"I know that!" Cora yelled. The boy backed up a little.

"You can't," he shook his head. "You just can't."

Cora looked at her feet and held out the root. She didn't watch him take it. "You better actually give it to the Pennebrows and not just keep it for yourself," she mumbled. The boy cleared his throat and shifted the root from one hand to the other, but Cora kept her eyes on the buttons of her shoes. She waited until she saw the boy's feet turn away, then walked to her father's milk shed and shut the door behind her. Dragging a limestone and clay block away from the tin pails, her stomach rumbled. She sat down on the big brick and started to cry.

"Hi," Cora pushed aside the linen curtain and kneeled in front of her bedroom window. "I knew you'd come back." Her breath fogged the glass in front of her face, and the girl slid a couple inches to her left to look out of a clear spot. The rabbit sat still in the center of the yard. "Daddy says there are so many of you, the chance of me seeing the same one twice is 'astronomical', but I'm so sure you always seem the same."

The rabbit twitched its nose.

"But really, even if you aren't the same all the time, I don't mind because I like you all. I'm so sorry people eat you. I would never eat one of you. Never ever. Not even if I was starving. I mean, *really* starving. But the people who eat you, they aren't bad people. They're just hungry. You know what it's like to be hungry, don't you?"

The rabbit leaned to one side and used its long hind leg to scratch the back of its ear.

"I'm sorry," Cora folded her arms on the windowsill. She closed her eyes and pressed her forehead against the glass, and when she opened her eyes again, the rabbit was gone.

"C'mon little lady, wake up," Cora's father smiled and laid a yellow, cotton dress across the foot of the girl's bed. "We have to try and look smart today."

"What?" Cora sat up in bed. "My yellow dress? I'm wearing my yellow dress? What's happening?"

"A man is coming to town, he's arriving today. He's supposed to be an expert in the rabbit problem. I guess he's seen it before."

"Oh," Cora frowned at the dress. "Why do I have to wear my yellow dress for some rabbit-man?"

Cora's father rubbed a hand over her hair. "Because we want to look educated, not like some bumpkins. People don't think you're intelligent if the first thing they see you in is work clothes."

"But I would never wear my good dress just around the house and fields. And I bet no one else at the meeting will be dressed formal-like," Cora looked toward her chest of drawers. "I can wear my knickerbockers," she pointed, "and my big collar shirt, it's all starched and everything. That would look more respectable. I bet that's what girls in the city wear," she peered at her father out of the corner of her eye.

"More like what the boys in the city wear," he smiled and kissed her on the forehead. "But I think that will do just fine. Wash up and get dressed. I want to have a chance to talk to the Constable before this man arrives."

Cora watched her father leave. She got up, stood in front of where her dress lay on the bed, and skimmed her hands over it, rearranging the creases on the skirt. She folded the dress into a square and carried it back to her chest of drawers, taking care to keep the cloth smooth as she placed the dress in the bottom drawer under the linens. She washed nervously. Every few moments Cora ran to her window to look for her rabbit, and each time she was both disappointed and relieved he wasn't there. 'If you're going to hide, today's the day,' she thought. She pulled on her thickest socks, the ones that didn't have any holes, and the short, puffed trousers. 'But I've got to think of some way to save him,' she thought, 'all of them. Or,' she paced her bedroom floor, 'at least one. At least mine. Ah, how can I say just mine? I've got to do something for them all!' She wet her palms and smoothed them over her chestnut-brown frizz, flattening the waves at her crown and tucking the hair behind her ears.

Cora stopped in the kitchen doorway. A stack of large, parchment sheets covered their slated wooden table, hanging over its edges like a tablecloth. She looked to the side and saw the sugar and salt cups, which had barely left the table during her twelve-year life, pushed next to the wash basin on the wooden ledge. "What are those papers?" she said.

Cora's father put his hands on her cheeks. "Listen Cora, this is very important, and it has to go well. You don't want the rabbits to be hurt, do you?"

"No," Cora shook her head.

"I want to try and fix it so they aren't, and it will be a challenge. But what I want to tell you is this," the man kneeled down so he and his daughter were eye to eye. "Don't talk to this man. Don't address him. I know it will be hard, and I know whatever you'll be thinking to say he will probably deserve. But we have such a small chance, and if you talk, and say all those things I know it will be paining you to say, our chance will get smaller and smaller, until there's no chance at all. I think you're the smartest girl in the world but this time, you'll have to just trust me and be quiet. Can you do that?"

"Yes," Cora nodded.

"Just trust me, believe in me, because right now, I am

the only chance your rabbits have."

"I will. I trust you. Daddy," Cora put her hands on her father's arms, "do you want me to stay here?"

"No. You need to see this, all of it. Because if, God forbid, we don't succeed, you will need all the knowledge you will get today. And I need you there for moral support," he hugged her with one arm as he used the other to grab one of the sheets sliding off the table. "Are you ready?"

"Yes."

Cora's father gathered up his parchment pages and rolled them into a long, stiff paper cylinder. Cora held his hand as they walked out into the dirt road, but the man stopped and started unrolling the papers. "Oh, honey, would you run back to the house and look in the top cupboard drawer in my bedroom? I think I left the small outline in there." The man crouched and laid the open sheets across his knees, flipping pages and changing the order, moving back ones to the front and front ones to the back.

"Oh yup, I'll be right back!" Her heart thumping from the seeming desperation of their task, Cora ran as fast as she could, much faster than she even needed to, back into the farmhouse. She stopped short in front of the old oak cupboard and yanked the top drawer open so quickly, it almost dropped to the floor. Next to her father's tin moneybox was one of the strange papers. She tipped her head and scrutinized the rows of words and dashes before pulling the sheet out and banging the drawer shut. Running past their bare kitchen table, Cora threw the front door closed behind her with such force, it bounced back open. But she was already off down the dirt path, and didn't see.

The little town was awash with commotion. Cora never knew there were so many people living near her. No wonder the rabbits were such a problem. Keeping silent would be easy in the face of such an overwhelming crowd; the loud, bustling hum of the usually quiet surroundings daunted her. She ran off to scan the north field while her father knocked on the dark, glossy door at the right side of the cobbled courtyard. Unlike most of the weather-beaten, gray wood buildings in the town, the Constable's office was new mahogany, with clean, even slats. Streamlined and modern, it was a stark contrast to the old-world style of the farm homes that had been handed down for generations.

With all the noise, Cora expected most of the rabbits to be in hiding, but there were none visible at all. That was very odd. She turned back to the town, and saw the Constable shaking her father's hand on the office steps. The two men stood close together as they spoke. Cora could tell her Father was nervous, he dropped half the sheets he was holding. Over the buzz of the crowd, Cora heard the sound of several horses approaching, moving in unison. The only carts in the farm town were one or two horse drawn at the most, and the army-like din that approached quieted the chattering townsfolk, announcing the sound of many but the arrival of one. Cora leaned back against the fence.

The coachman rushed off his stoop and ran to the front door of the stagecoach, with his stockwhip still bobbing in his sweaty grip. But before he could take hold of the door, a whitish, sinewy hand popped out of the window. The hand flicked its wrist in the coachman's face. He scurried back up to his box seat behind the horses, and sat, hunched, without looking at the crowd, while the stagecoach door opened. And the man—the other man—stepped out of the dark, walnut coach. He was lean and knobby, with pale skin that clung and wrapped around his bones like a wet sheet. He reached up to smooth his fingers over the crunchy, white wisps on his head and when he did so, the cuffs of his stiff, black frock coat crawled back to expose two ropey, blue-veined wrists. The man pinched the edges of the cuffs between his fingertips and pulled them back down, shifting his shoulders under his clothing.

The man raised a hand to the crowd, and forced a smile. There was a moment of silence, followed by a smattering of applause. The man smiled bigger, as though the amount of applause he heard was much greater than what Cora heard. Closing his eyes, he spread the fingers of his open hand, and the clapping stopped. He walked to the second, rear door of the carriage and pulled it open. The head that came out was that of a girl, a teenager, maybe sixteen. Her grungy, off-white bonnet cast a shadow over her eyes; Cora only saw pink lips and a couple chunks of greasy, light brown hair. Cora watched as a flat, brown slipper emerged from the carriage, the dirty, light blue dress lying stiff and heavy against the girl's broad calf like paper. The girl stooped as she stepped onto the light dirt, and when she turned she stayed hunched, but still her thick cotton dress hung out so far from her legs, it cast a shadow over her feet. Something under her dress—no, her stomach, it was swelling—

Pregnant. The girl was pregnant. It was painfully obvious to everyone. She moved to the man's side, positioning her feet alongside but six inches back from his. He didn't look at her once. Cora still couldn't see the girl's eyes. The man spoke.

"Ladies and gentlemen, I have come to rescue you from the vermin. I have come to smash them down, conquer them, and annihilate them all for you, so you will finally be free." The crowd didn't know how to respond to the man's dramatic address, but there was a murmur of assertion.

"I have come from the far away land of Australia," the man gestured upward, "where there were vermin so numerous the likes of which you have never seen. They tore through the fences, they ripped up the crops. And when their bellies were full, still they ripped up the crops, just for their own gratification. Just to lay waste to the people's toil and ensure everyone was left hungry. But my friends," he raised both his hands in the air, "if you put your trust in me, I will stop this plague and restore peace and prosperity to your homes and families here, just like we stopped the demon vermin in Australia."

The crowd erupted into a cheer. Cora felt a sickness in her gut, and scanned the crowd for her father. She ran, bumping between big arms and dirty elbows, until she reached her father's side. Cora tugged his sleeve and looked up at him, and when he turned down to her, she saw his face had gone quite white.

"Pastor Harding," the Constable bowed and extended a hand, "may I present Wayne Clyde, our town milkman?"

The Pastor turned from his new fans and tilted his head slightly at Cora's father, before peering down at Cora. She beamed and did a curtsy. Cora's father hadn't warned the girl to guard her expressions against showing her hand, but she had figured that out for herself, assuming that scowling would be nearly as bad as speaking out. Her father knew, or thought, that the man would pay little notice to his daughter beyond a polite introduction wherein he would see the girl was clean, neat and respectful, which was all men like that wanted or expected from children.

"Pastor, it is such an honor," Cora's father shook the man's hand. "And how good of you to travel so far from home on our account."

"But I am not native to Australia," the man smirked. "Can't you tell by my accent?"

"I beg your pardon, sir. I should not have assumed," Cora's father nodded a bow again.

"You're a country boy, then. Don't travel much?" the man squinted and showed his teeth.

"No sir, opportunity has not permitted me. I have lived here all my life. But as a reading man, I have found much to learn about the world in books."

"Not enough, apparently. Although books are only words on a page, and thus don't allow any man to learn much about regional accents. I am from the United States. Virginia. Not that it matters. And remember, sir, opportunity is what you make of it. Don't blame fate for denying you what hard work and perseverance would

12

undoubtedly reward."

"Yes sir, you are quite right," Cora's father said. The Pastor began to turn away, and Wayne Clyde had to step forward to be heard. "Oh no, sir, I—"

"Yes?"

"I wonder if I might take up another moment of your time. You see, I have been sketching some plans—"

"Plans?"

"Ideas. About erecting a large fence around the town, to keep the rabbits out."

"A fence? How archaic! We are not heathens, my good man. This is the twentieth century. Would you have us erect a great wall? Seal ourselves away from the rest of the world? Would you have us work harder to arrange our lives around that which is troubling them in the first place?"

"No sir—"

"Well, we have more modern ways to eradicate our problems than hide from them behind a fence."

"Oh yes, there are many ways to approach a problem. But perhaps sir, if you looked at the plans you might see this idea as a viable option. I was trying to think of a plan that would realistically work, and the added benefit of this one is that it would be gainful to all and harmful to none."

The Pastor put one hand in his coat pocket. "Oh I assure you, none of what I will do will bring harm to you or anyone in this town."

"I mean, sir, not harmful to people or rabbits."

"Not harmful to rabbits! Are you joking? The intent of your salvation is to *be* harmful to rabbits. Spending time,

13

energy and manpower to preserve life in the antithesis of all we're fighting against is not only absurd, it's immoral."

"But sir, isn't it true that a great fence is what is being planned in Australia right now to keep the rabbits out? Why would you oppose a precedented tactic taking place in an area whose rabbit problem far surpasses ours?"

"The problem is the problem, regardless of its size, and—" the man leaned closer to Cora's father, "where did you hear about that?"

"I read it, sir, in a paper."

"That reading again. It will get you into trouble, young man," the man said. "Listen to me, reading means nothing. What you have read means nothing. I am the one who has traveled the world, seen firsthand the destruction and wickedness these monsters can bring. Look at this girl," he grabbed the hand of the pregnant girl and jerked her forward. "Look at what became of her. Would you wish such a fate for your own daughter?" Cora saw the girl's pale blue eyes emerge from the shadow. The two girls looked at each other.

"But, surely you can't blame the rabbits—for the decisions of man?" Cora's father whispered.

"She was a God-fearing child before the vermin came, and look at her now. How can you deny what I have seen with my own eyes?"

Wayne's mouth hung open. He looked at the man, looked at the pregnant girl, then looked back at the man again.

"The rabbits will be stopped, and I would advise you to never press your pagan intent on me again. Go back to your books, and leave the real problems of the world to me," the man turned and gripped the pregnant girl's hand. She gave Cora one more look before he dragged her away. The Pastor cast a glance over his shoulder and Cora couldn't help it, she scowled. And her father didn't notice, but the Pastor did.

"He's insane," Cora's father breathed. "He's stark, raving mad."

"But Daddy, he has all the control. What is he going to do? What are we going to do?"

"Tell people. Don't worry, once everyone realizes how mad he is, they'll laugh him out of town."

Cora got out of bed the next morning and ran to her window, scanning the grass for her rabbit. Nothing. She dressed and went to the kitchen for breakfast, but found her father was gone, and that he'd left a note for her.

Cora—
     Went out to talk to the Constable. Be back soon.
Love, Daddy

Cora heated some bread with jam and carried it outside. The big yards of all her neighbors were empty. She looked around and squinted toward the sun; it was nearly seven a.m. She had overslept, yes. Had everyone else, too? Then Cora noticed a dull, even roar in the distance. She was moving toward the sound when her father, alone, came rushing at her down the path.

"What's that noise?" she said.

"Come with me, Cora," her father put an arm around her shoulder and hurried her toward the house. "I want you to stay inside today."

"But why? What's wrong?"

"Just, stay inside. I'll tell you later."

Once inside the house, Cora sat down in one of their scratchy kitchen chairs and folded her hands on the table, waiting. But her father barely looked at her. He just walked to his room, and shut the door. Cora sat at the table for a few moments, looking back and forth between her father's door and the chair across from her, where he usually sat. She stood and walked toward her bedroom, passing her father's room slowly. She thought she heard him... crying.

"Daddy?" she touched the doorknob. "Are you ok?"

"Some other time, Cora, please."

Cora tried to open the door, but it was locked. She rattled the knob. "Dad? Please let me in."

"Go to your room, Honey. I'll be there in a minute."

Cora walked to her room, sat on the bed, and waited. And waited. Time passed. The sun moved across the wall and Cora sat, her eyes fixed on the empty, open doorway. She didn't move and scarcely thought, just focused on her father walking in. But he never came.

When Cora woke it was dusk. She was lying back against her pillow, and her father had shut her door. She dragged a knuckle across her eyes and sat up, remembering the morning's events. Flipping her legs over the side of the bed, she gasped.

A rabbit was sitting in the middle of her floor. Just

sitting there. Cora looked around the room and back at the rabbit. She opened her mouth to call her father, but thought better and closed it again. She leaned toward the rabbit.

"Hello?"

The rabbit stared at her.

"Uh, how did you get in here?" she said.

The rabbit hopped a step closer to the bed. Cora put her hands against the mattress and eased herself to a half-standing position. When the rabbit didn't flinch, she slowly crouched down next to it and laid a hand against its back.

"You're not scared of me at all, are you?" She gave the rabbit a gentle stroke. She saw the rabbit's jaw shifting and heard a little chattering noise. She pet him, rubbing her hand over his ears and his soft, but slightly bristly coat. She began to look around the room again. "I wonder how you *did* get in here." Cora picked up the rabbit. She was surprised by the ease with which the animal allowed her to handle him. Why wasn't he more skittish?

"Dad?"

Cora's father was sitting at the kitchen table with his back to Cora's room. He turned around. Cora smiled apprehensively.

"I—I found the present you left for me," she lifted the rabbit closer to her face. Her father stared.

"Do you like him?" he asked.

"Oh yes. I love him. And he's so nice. He really likes me too, I think," she rubbed her cheek against the rabbit's ear.

"Where was he when you found him?" the man looked past his daughter, toward her room.

17

"Just sitting, in the middle of my floor, as nice as can be."

"Well, that's a good thing, then. If he'd hidden under your bed, you might not have found him right away!" her father smiled.

"Yup, I was surprised. Do you want to hold him?" she held the rabbit out toward her father.

"No, not right now. Some other time when he's more settled. He seems quite taken with you."

Cora smiled, and turned to walk back to her room. "Daddy?"

"Yes?"

"Thank you, so much."

"Well, don't thank me. You certainly deserve it."

Cora put the rabbit back on the floor, where she'd found him. She spent a lot of fuss and bother making him a bed out of a little wooden crate and some soft hay. The rabbit hopped next to the bed and started munching the hay, and Cora cooed, chuckled and spoke to the animal while she brought it a dish of water and a piece of lettuce. The rabbit seemed quite happy, and Cora lay on her side on the floor, watching him eat. She played with him until her father told her it was time for bed, and the girl fell into a joyful sleep. When she woke up, she found the rabbit had snuggled in bed next to her, with his head under her chin. How impressive, she thought, that he could jump up onto the bed.

Cora's father told her she must keep the rabbit an absolute secret from everyone, for the rabbit's safety, and that hopefully the animal didn't mind spending most of its time indoors. He built a large, shed-like box with no top and no bottom, but a little door so Cora and the rabbit could play safely 'outside', enjoying the sun and grass while concealed from the townsfolk. He put it in the bare yard to the cow pasture, where no one but Cora and her father ever went anyway. He even built the rabbit a cage to fit under Cora's bed—concealed behind her long bedskirt—so the animal would be safe and hidden when they were out of the house.

The girl hadn't had the heart to ask her father again about the day he came rushing back from the mysterious noise in the town. He had been so kind and focused on fixing a place in their life for the rabbit he'd given her; Cora didn't want to seem ungrateful. But as her father turned a head of lettuce around and around in a bowl of water, Cora spoke.

"Daddy?"

"Yes?"

"What is going to happen to the rest of the rabbits?"

The man sighed. "Nothing good, I'm afraid."

Cora shifted, waiting for the rest of his reply, but he was quiet. "Isn't there something we can do?" she said.

"I wish there were. I would love to think of some way, but the fence idea was the best I had. And I am only one man. The townspeople," he paused, "they already think me a threat now, or a madman, or both. They won't listen to a thing I say, and I dare say my safety is best preserved if I lie low for a while." He looked into the bowl. "I'm sorry."

"Your safety?" the thought hadn't even occurred to her.

"It was that man, wasn't it?"

"No, actually," Wayne said, "it was the people. They just turned on me. They were so agitated about everything and—" he cleared his throat, "the man, Pastor Harding, he stayed them, protected me. Like a father stopping his child from squashing a bug."

"The people are crazy!" Cora said. "How could they? That's terrible!"

"People are terrible when misguided. And how to guide them better, I do not know," Wayne kneeled to face his daughter. "I know it might seem to you that I am doing nothing but—"

"I don't think you're doing nothing," Cora said. "You're doing a lot. You're doing a lot for *my* rabbit," she smiled.

"That is because it is in my power to do. I know what you're thinking, you think bad of me for not having a plot to save the rest—"

"No!" Cora shook her head hard and her dark curls flew back and forth.

"It's okay, you don't have to say that. I know you, and I know how things appear. I used to envision more beyond my power, but it's hard now. I'm older. And tired. Sometimes you get tired of fighting, and you just want things to be easy. You'll understand, someday."

Cora blinked.

"If it were just me, things would be different. But I have to stay safe for you because without me, you are alone. I will not leave you alone."

"Daddy?"

"Yes?"

"What you're doing for my rabbit, that's a risk."

"Yes, it is."

"Why are you doing it?"

"For you." Wayne pointed at Cora's bedroom, "That rabbit is special."

"Is he?" Cora said. "I mean, I thought he was. It's just different hearing you say it."

"It is obvious, even to me. What I am doing now may not seem like much, but you'll see—someday I'll do something for you that's really great."

CHAPTER TWO

THE NECKLACE AND NELLIE

Cora lay on her stomach on her bedroom floor, with her hands folded under her chin. The rabbit hopped up to her and put its nose against hers. Then it walked around her side and hopped up to sit on the small of her back. Cora giggled and covered her mouth, trying not to make a noise. The rabbit stood up on its hind legs and looked around the room. Cora tried to hold still because if she shifted at all, she could feel her pet wobble. The rabbit jumped down and took off running circles around the floor, around her, kicking out his back feet, which sent his hindquarters weaving and bobbing behind him. Cora laughed. The rabbit leapt again, jumping as he ran, and then flopped down on his side, stretching his legs out behind him. He plucked a stray piece of hay off of the ground, and Cora beamed at the sight of the hay getting smaller and smaller, until it receded into the rabbit's mouth.

Cora and the rabbit lay like mirror images, bookended

in the bright afternoon light that shone through Cora's window. Cora reached out cautiously and laid her fingertips on the rabbit's small front paw. The animal lowered his head, and rested his chin against her knuckles. He blinked. Cora inched closer and placed a soft kiss on the bridge of the rabbit's nose. The rabbit clicked his teeth and pressed his nose into Cora's chin.

A gunshot. The noise shattered the still afternoon and the rabbit bolted up, jerking his head around. The sound was a ways away, but Cora startled too. The rabbit ran frantically around her room now, not hopping but stomping his back foot and honking with a squeaking sound.

"It's okay, it's okay, it's far away. It can't hurt you," Cora got up on her knees and waved her hands over her pet. The rabbit stopped in front of Cora and looked her in the eye. "What?" she said. "What is it?" The rabbit looked toward the window, and back at her. Then at the window, then back at her, again. Cora followed his eyeline to the window, afraid of what she'd find, but all she could see was her own yard, just how it always was. "I don't see anything," she turned back to her rabbit. He directed her gaze to the window again.

The grass was clear, bright and sunny, picturesque in their little microcosm and the rabbit stared into it, past it, searching the horizon. Cora looked too, to try and see what he was seeing. There was nothing, but the longer she looked, the more Cora felt her thoughts reaching into the unknown going on so close. And images came to her, of her father locking himself in his room, of Pastor Harding, the rabbit man, and of what more—she could only imagine. Who knew what was going on beyond their reach? She began to feel ashamed for not thinking of it. Not for trying to avoid it, for she really couldn't begin to imagine what to do, but she was ashamed she had found hiding from everything so easy. The rabbit came to her side and sat down with his hip up against hers.

"All your family, and all your friends, they're out there, aren't they?" she said. The rabbit stared ahead. Cora put her hand on the animal's tiny shoulders and they watched the far away hills together, thinking.

Cora pulled a cart filled with blocks of butter and cheese, and pails of milk. She could feel the disapproving scowls that surrounded her, barely concealed behind windows and hat brims. Each of the customers on her route, her neighbors, thanked Cora with polite courtesy as they snatched up their order, only to shake their heads and sneer as soon as her back was turned.

The pregnant girl sat pressing her bare feet into the grass of Pastor Harding's new yard. She smiled, watching the blades of grass move between her toes. Across the street, two adolescent boys observed her, giggling and pointing at the lace petticoat visible against the girl's pale thighs, under her knees. They were whispering to each other, red-faced, but even as their sneering grew louder, the girl seemed completely oblivious. Cora looked back and forth at the scene and the boys began to gesture.

"Hey, get out of here!" Cora ran to the boys and shoved the larger one in the center of his chest.

The boy looked Cora up and down, "Oh? What're you

going to do?" he gave her collar a little tug.

"I suppose you want the Pastor to see you?" Cora folded her arms over her chest.

The boy took a step back. "Ah, she's a fat cow anyway," he sneered at the pregnant girl. But as he and his friend walked away, he peered toward the cottage window.

Cora waited, hoping the pregnant girl would notice her. She shuffled back toward her cart and as she passed in front of the grass, Cora curved closer and slowed to a saunter by the girl's feet. But it wasn't until Cora lifted the cart handle that the girl looked up.

The pregnant girl walked over to Cora and stood before her, ethereal and unmoving. Since the girl was older than she was, Cora waited a moment for her to speak first, but the girl was quiet. For all Cora knew the girl was mute, but she almost didn't seem real.

Cora lifted one of the pails off her cart. "Um, this is some milk for you," she over enunciated the words. "You can have it—here," she held the bucket forward, pantomiming her meaning. The girl spoke.

"Hello."

"Oh, hi," Cora said.

The girl took the pail. "Thank you." She brought it to her lips and took a sip. "It's good."

"Thanks. Or I guess you should thank my Dad. Or the cows, heh."

"I'd like to," the girl said.

"Oh?" Cora fidgeted with the hem of her shirt. "Uh, how do you like our town?"

"I don't know, yet. I haven't been here long enough."

25

"Oh, yup."

The door to the cottage behind the pregnant girl swung open. "Do we have a visitor, Nellie?" Pastor Harding strode across the grass. Cora jumped.

"Begging your pardon, sir," Cora said, "I just thought your—"

"Niece," the Pastor said.

"Your niece might like to have some of our local milk. Good health for the baby and all."

"Yes, good for health. Although, I wouldn't concern myself with the 'baby' if I were you. You see, it's not polite to do so."

"My apologies, sir," Cora bowed. Underneath her blanket of dark waves, she scowled.

"You are the milkman's daughter."

"Yes. Proudly, sir."

The man laughed a little puff of air through his nose, "Yes, I expect so. We should all be so proud of our fathers."

"Yes sir." Cora held her bow and waited for the Pastor to say something else. The muscles in her legs began to quiver as she struggled to stay upright. Finally, she stood back up straight and pushed her hair out of her face. The Pastor was scrutinizing her, running his fingers and thumb along the pocket edge of his black coat.

"Don't you ever wear a dress?" he said.

"Not when I'm working, sir."

"Hm," the man puffed through his nose again. "Yes, well, move along," he waved his fingertips. "You can come back for the pail."

26

"Yes sir," Cora pulled her wagon away, and watched the pregnant girl walk around the side of the Pastor's cottage.

"And girl," the man said. Cora turned around on the road. "You needn't concern yourself with charity here. We have brought our own milk along with us. You shall have to find some other way to plump up your little ego, elsewhere. But thank you for the sample."

Cora thought she should wince at the comment, but for some reason, she felt quite calm. "You're welcome, sir." The Pastor hardly seemed to hear, and disappeared back behind the cottage door.

The tin pails rattled as Cora pulled her cart away. Nellie watched the young girl move along the road, slow, determined and sad. Nellie stood, bouncing her knees under her dress, waiting until she heard the Pastor's feet hit the floor of the lumber room.

Cora heard the sound of someone running at her back, and she wheeled around. Nellie was kicking up clouds of dust as she sprinted down the small road. She almost skidded when she stopped in front of Cora.

"I'm not a beggar," Nellie blurted out.

"No!" Cora waved her hands in front of her. "No, of course not. I didn't mean—"

"What I mean is," the girl reached into her shirt, her hand fumbling under the cloth at her chest, "I have something for you. For trade. To thank you."

"Oh! Well you don't have to—" Cora stopped because whatever the girl had to give her, she wanted it very much. Nellie pulled her fist out of her dress and yanked a black,

27

looped cord over her head. She opened her hand to Cora. In the middle of the girl's taut palm lay a shiny stone, tan and brown with swirling patterns that wove and looped into one another like a fingerprint. A rounded bit of thick, copper wire stuck out of the stone's top, and laced through that was the cord.

"It's special," Nellie said. "Go home, then put it on. It will give you a better understanding of the one you love. Whoever you see first."

"Wow, thanks," Cora reached out and took the smooth, tan stone. It was warm. "Thank you, very much. I really appreciate it."

"That's ok," Nellie smiled. It was the first time Cora saw her smile.

Cora put the necklace into her pocket. "Well, thanks. Bye."

"Bye."

"I know your—"

"Uncle," Nellie said.

"*Uncle*—said you had milk with you, but if you ever need anything from me, just let me know."

Nellie cocked her head to one side, "I will."

Cora started back down the dirt road. Slow, determined, but, Nellie thought, a little less sad.

"Hi Daddy!" Cora ran past her father in the kitchen.

"Hi Cora," he called back. The girl was already in her room.

"Oh my gosh, you won't believe what happened to me today!" Cora said to the rabbit as she pulled open the door of his cage. "The girl, the one I told you about, I talked to her! I gave her some milk. She gave me this," Cora pulled the necklace out of her pocket and held it up to the rabbit's nose. He sniffed it, and rubbed it with his chin. "She said for me to wait until I got home to put it on," Cora pulled the necklace over her head and centered it at her chest. "She had been wearing it," Cora looked down at the stone. She lifted it to her nose, and smelled it. She ran to her mirror. "It's beautiful!" She squatted down to give her rabbit a little pet. "I'll be right back—ooops," Cora picked up the stone and dropped it under her blouse, just as Nellie had worn it. She walked out of her room, into the kitchen.

"Hi Daddy."

"Well, 'hi' again," Wayne set down his cup of coffee. "How was your day?"

"Good," Cora sat next to him. "What'cha' doin'?"

"Oh, just organizing the stock list."

"That's nice. Daddy?"

"Yes?"

"Why did you lock yourself in your room that day and never come out?"

The man's face went sullen. "Cora, that's complicated. I would rather not talk about it."

"Oh," Cora looked at her thumbs.

Her father put his hand on hers, "We haven't seen each other all day. Can't we talk about something cheerful?"

Cora tried to smile. "Of course, Daddy. I'm sorry."

"Naw, don't be sorry," he rubbed her head. "Never be sorry for asking questions."

Cora shifted in her chair and waited a polite amount of time before she went back to her room, saying 'rabbit was waiting.' She shut the door behind her and sat down on the floor next to her rabbit, pulling the necklace out to look at it.

"Maybe it's not working right," she frowned, and ran a hand over the rabbit's fur. "Rabbit, I thought Daddy would finally talk to me, like he used to. I know he's just trying to be nice, but I want to know things. I don't know what to do. All the things in the town, everything that day, I don't know what to do," Cora lay down and hugged the rabbit, resting her forehead against his back. She felt the rabbit put a little paw on her wrist, and then she heard a voice—

"I'm sorry."

Cora buried her face in the rabbits fur. "I know."

"Little girl—"

Cora heard a rapping on her window. The rabbit leapt up, tossing the top of the quilt back, and hopping onto Cora's chest. Cora sat up in bed and lowered the rabbit to her lap.

"What? What is it?" Cora said.

"It's Nellie," the rabbit said, "the girl who gave you the necklace. Look."

Nellie moved her face closer to the window and a faint glow outlined the pregnant girl's nose, cheeks and forehead. Without her bonnet—her light brown hair stuck, lank, against her crown—Nellie's pale eyes looked even more huge peering in from the black outdoors.

Cora struck a match and lit the oil lamp on her bedside table. She scooped the rabbit into one arm and held him against her chest as she pushed the window open with her other hand. Nellie's fingers came over the sill.

"What's wrong?" Cora said. "Are you ok?"

"I ran all the way," Nellie gasped. "I got a message from my beloved—he's here! He's here to see me! I don't know how he did it, but he left me a message to find him. Here—" she threw a folded scrap of paper into Cora's hand. As her pale arm came in through the window, Cora saw a cluster of little, blue bruises up the girl's forearm. "Do you know where that is?"

Cora read the note. "Yes. I haven't been there recently—Daddy doesn't want me to go there anymore—but I can find it."

"Will you? Can you take me there? I don't know where anything is here. Pastor Harding never lets me out of the yard."

"Uh, ok. Now?"

"Yes, now. Please," Nellie looked over her shoulder. "In fact, as fast as we can go. Is that okay?"

"Sure, let me get dressed," Cora placed the rabbit back on the bed.

"Can I come?" the rabbit said. Cora looked at Nellie.

"I didn't know you had a friend," Nellie smiled, "What's your name?"

"Cora," Cora said.

"Basajaun," the rabbit said.

"Oh, I thought you meant—" Cora stopped and turned to her pet. "Hey, you never told me that."

"You never asked," Basajaun said.

The two girls started down the hill with the rabbit hopping next to them. He was flipping his head left and

31

right because it'd now been some time since he'd been out so far, too. Cora wasn't used to finding her way around town in the dark, but she found everything looked nearly the same, just shadowed in deep blues and greens.

"Is your beloved from Australia too?" Cora asked.

"Yes," Nellie said.

"How did he get here?"

"I don't know."

"When did you get the note? Was it a special wire?"

"No. I wrote it," Nellie said.

"Huh?" Cora stopped and turned to the teenage girl.

Nellie kept walking as she spoke, forcing Cora to run alongside to catch up to her. "It's his words, but I wrote it. I knew he was near," Nellie took a deep breath and her lids began to droop. "When I lay in bed at night, I could hear him calling for me. I sat on the chair in my room with a wood block on my lap, put a piece of paper on it, and held a pencil. I asked him how I could find him."

"Oh," Cora looked at the piece of paper. It had been in her palm, but now she fingered it between her thumb and forefinger. Basajaun looked at her.

"At first I wasn't sure about asking you to come with me," Nellie said, "but then I thought, 'How lonely do you have to be, to come to me?'"

Cora led them toward an old thicket where she used to play. "We can cut through here," she said. "It's dark but it will be quicker than going around." She was counting on following her old landmarks within—the big and little 'mama and baby' boulders nestled side by side, the tree with the 'v' shape—but Cora hadn't anticipated on the unfamiliar overgrowth that had popped up during her absence. There were some plants she remembered, but her usual paths were dense and obscured. The two girls wrenched bramble and tree-limbs aside, cracking small branches and pulling out the little, picky thorns that got stuck in their clothes.

"We'll take a different way back. I'm sorry," Cora said, and wondered why she had expected everything to remain unchanged while she was away from it. Nellie didn't reply. She seemed unfazed by the dark, the distance, and the tenacious bramble that crackled and poked every time the girls moved. Cora didn't think there was any obstacle in the world that could deter the pregnant girl from reaching her destination that night.

Just when Cora was beginning to worry she'd gotten them lost, she pushed aside a final cluster of shrubs and stumbled onto open ground. She was turning a circle to get her bearings when Nellie began running in a zigzag pattern across the patchy clearing.

"He's not here," Nellie said. She ran a little more, just to be sure.

"Are you sure this is it?" Cora studied the scrap of paper.

"It is," Nellie said. "I can feel it," she closed her eyes toward the sky.

"We could wait a little while, I guess," Cora sat down in the grass.

"No," Nellie frowned, "he won't be here, tonight. He may be in some sort of trouble. I'll just have to wait until he calls me again," the girl walked back to the thicket, and pulled aside the brush.

"Oh no," Cora pointed toward some short trees. "That way will be easier. And it probably won't be that much longer since we won't be fighting the plants. But, are you sure you don't want to look around some more? The clearing goes further down the hill, and we came all this way."

"It's no use," Nellie said, and walked in the direction Cora had pointed.

Cora and Basajaun shrugged at each other and followed Nellie, keeping a few feet behind. Basajaun nudged Cora's leg and she lifted him up. She felt his breathing slow as he fell into a half-sleep in her arms.

"When was the last time you saw your beloved?" Cora said.

"In Australia, before Pastor Harding took me away."

"Is he really your uncle?" Cora stared at the back of Nellie's head. Nellie didn't reply. "Do you like him?"

"No. Do you?"

"No, of course not," Cora said. She waited for Nellie to say more. The pregnant girl's shoes shuffled against the grass. "Do you miss him? Your beloved, I mean?"

"All the time."

"I'm sorry," Cora hugged Basajaun close and he rumbled a contented little grunt.

"Me too," Nellie said. "He's coming for me, though. I know he is. He will find me before the baby is born. The baby is for him. So long as I have the baby, he will find me. And we will finally be together."

"What about the Pastor?" Cora asked. "Will he let you

34

go?"

"Then, it won't matter," Nellie said.

The two girls were walking in silence when Cora noticed an acrid, oppressive odor. She stopped. "What's that smell?" she said. Basajaun's ears shot up.

"What is that?" he barked, shaking, and kicked his back feet off Cora's chest, bolting out of her arms.

"What?" Cora flipped her head around. "What's—? Oh my God—"

The pile was massive, near a thousand. More, over a thousand. Shapes at the top of the mound were discernable in the moonlight, but lower and closer to the ground the outlines meshed into mass of dark brown. Basajaun's eyes moved over the pile, then stopped at its center, glassy and stunned. He was so small compared to the mass of bodies that lay heaped against the night sky.

"Who has done this?" he yelled. "Who?" He let out a piercing cry. It seemed loud enough to shock life into the lost but after the ringing stopped, the rabbits still lay motionless.

Cora kneeled and put her arms around her rabbit. "Oh Basajaun, I'm so sorry," she hugged him and tried to pull him to her but he stayed rooted, muscles rigid, staring at the pile of death. Cora slumped forward and put her hands over her face.

"Are they not even eating them?" she cried to Nellie. "Are they just to *lay* here like this? Why?"

"Pastor Harding says no-one is to eat them," Nellie spoke low, "for to consume their flesh would make one subject to all the animal's same urges and weaknesses."

"That Pastor is a horrible, horrible man!" Cora reached for Basajaun and he pulled away. "How could he slaughter them like this? They are living things! They think, and feel, and they are a million times more noble and admirable than he is!" She pointed to the pile, "He should be there, not them!" Cora tried to stifle her angry gasps, and waited for Nellie's response. The teenager folded her hands at her chest and bowed her head. Her sleeves fell to her elbows and exposed again the cluster of bruises on her arm. Fingerprints.

"We should've done something," Basajaun growled. "We should've done something!"

"I didn't know," Cora said.

"Yes, you did," Basajaun hissed. "*You* could've done something."

Cora looked at the ground. "I didn't know what to do," she whispered, and choked on her tears because she felt too ashamed to cry.

The two girls and the rabbit stood. Each of them thought a few words for the deceased—regret, apologies, promises. And after a while, Nellie turned and walked slowly down the path. Cora's eyes were still on the ground. Basajaun stared at the profile of his friend and nudged his nose against her leg. Without looking at him, Cora picked him up and followed after the pregnant girl. The three of them walked home in silence.

Cora brought Basajaun his breakfast on a little plate. She set it in front of him and took a few steps back to sit on the floor. He munched a piece of lettuce, staring into her.

For the first time since the previous night, he spoke.

"That Nellie, she is strange, isn't she?" he said.

"Yup," Cora pulled a lock of hair in front her face and studied it. "I don't know what to think of her. Do you think she's crazy?"

"Yes," Basajaun said. "But I like her. She's nice. I feel a kinship with her, or comfortable, or something like that."

"Me too. I don't know why."

Basajaun sat next to his plate. "If she did make it all up, and imagined her beloved was coming from so far away simply to find her, that's very sad."

"I know. But she had to have made it up, right?" Cora said. "What she said, it's not possible. And then he wasn't even there. It is very sad. He probably abandoned her and never thought of her again," she fingered Nellie's necklace under her shirt. Basajaun folded his feet under himself and Cora edged closer to stroke his back. "I didn't even know your name, Basajaun. Tell me about yourself, about your family. There must be so much to know."

"Too much. But haven't you wondered how I found you?"

"I guess, yes. But I had been watching you for so long, and you came to me sometimes. It seemed to follow."

"My father told me about your father," the rabbit said. "He said your father was a great man, and not like the others in the town."

"Really?" Cora said. "Really?"

"Yes. It was him I came to the house looking for, but I found you first. You were friendly and soothing. I liked you right away. And then you gave me food, I couldn't

37

believe it. By the time I found your father, I was already so focused on you that I… he was very nice, your father, very good. But he didn't look at me the way I imagined he looked at my father, the way you looked at me. Like you knew me."

"So you let him bring you in to be with me," Cora tipped her head at the rabbit and smiled.

"What?"

"To be with me, to live here. You let him bring you in and put you in my room. I'm so glad he did," she smoothed Basajaun's ears.

"Oh," Basajaun said. "Yes."

"What? What is it?"

"I'm sorry, but your father didn't bring me in. It was Nellie."

"What? But I thought—how did she get in?"

"I don't know, I was sleepy when she found me. She meant me for your father too, I think. As far as I can remember, she just came in the front door. But then his room was locked. She left me in the hall in front of his bedroom, but when I was alone I saw your room was open, so I went in. I recognized you." Basajaun watched Cora trying to work out what he was saying. "Did your father tell you he was the one who brought me in?"

"Yes. Well, maybe. I don't know," Cora's face scrunched. "I thought he did it. I *assumed* he did it, for forgiveness or niceness for leaving me alone. He just let me think it, I guess."

Cora frowned, and Basajaun felt sorry for letting out the truth. He moved closer to her. "Your father is a very good man, Cora. You should think well of him."

"I do," she said. "I really, really do." But she grew quiet, and looked doubtful.

"I felt so ashamed of myself last night," Basajaun said, "living this happy life with you. Forgetting all my kind and leaving them to die. Pretending not to think about them or that they exist. It hurts, to have done such a wrong. Hurts, and something deeper I can't explain."

"What can we do? You are just a rabbit, and I am just a girl. I feel so powerless."

"I am a prey animal. When I see someone bigger or stronger than me, I flee. I have bravery, but to use it like a man would be foolish. What good does honor do me if throwing myself into danger causes me to fail? Having the sense to run from a force that could lay you out in one blow does not make you a coward. No, we need a strategy. A plan. Although I think if I had the chance, I could kill him with just my paws, and I would dance in his blood."

Cora started at Basajaun's comment, but she couldn't blame him. And it was no less, she thought, than what the Pastor deserved. Still, the bloodlust in the small animal's voice frightened her a little.

"Cora, I have to talk to you."

Cora laid a plate on the wooden counter-ledge and turned around, drying her hands on the kitchen cloth. She had been hoping to avoid her father that morning, or at least until she got her thoughts straight. "What?"

"Did you—" Wayne touched his jaw, "well, do you have enough money?"

"Money? What do I need money for?" Cora tossed the cloth onto the plate. "I mean, yes, I have enough. What's wrong?"

"Cora, did you take some money out of the cupboard in my bedroom?"

"What? No. I don't even know where that is," Cora paused. "How could you think I would do that, anyway? You think I would steal from you?" She had never before addressed her father with such an indignant tone.

"No, honey. It's just, it's gone. I thought maybe you needed some money to go out with your new friend," he kneeled.

"Basajaun?" Cora said. 'Ooops,' she thought.

"What?"

"I mean, my rabbit," she replied quickly. "That's what I decided to call him."

Her father smiled. "Wherever did you think of a name like that?" Cora shrugged. "No, I meant that girl who came with the Pastor. The pregnant girl."

"Oh. Nellie," Cora said.

"Nellie?" her father said. "Yes."

"What do you think of her?" Cora asked.

"She seems a nice girl. I feel bad for her, trapped with that Pastor. I think it's good you're making an effort to be kind to her. She seems such a sad and lonely thing."

"Have you talked to her?"

"No. Pastor Harding doesn't let her speak hardly at all. At least not when he's appearing. Lord knows what they talk about when they're alone."

"I can't imagine they talk at all," Cora said. "But the

40

money, Daddy. Some money is gone?"

"Yes, missing. I don't know where it went. I dare say someone might have taken it, but I don't know how. We'll have to get an extra lock for the front door, and be more careful to be sure we don't leave any windows open."

As soon as she had a moment to spare, Cora brought Basajaun to their secret, outdoor playhouse next to the cow pasture. She had things to tell him, although she regretted she still hadn't come up with anything that resembled a plan to deal with the real problem, the one that mattered.

"What do you think, Basajaun? If Nellie got in the house to bring you to me, she easily could've gotten in to take the money."

"Nellie would never steal, I'm sure of it," Basajaun shook his head. "What would she do with it, anyway? How could money help her?"

"I don't know."

"What about the Pastor? He could've taken it."

"Yes, it could've been a ruse," Cora said. "That whole thing was so strange and suspicious. If Nellie and the Pastor were working together, it could've been a trick to get me out of the house so he could take the money."

"But your father was still home," Basajaun said, "and the money was in the cupboard in *his* room. Getting you out would be no benefit to the Pastor to steal it."

"That's true. But Nellie has ways into the house." Cora pointed into the grass, "She could have gotten it at some other time."

"It's not Nellie," Basajaun said again. "It's just not. And she wasn't able to get into your father's room the day

41

she brought me in your house, anyway. Why don't you trust her?"

"I do. In my heart I do. It's just hard to because, I don't understand her. She's so strange. She's so pretty. And she didn't even seem sad when we saw—you know—"

"She was sad. She just shows her sadness in different ways," Basajaun said. "It could be the Pastor though. You know, some other way. But we need to know more."

"There's a town meeting about it tomorrow," Cora said, "and I'm going to go."

"Your father is letting you?"

"Oh he opposed me on it, boy did he ever. But I'm going. He can't tell me what to do, anymore," Cora folded her arms over her stomach.

The rabbit leaned closer to her, "Be careful, Cora. Don't do anything rash."

"How else are we going to learn more about what's going on? I'm not just going to sit in my house and hide anymore. And you want me to go. You can't deny that."

"You're right," Basajaun said. "I just worry. Remember, being headstrong and loud does not make you a hero."

"Yes, but closing your ears and eyes to all evil does not make it go away," Cora replied.

CHAPTER THREE

THE CHIEF

Cora was reaching for her father's hand when she stopped, curled her fingers a little, and put her hand back by her side. They were rounding the final turn before the town square, where the dirt road turned to stone and opened out into a wide circle, surrounded by the official buildings. Cora hadn't been there since the first day the Pastor arrived, and she looked at everything now with a new eye. It seemed not so large, not so strange, not so bustling. The noise of the crowd ebbed away into the backdrop of Cora's awareness, and became nothing to her but a quiet drone. Her father's steps slowed as he and Cora made their way through the crowd, so Cora grabbed his hand and led him closer to the front. The Pastor came up onto the platform, but Cora noticed he was alone. Where was Nellie?

"There is a thief in our midst," the Pastor raised his hands over the crowd. "Reports have been made, to me, that saved funds from several homes in the town have gone missing."

"We never had no trouble with thieving before," someone in the crowd yelled.

"No, who would steal from their own? Everyone knows everyone here," called out another.

"I know that too, and have taken it under consideration," the Pastor said. "Which means only one thing," the man paused to take in the crowd's baited apprehension. "That either someone here has turned on us, or there are external forces at work."

The crowd erupted into a wave of murmurs. 'What?' and 'Who?' and 'What do you mean?' bandied about in the air. The Pastor put a hand up and the crowd was silent.

"The rabbits," he hissed, "the plague. First they take your food, then the money that would fund more food goes missing. What are we to assume?"

Cora gasped. Was he blaming the town thefts—on the rabbits? She looked at her father, and he stared down at the ground. Cora turned toward the stage and called out, in her loudest voice, "Why are you not letting the townspeople eat the rabbits?"

"What?" The Pastor put a hand over his brow, casting an eye into the crowd. "Who said that?"

"I did," Cora said. "Why aren't you letting the townspeople eat the rabbits?"

The Pastor put his palms together, resting his fingertips against his wrists. His lips barely parted as he spoke. "Because to consume the vermin flesh would make one subject to all the animal's same urges and weaknesses," he said, and turned to continue his address.

"But they had been," Cora spoke again. "The people had been eating the rabbits long before you arrived, long before there was a problem, even. Food is short, and the rabbits eat the food, so the people eat the rabbits." Now all eyes were on Cora. The crowd watched her tawny profile, surrounded by dark waves. Then they looked up at the Pastor, waiting.

The Pastor bent his knuckles, turning his fingertips in and digging his nails into his wrists. His face was stony. "This was already discussed," he barked, "at the last meeting. Eating the flesh of the vermin allows their hold to continue, even after their death. You said yourself that you ate them before there was a problem. *Before.* Now they run rampant, ruining your lives. I would think the logic is obvious, even to you."

"But that isn't logic," Cora said, "it's coincidence. It doesn't follow, not at all. Eating rabbits does not make there be *more* rabbits. That just doesn't make sense."

"Silence!" the Pastor yelled and pointed at the girl. "You know *nothing.* You have *lived nothing.* Experienced nothing. What you call logic is clouded by inexperience and an undeveloped brain. I have seen the world and dealt with real problems, not lived under a thicket roof being spoon-fed the idealized ramblings of a failed attempt at manhood."

Cora's father stiffened. "My father is a great man," Cora said. She wished it were still true, but her feelings were her own, and private.

"Well then, if you say one more word, child, I will find

45

your father in contempt, and a traitor to the safety and stability of this town," the Pastor said. The crowd turned back to Cora. She was quiet. The Pastor curled his upper lip, showing his teeth. "We should all be so proud of our fathers."

Cora played the morning over and over in her mind as she cut a large brick of cheese into big squares, next to the water basin on the wooden counter. She was arranging the squares back into a block shape when she heard a rap at the door. She looked at Basajaun and he ran out of the kitchen, into her bedroom, and hopped under the bed, into his cage. Cora was about to put the knife down onto the cutting board, but instead she flipped up her apron to reveal the folded hem on its underside. Using the blade, she sliced open a few stitches and slipped the knife into the hem, dropping her apron back down over her legs before she went to the door.

"Who is it?" she called through.

"It's Henry," a boy's voice replied.

"Henry? Who's Henry?" Cora cracked the door. A freckled face peered in through the slit.

"Me. I'm Henry. I live across the street. Remember?"

Cora opened the door and saw the farm hand from the big grain farm standing before her. Dirty and sinewy, and only about two years older than she was.

"Oh, it's *you*," Cora sneered. "What do you want?" She put out her hands. "As you can see, I have nothing for you to kick out of my hand today."

"No," the boy said. "I just came to talk. Friendly-like. I

swear."

Cora wrinkled her nose at him. "What about?"

"About what you said to the Pastor today." He leaned closer to her and whispered. "About eating the rabbits. I agree. I mean," he looked behind him. "Can I come in?"

"No," Cora said. "My father will be back soon from milking the cows. Wait outside. I'll be right there. I have to get a sweater," she closed the door in his face. Cora ran to her bedroom, and kneeled down to look into Basajaun's cage. He sat centered in a little pile of hay.

"Be careful," he whispered.

Cora closed his cage and hooked the latch. "Don't worry, I'm prepared," she said, and pulled the knife out of the hem of her apron. Throwing the apron on the bed, she opened her bureau and searched for the thick, cable-knit sweater that used to belong to her mother. It was the muddied color of faded, old khaki, and smelled like the inside of a drawer. Cora checked the sweater's pockets and, just as she'd remembered, they were nice and deep. She put the sweater on and dropped the knife into the right pocket.

When Cora stepped back outside, Henry was gone. She tiptoed toward the left side of the farmhouse and saw the boy, leaning up against the side, chewing on a long stalk of grain.

"Where should we go?" he said.

"This way," Cora waved her hand over her head as she walked away from Henry, toward the cow pasture. "There's a tree. No one can see us if we're on the other side of it."

47

The two children walked in silence. Henry kept looking at Cora and she stared straight ahead, feeling the weight of the kitchen knife bouncing against her hip. When they reached the tree Cora put a hand up against it, and waited for the boy to speak.

"What you said, about eating the rabbits, you're right, you know," he said.

"Of course I'm right," Cora said. "Is that all you wanted to tell me?"

"No. I just want to talk to you because, well, you're right. But no one else seems to be questioning it. I've been thinking it. Other people must be thinking it, I don't know," he kicked the grass in front of him, and a few blades tore up around his wrinkled boot.

"Well, you must talk to lots of people," Cora said. "What kinds of things are people saying?"

"Nothing! That's just it!" Henry paced back and forth. "Nobody will say a damn thing! And I'm afraid to say anything because *I* don't want to be lynched! So everyone is just hungry. Hungrier! It's worse than ever before!" He plopped down on the ground. Cora folded her arms and stood over him, and Henry gestured into the empty air. "So I went, I went to the termination site. And I waited an hour in hiding, I wanted to be there early so the meat would be fresh. I thought if I prepared it and got it ready to cook, or even cooked it myself, I could bring it to my family and a few others who really needed it, and who hopefully wouldn't have judged me for my actions. I only took a couple but when I skin—" he looked at Cora, "I mean, when I, uh, opened them, they didn't smell right. I tore off

48

a small piece of the meat and cooked it with a match, but when I took a bite, it tasted bitter. Or like a bad medicine, or fertilizer or something. It was bad. They are poisoning the rabbits somehow and all the meat is bad. And the Pastor has prohibited hunting and trapping them by law. He has just taken control of everything and it's a mess!"

Cora sat down next to her neighbor. "I've been to the termination site, too," she said. "Why is the Constable letting all this happen? Couldn't he just get rid of the Pastor? We'd be no worse off than we were before, and better than we are, now."

"No one can get to the Constable. He's always either with the Pastor or he's not around. He's never in his office. I don't know what's going on." The boy and girl sat, looking at the wide, open field. Henry pulled up a blade of grass and flung it out, hard, but it twirled before him and landed at his feet. "I couldn't believe you said the things you did. I couldn't believe the Pastor didn't come down into the crowd and wring your neck where you stood. Is your father proud of you, or angry at you?"

"He's worried about me," Cora said. "He was angry, not because he thought I did a bad thing, but because I put myself in danger and made myself a target, he said. We had a little bit of a fight. He yelled at me. I yelled at him," Cora put her chin on her knees. "I've never yelled at him before."

"Oh," Henry said.

"Tell me," Cora said, "is Nellie usually at the meetings?" she was about to correct herself and clarify who she meant by saying, 'the pregnant girl', but Henry spoke.

"Yup, she usually is. I noticed she wasn't there today."

"Do you know her?"

"I've talked to her a few times. I brought her some bread. I offered to help her weed the little flower patch left over by the cottage."

"Oh," Cora scrutinized him. "How did you meet her?"

"Just introduced myself to her," he shrugged. "She's outside all the time."

Cora studied him some more. Henry could see her eyes moving all over his face, searching for something. "So you don't know where she was today?" she said.

"No. It made me wonder. It's probably nothing, but I was going to go look for her after I talked to you. Do you want to come?"

"Oh," Cora said. "I guess so. Yup."

"Okay," Henry got up, "we can go now."

But as the two of them approached the back of the farmhouse, Cora heard a tinny, rattling noise coming from her room. It was faint through the brick walls, but for it to carry to the back yard, Cora knew it must be fierce. She took off running. "I'm sorry," she called over her shoulder, "I can hear my father, he needs my help. He'll be angry. I'm sorry!"

"Do you need help?" Henry called at her back and began to follow her. "Do you want me to come in?"

"No!" Cora yelled louder. "No, it's best if I go alone. You go look for Nellie. Come back and tell me what you know. I'm sorry!" she slammed the door.

Cora yanked the knife out of her pocket. Her heart was

50

pounding as she threw open the door to her bedroom. It was empty. She felt sick. She dropped to the floor and pulled up the bedskirt, prepared for the worst.

Basajaun was gripping the chicken-wire mesh with his teeth, pulling his entire weight against it so his whole cage rattled and shook. Each corner of the cage rose up, one after the other, as the whole thing trembled and rocked like a jumping bean.

"Basajaun!"

The rabbit looked up and saw Cora. "Thank God you've come. We need to go! We need to go *now*!"

Cora reached under the bed and unlatched the door to Basajaun's cage. "Where? What's wrong?" she said. Basajaun jumped out.

"My father has summoned me. He wouldn't do this unless there was major trouble. Really Cora, we must go! This is important!"

Cora looked at the window. "But it's day! You can't be seen out, much less with me."

"You can hide me, carry me, anything."

Cora sprinted out to the milk shed and grabbed a large pail. When she ran back in the house she pulled open the door to the high kitchen cupboard, and dragged out a wide cheesecloth.

"How did he summon you?" she set the pail next to the rabbit.

"He sent a footman to stomp beneath your bedroom window. It was a great risk." Basajaun allowed Cora to scoop him up and place him in the bottom of the pail.

"How will you direct me?" she said. "I don't know

where to go."

Basajaun stared up at her from inside the tin bucket. "Since you're human, the meeting place will be inside the giant pine, near the wild rhubarb. Do you know where that is?"

Cora held the cheesecloth up at her chest. "Yes, but—human? He wants to see me?"

"Yes. There's no time to explain. Just be very, very respectful. My father is the head of the rabbits."

"The head?"

Basajaun sighed. "The *Chief*."

Cora's eyes were wide. She was waiting for Basajaun to say more, but he just stared at her. She laid the cloth over the top of the metal pail.

When she arrived at the large pine, Cora looked around. "We're here," she whispered.

"Go inside," Basajaun's little voice floated up out of the covered bucket. "In between the branches, under them—you know—where the trunk is. Go inside."

Cora got down on her hands and knees and peeked in between the prickly branches. She didn't see anyone, or anything. She placed the bucket on the dirt in front of her and pushed it inside, then crawled in herself. The pine needles rubbed her face and snagged her sweater. There was barely enough room for an adult person to crouch but Cora was small and found that, even kneeling, she fit rather well; concealed from view within the branches of the enormous tree. She lifted the cloth off the pail and Basajaun's little nose came over the top. Then his head. He peered all around their surroundings before he jumped out, and a small cloud of dust puffed over his legs as he hit the ground. Basajaun sniffed the air and slapped one of his big hind feet against the dirt, 'thump'. He moved his head up and down, examining the inside of the canopy, and did the same thing again, but twice in quick succession, 'thump thump'. These were gentler, quieter thumps than the ones Cora had heard Basajaun make in her own room. Cora waited.

A rabbit jumped out of nowhere; or at least what seemed like nowhere. He must have been concealed somehow in the layers of the pine branches. He hopped in front of Basajaun and Cora, on the other side of the tree's massive trunk, and his body shimmied as he shook out his fur. After giving his ears a final flap, he stared at them.

The new rabbit sat staunch like a soldier. His shoulders pressed into the fleshy roll of fur around neck and chest, and pushed it up around his jaw like a ruff. He was larger than Basajaun but mostly Cora thought he seemed more serious.

"Basajaun," the rabbit said.

"Hello Artulyn," Basajaun said.

"You wait," Artulyn said. "I'll bring the Chief."

The rabbit hopped off and Cora turned to Basajaun. She was full of things to say and anxious for him to explain, but Basajaun refused to look at her; he was absolutely still and silent. Cora rocked a little and leaned forward into Basajaun's line of vision, but he didn't budge. Finally Cora turned her own head forward, sitting still. It was then that she realized Basajaun seemed nervous. Without looking she reached her hand to the side and stroked his front paw. Two small strokes, before replacing her hand in her lap.

Artulyn returned, and bowed at the girl and the rabbit waiting. Basajaun bowed back, and so did Cora. Then out of the pine brush came the largest rabbit Cora had ever seen.

Basajaun's father, the rabbit Chief, was big, heavy and square. His skin looked coarse and loose, but it moved over a body of pure muscle, dense and compact. He sat before them in the same manner Artulyn had, but when he did it the effect was not only stoic, it was absolutely stunning. The rabbit was regal and severe and even though there was a ferocity in his manner, Cora could also see that he was old and wise and full of experience. Full of diplomacy, debate, authority, and regret.

Basajaun lowered his head until his chin rested flat against the ground. Cora tried to imitate him even though she had to put her hands down to steady herself, so her face didn't fall into the dirt. She stretched her neck out in order to place her chin against the earth. She tried to keep her eyes downcast, but soon wondered if that seemed disrespectful or odd, so she looked up at the formidable rabbit before her. He spoke.

"You may rise," he said, "but thank you." He looked back and forth at Basajaun and Cora before turning to his son. "This is your human? But this is just a little girl. Where is the man?"

"He wasn't available to me, sir," Basajaun said. "But this is his daughter. They have the same blood."

The rabbit looked Cora up and down. "Forgive me,

dear, I mean no disrespect. You are just not what I was expecting."

"Oh, that's all right—sir," the address felt strange in Cora's mouth. She hoped it didn't sound forced.

"Is it long until you're grown then?" the rabbit asked.

"I'm afraid so," Cora said.

"Well, no matter," the rabbit eased into the low, sitting position Basajaun so often used, with all his paws on the ground and his back rounded up like a puff of bread. He shifted as he moved one front paw on top of the other and Cora noticed just how old he really was. Thinking this, she stared at the rabbit Chief too long and he shook out his ears, flapping them loudly in an effort to stave off that unfamiliar projection of doubt, and the new vulnerability he sensed others perceived in him since his advancing age. "What kinds of things can you do?" he asked gruffly. "What are your skills?"

Cora opened her mouth, and nothing came out. What on earth could she tell him? That she could milk a cow? Pull a dairy cart? The rabbit's hopeful eyes looked into hers, waiting.

"She has empathy," Basajaun said suddenly. "She understands people, and how they think and feel. She draws them in to her. Anyone. Anyone who talks to her long enough will trust her."

"That is useful," the rabbit Chief nodded.

"She can prepare for danger," Basajaun went on. "She moves with ease from neutrality to being ready to fight. She can do it without stopping to question it, without stopping to let fear immobilize her."

"Very good," the old rabbit seemed pleased by that answer.

"She can find things," Basajaun said. "She remembers where places and things are and can find them again, even in the dark. Anywhere she has been, she can imagine again how to get there."

"Good," the rabbit said again. "Those are all good skills. We will be proud to have you on our side. Now, what is your plan against the enemy?"

"Our plan is to kill him," Basajaun said.

Cora whipped her head to the side to look at her rabbit friend. He didn't meet her gaze.

"That is the only recourse," Basajaun's father said. "What is your plan to carry this out?"

"Well, we must do it in such a way that his death will diffuse the threat to us, so that the humans do not just replace this enemy with another. Another who would no doubt carry out our demise with even more zeal due to his predecessor's failure," Basajaun was sitting up straight and stern, just like his father.

"Yes," the Chief nodded.

"However, some of the human's trading funds have gone missing," Basajaun said. "Someone is taking them. If it is the enemy, which I highly presume, all we need is a plan to expose him. Once the humans find out he is stealing the funds, they will have no further use for him."

"And if he isn't?" the Chief said. "If he isn't the one stealing, I mean."

Basajaun hunched and looked at his father out of the corner of his eye. His voice became less sure. "Then we make it seem as though he is?"

The large rabbit sat and stared, and stared, and stared. He looked down, thinking. Basajaun lowered his own head even more, nearly resting his chin against the ground again. He closed his eyes. Cora tilted her head down and closed her eyes, too. She waited for someone to break the silence, and the time seemed to pass terribly slow. Finally, the Chief rabbit spoke.

"Yes," he sighed. "For the enemy is guilty of so much else, it does not matter."

"Just as you say, Father," Basajaun bowed.

"Good work, son," the Chief replied. "Will you and your human friend be available if I need to talk to you again?"

"Oh always, Father. Always."

"Good. Take care. Take great care," the old rabbit turned to leave.

"Father?" Basajaun said.

"Yes?" the rabbit said over his shoulder. He turned to Cora, "Oh yes, thank you too, dear child. Thank you for all and anything that you do."

"Oh yes," Basajaun said, "yes but I also have a question." The Chief turned his body back around to face them. Basajaun stumbled over his words. "The call," he said, "the emergency, has something happened?"

"The north field is wiped out," the old rabbit replied. "Some had moved to the opposing sides but most numbers did not, or were not able." Basajaun was quiet and swallowed hard. For the first time since they'd arrived, the big rabbit stared deeply into his son. "You stay with this girl," he said, and gestured a paw at Cora. "No matter what happens, I want you with her. I want you safe."

Basajaun took a step toward his father. Then another. But then he hesitated, and in that moment the hulking rabbit hurried away. Artulyn glanced back before he followed. The dark pine brush rustled as the two wild rabbits disappeared to the other side, then lay as still as before the animals had come. Their passageway was now imperceptible, no different than any of the branches in the surrounding awning, but Basajaun sat in front of it for a long, long time. And when Cora reached for him, Basajaun leapt sideways away from her, kicking out his back feet and sending a cloud of dirt in her face. She reached again and the rabbit jumped again, snorting this time with a grunting sound. Cora wiped the dust off her face with her arm and crouched down to extend a single hand toward her pet. Basajaun jumped into the bucket. He bowed his head and buried it against the side of the metal, hiding his face under his shoulders, and became just a rounded, brown back and a little pair of flat ears. So Cora picked up the bucket, wrapped her arms around it, and hugged it close. She brought it up to her chest, lowered her face inside, and kissed him. Then she laid the cheesecloth back over the top.

Cora was backing out from under the tree when something grabbed the back waistband of her short-pants and yanked it upward. She instinctively let got of the bucket as she lurched forward, for the force pulling at her waist almost turned her upside down. Her palms dragged against the dirt as she was wrenched away from the pine.

She fell on her hands and knees, and someone grabbed her arm and pulled her to her feet. She gasped as that person threw her up against a tree. It was the Pastor.

"What were you doing under there?" he barked at her.

"Look—Looking for roots," Cora sputtered.

"You idiot child. There are no roots under there!" He looked around. "Where is your father?"

"What?" Cora said. She pulled against his grip but it didn't budge. "Let me go!"

The Pastor grabbed her face, pressing his fingers and thumb between her cheeks and jaw. The heel of his hand leaned against her throat and as it began to bear down, Cora coughed. The Pastor's face moved closer to hers. "Where is he?" he snarled. "I know he put you up to this!"

For the first time, Cora stared into the man's eyes. They were beady, fierce, crazed and glistening. And not only that, they were absolutely cold; like a dark hall that never ended, and led nowhere. Such hatred. Cora had never imagined what it would be like to be hated so much, or to feel such fear at the hand of a man. So frightening. He was the most frightening thing she had ever seen.

"Answer me!" he yelled.

Cora's breath came out in short gasps and she shook, her head trembling no matter how hard she tried to hold it still. She flung her hands against the tree behind her and pretended to struggle some more, but threw open the edges of her sweater as she did so. She reached into her right pocket, and pulled out the knife.

She closed her eyes and thrust the knife forward. She imagined she was plunging it into a block of cheese, and felt the familiar combination of resistance and yielding as the knife sunk in. She cried out as she did it, although she didn't know why. She felt the Pastor's hand release her face and she leapt away from the tree, pulling the knife back out as she did so. It moved smoothly, as though it were coming out of butter. Cora opened her eyes.

The Pastor was staring at her, stunned. He looked down at where the knife had come out from under his ribs, where blood was spreading out and darkening the fabric of his corded coat. He looked back at Cora, and his face flushed with a terrible rage. He reached for her. "You little bitch!"

"Ahh!" Cora yelled again and swiped the small knife from right to left with all her strength. She barely saw it slice open the Pastor's palm as she turned and stumbled in the opposite direction. The momentum of her strike had rotated her small body a half-circle on the grass.

She panted as the Pastor came at her again. He bared his teeth but instead of laying another strike, Cora began to shriek as loud as her voice could carry, screeching, "Let me go! Let me go! Let me go!"

"Shut up!" the Pastor hissed, and ran at Cora's back. He wrapped his arm around her chest, pinning her arms at her sides, and lifted the girl off the ground. Cora kicked her legs in the air and screamed with all her might, and the Pastor clamped his bloody hand over her mouth. The blood tasted like metal, but Cora forced herself to bite down. The Pastor screamed and Cora bent her knees, put the soles of her shoes against the man's thighs, and pushed. The Pastor let go and, arms flailing, Cora fell flat on her face, on the ground. She spit the Pastor's blood into the grass and began screaming again.

"Let me go! Let me go! Let me go!"

"You idiot!" the Pastor gripped his wounded hand with his free one. "I'm not even holding you right now!"

"Let me go!" Cora screamed again. "Let me go! Let me go! Let me go!"

The Pastor cast his eyes over either shoulder. He hunched, and ran at Cora with his bloody hand aimed at her mouth again. "Stop it! Shut up!"

This time Cora ducked and hopped back. "Let me go! Let me go! Let me go!" she yelled.

"You're insane!" the Pastor said. But he started looking around the clearing. He thought he heard the snap of a twig. He flipped his head nervously from side to side. Cora took a deep breath and let out a piercing, wordless scream.

"Ahhhh!"

The Pastor gave Cora a final glare, and ran off in the direction he had come. Cora kept screaming, until she was sure he was gone. Then she stood, panting, wild-eyed and shaking all over. She ran back to the pine and clamored at the sharp branches, yanking them aside with her bare hands. The pail was still lying on its side and she could barely reach the handle. She strained against the tree, the needles pressed into her face, and finally she snapped up the bucket, and dragged it out.

It was empty.

CHAPTER FOUR

HENRY AND THE GRAIN CELLAR

Henry's short, dirty fingernails scraped the windowsill. He could just fit the toe of his boot in the cement grooves between the rounded stones, and create enough leverage to pull himself up. A white-gold light was appearing when he slipped, and the stone ledge raked his fingers as he fell backward onto the overgrown flowerbed.

"Hello? Who's there?" Nellie pushed the window open. She craned her face into the dusk wind and peered up the empty road. She leaned out further, straining to see the cottage front door. "Pastor, sir?" she said, but there was no one there. Nellie gasped and held perfectly still. "Maju?" she whispered.

Henry was shaking out his head from the fall, and brushing the torn up plants off of his wrists and ankles. "Hello," he called, in a hush. "It's me, Henry."

"Who?" Nellie said.

"Henry," he stood and stretched toward the girl.

Nellie glanced down below her window. "Oh, it's you."

"It's me," the boy said. "I wanted to check that you were okay." Nellie didn't reply. "You weren't at the meeting, today."

"No," Nellie said.

Henry grabbed the windowsill again and pulled himself up, until he and the pregnant girl were face to face. "Do you need anything?" he said. "Are you okay?"

Nellie was staring past him, toward the darkening yard. "I was looking for someone," she said. Her eyes moved back to his face but still she seemed to look past him, through him, at him, all at once. "Do you really want to help me?"

"Yes, I do."

The dark circles below the girl's eyes reflected a blue tint onto the shining whites above them. "Can you get me out of here?"

"Yup," Henry reached for her hand, "Come on, you can climb out. I'll help you."

"No. I mean, do you have somewhere I can go? Somewhere you can hide me?"

Henry rubbed his hands against the stone, thinking. "Yes, I do."

"I want you to be sure," Nellie said, "because once I leave here, I can never come back. I'll be relying on you."

"I'm sure," he reached for her hand again.

Suddenly, a door slammed. Nellie threw the curtain back over the open window. "Go!" she whispered, and pulled the window closed.

Henry dropped down until he was hanging at arms'

length, so that when he let go of the sill, his feet plopped noiselessly onto the foliage. Flattening his body against the cool stone, he listened. He could hear footsteps and random grumbling. No, it was cursing. An angry voice sloshed a pan of water. "Come here!" it yelled. Henry heard Nellie's feet trotting over the floorboards. He followed the sound, running alongside her footsteps, and imagined the two of them moving parallel. Together. Henry put his hand out, and wished he could reach through the stone wall, to the girl who was on the other side. Nellie's feet stopped where the voice was the loudest.

But Henry could no longer make out what the voice was saying. He leaned against the side of the cottage, and as he did, a stone shifted next to his cheek. Henry jerked. He examined the stone and noticed that, unlike the other bricks, this one had a thin shadow circling its edge, creating a dark line between the brick and the old, solid mortar. He pressed his fingers against the stone and rubbed back and forth. The stone jiggled. Cramming his calloused fingertips into the mortar seam, Henry took hold of the brick, and pulled. To his amazement, it slid out. He placed the brick next to his knee, and held his breath as he peeked into the small, open recess the stone had left. Reaching inside, he patted all along the bricked sides until he felt the solid, wood foundation that lay behind. He made a fist and pushed against the wood with his knuckles. No way through, no way even to see in. But the agitated voice inside the cottage rang through the wood foundation now that there was one less layer to contain it. Henry put his ear to the hole and listened.

"Treat it!" the Pastor growled over the sound of sloshing water. "No, treat it properly, you witch!" Footsteps darted across the floor. Henry heard the Pastor wincing as sliding and rattling sounds came from the direction of Nellie's room. The footsteps returned.

"That's enough!" the Pastor said. "Leave those buttons! The wound is just there. Ouch!" the man winced again. "And here, after I ordered you to leave your pagan ways behind, still you brought the plants with you. You're a wicked, wicked girl."

If Henry didn't know that Nellie, or someone, was attending to the Pastor, he wouldn't have guessed, for the girl had yet to say a word.

"Well, this is the last time," the Pastor said. "Who knows if there's a doctor in this town, anyway? Now, rewrap my hand for me. And you don't need to stuff any of that devil's moss in there. Just wrap it tight."

There were several moments of silence. Then Henry could hear more shuffling and walking about, doors opening and closing, and a chair being moved across the floor. The Pastor spoke again.

"Aren't you going to ask me what happened?"

There was no response.

"I'm not letting you back outside, if that's what you're getting at," he said. "You're not leaving that room; you can't be trusted."

Silence.

"You are a wicked heathen."

Henry felt his own heart begin to beat fast. Then, the Pastor yelled.

"I want that baby!" There was the sound of a chair being turned over and the man's heavy footsteps rushing across the room. "And I will keep you chained up in a *cellar* until it's born if I have to! I will have that baby!" Henry heard more scuffling, the sound of all four feet moving and jumping around on the cottage floor. He ran around to the front of the house. Raising a hand to knock on the door, he paused. His fingers were touching the knob when a familiar hand gripped him by the arm. Henry jumped.

"Henry, what are you doing, boy?"

Henry looked up at Sam, the head steam thresher operator from the farm, and Henry's superior. The man had freckles like Henry did, but a wide jaw atop a thick, tree-trunk of a neck and a wiry black beard. He was wearing a high-collar shirt with the top button undone, and gray, pinstripe trousers, which was the only outfit he owned outside of his farm clothes. He put a thick cigar between his teeth and grimaced to hold it in place as he looked down at the adolescent boy. It was beginning to rain.

Henry faltered. His voice was quiet. "There's trouble," he pointed at the cottage door, "I want to help."

Sam frowned. "Somebody else got there to help long before you did," he said. "And I'll not have you getting mixed up and making trouble with those people."

"Maybe you could—" Henry began.

"Listen," the man grabbed Henry's arm and dragged him toward the road. "I can find you a better'n than that, and one that ain't all fattened up already."

"No," Henry began to pull away. Sam yanked his arm

and gave the boy a little shake.

"No!" the man barked. "This is none of your business, and you'll not make it your business. What are you thinkin'? She ain't worth it! They all end up like her, every single one of 'em."

Henry looked back at the cottage. His eyes felt tight. He shook his head until the tightness went away.

Cora let go of the bucket as though it had burned her. It dropped onto the grass and rolled to one side, empty. Cora was shaking. She looked up, into the expanse of land that lay before her. "BASAJAUN!" she screamed, and her cry shook the very roots of the trees.

Cora took off running around the clearing, all the time screaming her rabbit's name. Her breath came out in short, labored gasps as she ran from bush to shrub, to grass, to tree, searching under and inside them all. She ran back to the giant pine and shoved her way inside, but in moments could see no one was there. Its emptiness taunted her; so still and untouched Cora could hardly believe what she had taken part in beneath its branches. She grabbed the hair at her temples, and rocked a little bit on her knees.

Cora burst out of the pine and snatched up the bucket. She began to run again, this time away from the grassy patch where she and the Pastor had come to blows only moments earlier. As she ran she saw nothing, and the branches of trees hit her in the face. In one hand she held the tin pail, and in the other she still held the bloody kitchen knife.

"Basajaun! Basajaun!" she cried, "Basajaun!" and then

she just screamed. Standing in an unfamiliar thicket, armed with a short, serrated blade and an empty bucket, Cora realized just how alone she was. Finding a small, wild rabbit in the midst of the entire outdoors was utterly beyond her scope, but it was the only thing that mattered. She needed help. She had no idea where Basajaun's father, the Chief of the rabbits, could be, but she knew she had to find him.

As the objective solidified in Cora's mind, the unfamiliar thicket became more familiar. She turned left and ran. Small slivers of rain began to graze her face, and she could hear the high, melodic 'plink' of the droplets of water hitting the light bucket. It hadn't even occurred to her to put the knife away, and somehow she felt it rooted to her hand, immobilized in her small grip. If anyone had tried to take it from her, she would've cut them. Cora had no real guess as to where to find the rabbit Chief, but the only place she could think to begin was the last place she had seen a rabbit other than Basajaun.

The acrid odor told her she was there. As pungent as it was it grew worse when she moved closer. Cora gagged. The sprinkling in the air had picked up to a full rain, and the cascading drops moved over the dense mass, making little, varying dents in its surface, and giving an eerie motion to the lifeless fur. Cora walked toward the pile. She couldn't help but look, but soon averted her eyes again when she saw nothing to aid her in her search. As she walked around the side of the heap, she put her forearm over her face to shield it from the heat that warmed her skin like a distant, black sun. She coughed and strained to yell a greeting, "I'm looking for the Chief, please!" she called. "He must help me find his son!"

"Cora?" a little voice said.

Cora blinked. She almost thought she'd imagined it. "Basajaun?" she said. She looked toward the back of the pile and saw a little black eye peering at her from the shadows. "Basajaun!"

There, on the ground, was her rabbit. Sandwiched within the heap of bodies, alive in the midst of death, only Basajaun's head and shoulders were visible as he sat hidden from the world of man in a camouflage that no one but Cora would have cared or dared to see past.

"Oh, Basajaun," Cora said. Basajaun laid his chin against the ground. Cora pushed her hands, wrists, and forearms into the carcasses until she felt Basajaun's hindquarters, and pulled him out. Cradling Basajaun in her arms she pressed him up under her chin, hugged him, squeezed him, and collapsed onto herself as she bent her body over him, until all that could be seen was a little girl, curled up in a ball, in front of a pile of dead rabbits.

"I thought you wouldn't want me anymore," Basajaun whispered.

"What? Basajaun," she lifted him up to her face.

"I didn't know what to do," Basajaun's voice shook, "At the first sign of danger, I flee. That is how it has always been. So I ran, I ran like I always did. But I didn't want to. I heard you screaming and I wanted to turn back, but I couldn't; I didn't know how. I couldn't make myself act or be different than what I knew. But this time it hurt. This time it wasn't natural, it was terrible. I couldn't do anything but run. It was making me sick, but I kept running. And your cries grew further and further away, and then I was alone. I had done the wrong thing, and I was all alone. So I came here to be where I belonged, where I deserved, with all the others like me who could do nothing but run and die and rot until they are forgotten because they never did anything that mattered."

"Basajaun, you—you—" Cora hugged the rabbit again. "I never expected," she buried her face in his fur. "I *never* expected."

"I should've done something!" he growled.

"No," Cora said, "You couldn't. That man would've killed you. Killed you! To run was the only thing you could do. It's not your fault, it's just not fair," she stroked Basajaun's back and rocked him back and forth. "You are a rabbit," she felt the animal flinch, and she pulled him out from her a little so she could see his face, "and that is a great, noble, wonderful thing to be. But a rabbit is an animal, and a rabbit is small. You *can't* act like something else. And you can't expect yourself to. You have to run, and you have to make yourself safe, because that is the only thing to do." Basajaun looked at the ground, and Cora leaned closer to him. She spoke quietly into his ear. "Don't ever leave me again. Don't leave me. If you do, I will always come for you, always look for you. No matter what, I will never stop looking."

Both Cora and Basajaun were soaked with rain, and if it weren't for that, Cora would've felt the wetness against her wrists from the tears in the rabbit's shining eyes.

Cora stood, and she and Basajaun looked up at the

night sky. When she knew she couldn't risk staying away from home any longer, she put Basajaun back in the pail, laid her sweater over the top of it, and carried him home.

When she reached the farmlands, Cora could see light glowing from her house. She stopped in the yard, took the knife out of the pocket in her sweater, and rubbed the dirty blade against the wet grass until it looked clean. Then she wet her hand and rubbed it over her face. When she looked at her palm, she saw the dark, dried flecks of the Pastor's blood that had been caked around her mouth. She rubbed her hand in the grass again. Cora put the knife back in her pocket and took a deep breath before she opened the front door. She hoped her father would be anywhere but in the kitchen.

"Cora!" her father ran to the doorway and hugged her tight. He put his hands on her shoulders and studied her at arm's length before pulling her close and squeezing her some more. "Where have you *been*?" he ran and shut the door behind her. "You didn't leave a note, nobody had seen you. What happened?"

Cora stood up straight. "I'm sorry, Daddy. I know I didn't get all the cheese cut and I know I wasn't here to help when you brought the milk up from the barn. But Henry had asked me to go on a picnic. And I'd never done, not with another kid, so I wanted to go."

Cora's father shook his head a little. "What? Are you— who's Henry?"

"The farm hand from across the street. The boy."

"Oh," the man looked at his daughter. Cora gripped the handle of the pail with both hands and held it daintily in front of hr legs. Her white shirt was wet, rumpled and tinted brown with dark splatters and spots of mud. There were deep dirt stains on the knees of her olive green knickerbockers, and her damp hair stood around her head in a halo of wild frizz. The girl's dirty cheeks were flushed and spotty, and her eyes were puffed as though she'd been crying.

"We had such fun," Cora tried to smile, "and he showed me all about how to plant the grain and how to tell flowers from weeds. But it began to rain so we got lost, and the ground was slippery so I fell. I'm sorry that I got my clothes all dirty. But I couldn't help it."

"That's okay," Cora's father was looking deeply into her.

"Henry's so nice," she smiled again, and then all the expression dropped from her face, "but I didn't think I'd be gone so long and I really missed you." Cora set the bucket down, ran to her father, threw her arms around his waist and hugged him as though she'd never let go.

"It's okay, honey," Wayne leaned down and put his arms around his daughter. "But next time let me know before you go off and do something like that. I was really, really worried."

"I will, Dad, I will." Cora hid her face in the man's shirt, so the tears wouldn't come. Finally she let him go, picked up the pail and began to walk toward her room.

"Cora," he said, "what's in the pail?"

"Just some flower clippings and seeds," Cora beamed. "I put my sweater over them so the rain wouldn't wash them away."

72

"Oh. Where's your rabbit?"

"Why, he's in here, Daddy," Cora stopped in the doorway of her bedroom and looked over her shoulder at her father. "He's in his cage."

"Oh. All right, sweetie," the man said. Cora went in her room, and closed the door behind her. Her father sat back down at the kitchen table, and laid his forehead in his hands.

Early the next morning, a knock sounded through the farmhouse door. Cora's father shuffled into the kitchen. The sun was bright when the man opened the door, and he recognized the young farm hand from across the street— wide-eyed, alert, and only two years older than his young daughter.

"Good morning, sir," Henry half-bowed and half-nodded, unsure which, if either, was the appropriate address. "I hope I'm not bothering you too early."

"No, it's all right," Wayne said. "What can I help you with?"

"Well sir, I was wondering if I might talk to Cora."

"Oh, sure. Come on in. Sit down, I'll go wake her."

Henry sat at the table, watching the man disappear into another room. He looked around the kitchen. It was neat and spartan, and looked very obviously to him like a place where a woman hadn't been in a long, long time.

"She'll be right out," Cora's father returned and sat across from the boy. "Cora told me you two had a right fine time yesterday."

Henry crossed one foot over his knee. "Yes sir, we sure

did."

"Ah," the man said, "until you got lost, of course."

"Oh yup," Henry nodded too emphatically. "Yup, we sure were in a pickle there for a while." He smiled.

"So, which one of you found the way back?"

The boy paused. "Cora did, sir. She's got a great sense of direction."

"She does at that," Cora's father said. "Even in the rain."

"Yup."

"And she said that you two even had to run after a sheep that got loose from Cartwright farm."

Henry swallowed. "Yup."

"But that you finally caught it."

"Yes sir," the boy looked past the man toward Cora's bedroom door. "That sheep sure was a mess when we caught it," he paused again, "with the rain and everything."

"Yes," Wayne nodded. "And you two were, too. You should've seen Cora when she got home—well, I suppose you did. She looked like she had been through something terrible," the man looked the young boy in the eye.

"Well—" Henry was drumming his fingers on his leg under the table when Cora's bedroom door opened. Henry smiled and breathed a sigh of relief. "Hey there!" he waved.

"Hi," Cora moved quickly across the hall. "You sure are here early."

"I hoped you two wouldn't mind," Henry said.

Cora turned to her father. "Is it all right if I go outside and talk to Henry for a few minutes before I start work?"

"I guess so," he replied, "but don't be long. And I want you to tell me before you go anywhere."

"Oh, I surely will," Cora kissed her father on the cheek, opened the door for Henry, and ran out after him.

Henry slowed on the path in front of Cora's house. "Keep moving," she ordered, "we have to go somewhere else to talk. Can we go somewhere on your property?"

"Sure."

The two children were stepping onto vast grain fields when Cora spoke. "Did you find her? Did you find Nellie?"

"Yes."

"Is she ok?"

"Yes, that's what I came to talk to you about. We have to—" Henry stopped. "What did you tell your father we did yesterday?"

"Went on a picnic," Cora said. "Why?"

"What else?"

"That we picked some flowers and stuff. Why? What's wrong?"

"Did you tell him something about us getting lost in the rain?"

"Yeah."

"And chasing a sheep?"

"What?" Cora said. "No, I didn't say that. What are you talking about?"

"Your father told me that you and I chased down one of the Cartwright's sheep, that had gotten loose."

"What? I didn't say that," Cora frowned. Henry waited for the rest of her response, but she turned to him and said,

"What about Nellie?"

"Oh," Henry sat down, and Cora sat beside him. "Ok. I went to Pastor Harding's cottage. She was there, in her room. She was ok."

"Did you talk to her?"

"Yes. She asked me to get her out of there, to hide her somewhere."

"Are you going to?" Cora's eyes were wide. "You must do it!"

"Yes, I will. I was going to take her with me right then, but the Pastor came home and she shooed me away. He was in a foul mood or, I guess maybe he's always like that. I don't know. He wanted her to help him, take care of him. You know, I think he was wounded! But he didn't say what happened."

Cora blinked. "Oh."

"But he kept ordering her around, and getting angry at everything."

"He is a terrible, terrible man," Cora scowled.

"And then—" Henry shifted around, and squinted.

"What?" Cora said, "What is it?"

Henry leaned close to her and spoke softly, even though there was no one else around to hear. "He said he wanted the baby. He demanded it."

Cora was quiet.

"Do you know whose baby it is? I mean, did she ever say?"

"Some boy, or man, back in Australia," Cora said. "She calls him 'her beloved'. She thinks he's coming to find her, but I doubt it," Cora paused. "What would the Pastor want with a baby?"

"I don't know," Henry said, "but it wasn't good. It didn't sound good, I mean. He said he was going to keep her a prisoner until the baby came out. I guess so he can have the baby?"

"We must get her out!"

Henry noticed Cora's use of the word 'we'. "Do you want to help me, then?" he asked.

"Yes," Cora nodded. "I can't be seen by the Pastor, though. Not ever."

"Why?"

"Because of what I said at the meeting!" Cora exclaimed. "You said it yourself, that you were surprised he didn't wring my neck!"

"Oh," Henry said, "right."

"Where are you going to hide her?"

"I'll show you."

Henry and Cora walked across the wide, golden-brown field. Cora didn't know much about growing grain, but she thought the field was very beautiful. It took longer to cross than she expected, and she could hear the mechanical puff-wheeze of the steam thresher almost a half-mile away. When they arrived on the other side of the growing area, Henry led Cora to a row of large sheds. He opened one of the dry, spring-bound doors and gestured for Cora to poke her head inside. There were bags and bags of grain, some huge, thick burlap, some thin, woven bags that were smaller. Cora turned in the direction of a 'whirring' sound, and saw a large, metal fan spinning in front of one of the mesh window screens.

"The fan helps dry the grain out," Henry said, "so moisture or mold doesn't grow."

"Oh."

Henry shut the door and walked further back away from the field, away from the massive grain sheds, to some short, box-like rectangles sticking out of the ground. He lifted the top of one. "Look," he said.

Cora peeked inside. Wooden steps led down into the box, down into the ground. It was very dark. "How deep is it?"

Turning and holding the hinged lid open over his head, Henry took a few steps inside. "Come on," he said, "see for yourself." Cora gazed disapprovingly into the dark cellar. "It's safe. I promise," Henry said. Cora placed a foot on the top step and felt it creak under her weight. She followed Henry down, and he closed the door over them.

The cellar was utterly dark and stank like must and mold. Cora heard Henry fumbling with something, heard a clicking of metal against glass. A low light appeared in the darkness, and the oil-lamp sent a soft glow over the side of Henry's freckled face. He smiled.

"These are the old grain cellars," he said. "In the 1800s, early-like, the previous owners of the farm used to store their grain in here. Back when my family bought the farm—some time ago, like seventy years—they tried to use these cellars, first. But the underground is so dank and damp. They lost a ton of the stock just from the mold, and from the buggers that would get inside easier since it was underground. Plus there was no way to keep the grain aerated, and that just made the moisture problems worse.

So once they had their savings up they built all those nice, airy, outdoor grain sheds I just showed you. With the fans and all."

Cora nodded.

"So I can hide Nellie in one of these!" Henry exclaimed, and held his arms out at his sides. "One of these old ones! Nobody goes down here anymore, we just use them to store old equipment parts and things. And there's ten of them. I'll figure out which one is the least used, the least likely for anyone to enter, and no one will ever suspect. Probably the most run-down one would be the best."

"Is it healthy, though?" Cora put her hand in front of her face. "It's so dank, like you said. Will she ever get any air? She's pregnant, you know."

"I thought I could kick the lid out a bit on whichever one she's in. Just some holes in the wood. That will let more air in and a little light too. And if the lid is damaged no one will think to use it for storage when there's plenty cellars left with perfectly good lids to keep out the wind and rain, so no one will go in."

"Will she be warm enough? Protected?" Cora said.

"I'll bring her lots of blankets. I'll do everything I can."

Cora crossed her arms and looked from side to side at the grain cellar's dreary interior. Henry leaned down into her view. "Believe me," he said, "it's better than where she is now. Much, much better."

Henry walked Cora back across the road. "Tonight, then," he said. "I'll meet you here at eleven." Cora nodded, and went back into her house.

"Did you have a nice talk with your friend?" Cora's father said.

"Oh, yes," Cora smiled. "Thanks."

"So, no plans for today?"

"No," Cora looked down at her waist while she tied on her apron. "He just came to say hello, and make sure I was all right after last night and everything."

"Ah," her father said. "He seems like a nice boy."

"Yes, he is."

The man breathed in. "I think it's good for you to have some friends."

"I guess so," Cora kept her head down and adjusted the cutting board on the counter.

"Cora?"

Cora turned to her father. "Yes?"

"Just, be careful."

"I will," Cora smiled. "I know to cut down, not toward myself," she laid a big brick of cheese on the cutting board.

"Yup," the man nodded, put on his straw hat, and walked outside.

Cora worked at a rapid pace. She filled the time with all the chores she'd failed to complete the previous day, and then was disappointed to see that she still had several hours before nightfall. So she went out to the barn and carried up pail after pail of fresh milk, pushed some bales around to reorganize and make more room in the hayloft, shoveled the manure out of the barn, and even washed out some of she and her father's work clothes. She did all this, but as she did it she was thinking too, about her altercation with the Pastor, and how she was going to save the rabbits. She was enmeshed in it now, and finding the bravery she hadn't had the opportunity to use, yet. When her father was winding down for bed, Cora went to her room and laid on her stomach next to Basajaun, as was her nighttime tradition, and watched him eat his hay.

"Who is this 'Henry' person, anyway?" Basajaun said, and the piece of hay in his mouth moved up and down as he spoke. "Can he be trusted?"

Cora put her chin in her hands. "Not in all things, but with this, yes."

"We should be the ones hiding Nellie," Basajaun said. "I don't know if I like another human being involved."

"She asked him," Cora said. "And honestly, I don't know if I have a good place I could hide her. The place Henry showed me is dismal, but at least she'll be hidden. And even if I could manage it somehow, Nellie wouldn't be safe with me, I know it. All hell will break loose when the Pastor discovers she's gone, and anywhere having to do with me will be the first place he will look. No, this is best, for everyone's safety."

"You're not jealous, then?"

"No," Cora glanced sideways at Basajaun and put her hand on Nellie's necklace, feeling its outline under her clothes, "I know I'm special to Nellie."

"Oh," Basajaun picked up another blade of hay off the floor.

"You'll wake me then? At ten-thirty?"

"Yes. I don't particularly like it all, but I understand your point—right now there seems no other way."

"Thank you." Cora moved a scrap of hay around on the

81

floor with her finger. "Basajaun, I wanted to ask you something else, too. About today."

"Yes?"

"When we met with your father, the Chief, why did you tell him those lies about me?"

"Lies?"

"You know, about my special skills and all that."

"Cora, nothing I said about you was a lie."

Basajaun sat on Cora's bed, staring out the window and watching the night world creep past. It was the first time he had stayed up a night in that room without his friend awake by his side, and in that aloneness his thoughts roared and vied for attention among each other—thoughts about his father, life, his own life, and hers, and everything that had happened since the evening Nellie left him so chancedly close to the little girl who slept. It was not usual for a rabbit to have so many thoughts at once. Basajaun shook his head and flapped his ears from side to side, and instead concentrated on the overshadowing dilemma whose outcome would surely affect all he could possibly consider and more: what to do about Pastor Harding. The rabbit's outline was illuminated against the dark sky as he watched the moon rise, and he thought about this dilemma for a long, long time.

CHAPTER FIVE

ARTULYN

Basajaun prodded Cora's cheek with his nose. "It's time," he whispered.

Cora sat up and rubbed her eyes with the heels of her hands. "Ok, I'm awake," she said. Basajaun watched her dress and didn't say a word. Finally, Cora picked him up and lowered him to his cage.

"Be careful," he said.

"I will."

"No, be *really* careful."

"I will," Cora said, "I really will." She tried to smile. She kissed Basajaun, and locked him in his cage. He looked up at her, kneeling over his chicken-wire cage, and for the first time in her presence, he felt very small. Cora let go of the bedskirt and it floated to rest in front of the cage, like a curtain. If Basajaun leaned his cheek against the cage bottom he could see a thin crack of the room, see Cora's feet walking over the floor like he always did, but still it was dark under the bed, and Basajaun was alone.

"I thought it would always be just us, together," he said. But Cora had already left.

Henry stood silhouetted on the gravel road, with his head bent. When Cora got closer, she could see the outline of a long stalk of grain sticking out of the shadow of his mouth. He threw it down when she approached.

"Hey," Henry said.

"Hey."

"You ready?"

"Yeah," Cora said. "Let's go."

The way to Pastor Harding's cottage was flat, wide, and absolutely still. Again Cora was struck by the difference of the world at night. The land before her was familiar, but empty. Expansive, and usually public, but now quiet and private, as though it belonged only to her and the boy.

"The poison," Cora said softly, "that they're using on the rabbits, what do you think it is, or looks like?"

"Dunno," Henry said. "Usually to poison animals, people use a powder, like strychnine, and put it on food, some sort of food that the animal would like to eat."

"Oh."

"I don't do that, though," Henry said. "I mean, I don't want you to think—"

"Oh no," Cora shook her head, "I didn't mean—"

"I think a person should use a gun or a knife. That's an

84

honest kill. Eating animals, it's the way. But I don't think animals should suffer or just be executed in a way that's disrespectful, dishonest."

Cora didn't reply. Neither of them could think of anything else to say. When they arrived at the cottage, the windows were dark. Henry strode in front of Cora to Nellie's window, and Cora watched him climb up and tap on the glass.

"Hello," he said, and tapped again. "Hello?"

Nellie appeared at the window. She pushed it open a crack and motioned toward the front of the house. "Go. Go to the front door. I'll be right there." The girl dropped the curtain back over the window, and Henry turned from his perch to signal Cora. She walked to the side of the house and put a hand up to help him down.

"Do you think it's safe?" he whispered. "Where's the Pastor? Will we wake him?"

"I don't know. I don't think Nellie would put us in danger if we're helping her," Cora said, more for herself than for Henry. "Could he be out?"

"Psst," Nellie was peeking out the front door. The two children approached the dark doorway, and a narrow beam of light came through the crack, diagonally segmenting the walkway. "Come in," Nellie smiled, "it's safe."

Henry moved toward the pregnant teenager's smiling face. She opened the door wider and stepped aside so Henry could pass under her upraised arm, which held the lamp. Cora didn't budge.

"It's perfectly safe," Nellie said again. "I swear."

Cora moved her knees a little back and forth, and

looked past Nellie into the cottage living room. It appeared innocuous enough. She went in, passing under Nellie's arm just like the boy had done.

Cora looked around the living area. The cottage had wood walls that gave its interior a warm glow. Even with a full lamp or two it didn't seem the room would ever really be well lit. It was cozier, Cora thought, than she ever would've expected. But that could've just been the aura she was feeling from the girl.

Nellie motioned for the two children to follow her, and in the next room she lowered the lamp over a bed. The swinging light rocked back and forth and an alternating light and dark fell over the Pastor's sallow face. Cora jumped back.

"It's okay," Nellie leaned closer to her keeper, "you won't wake him."

"What do you mean?" Cora said.

"It's a sleep tonic. Good for the whole night. Look," Nellie snapped her fingers in front of the Pastor's face. "He won't wake. I mixed it into his nightly glass of wine."

Cora looked down at the sleeping man. His lips were closed and his skin was thin, lying across the chiseled, bulbous bones of his face like soft birch bark. It was strange seeing a grown man sleep, doing something so passive and quiet. When she was very little, Cora had only imagined children like herself sleeping, or maybe young women. Even then she had known all people sleep, but she remembered the first time she saw her father sleeping, and how small and vulnerable he looked. Like himself, but also like someone else. Or, like himself, but in a side of himself that she had never before thought was there. And the Pastor now, the man she feared most in the world, lay completely defenseless beneath her and the other two young people; the people he thought he held complete sway and command over, and whom he'd scoff at and mistreat without a second thought. 'Right now, we could do anything we wanted to him,' Cora thought, 'even kill him.'

Cora looked at Nellie. "How did you know we were coming tonight?"

"I figured I'd just do it every night until you came," Nellie shrugged.

"But," Cora said, "I mean, I think it's good that you waited for us, that's really good. And we're glad to come. But, if you could do that—put him to sleep, I mean—why didn't you just run away before?"

"Where would I go?" Nellie said.

Cora looked back at the bed.

Henry hadn't said anything since he'd entered the room, but he leaned over the Pastor now and looked closely at the man's face. His eyes moved over the blankets, and he slowly lifted the edge near the Pastor's hip. Underneath, was the man's wrapped hand.

"What happened to his hand?" Henry said.

"I don't know," Nellie said. "He came home with that last night. There was a deep gash across his palm."

"Was there anything else?"

"A deeper wound in his stomach, that went in. A stab."

"Do you know what happened?"

"I didn't ask."

Cora peered nervously around the room, at what she could see in the low light. The Pastor had a bedside table and on top of it was an empty wine tumbler, a worn, leather-bound copy of the bible, a handkerchief, and a large ring of keys. A few of the keys were old silver or iron, some shiny new brass. Cora laid her palm on the key ring and shifted it. The long, heavy keys clacked together. There were a lot of them.

"What are all these keys for?" Cora said.

"They're old. Most of them belong to things he doesn't have anymore, or that aren't around, or that are far away," Nellie replied.

"Oh." Cora rubbed the keys against the table again.

Nellie walked out of the room, and Henry and Cora followed. In her own room, the pregnant girl opened a squeaky drawer to an old dresser, pulled out a long, cream-colored fabric bag and shoved in the few clothes she owned: a nightgown, another dress like the blue one she wore, another petticoat, an apron and a bonnet. The clothes fell to the bottom of the deep bag and hardly filled it at all, but then Nellie stretched out on the floor, leaning up on an elbow, and reached under the dresser. Cora heard a latch, a light 'thump', and saw the girl pulling something out from under the bottom drawer. Nellie kept her back to them, but Cora and Henry could see the small boxes and bundles of sticks the pregnant girl shoved into the sack.

"Okay, we can go," Nellie put the bag over her shoulder.

"Do you need any help?" Henry reached for it.

"No, it's fine," Nellie said. "It's better if I carry it." As they passed the Pastor's room, Cora glanced at his sleeping form in the bed. "Oh, yes," Nellie said, and pulled the man's bedroom door closed.

Out on the wide road, it was still dark. Cora and Henry were walking fast, but Nellie looked up at the stars.

"Oh my," she said, and turned slowly around and around, as if she were trying to take it all in. "I would have never thought a place like this was so beautiful."

Cora went to the girl's side and looked up, too. How beautiful it was, indeed, she thought. The surrounding nature of her familiar dairy route was so much a day-to-day part of Cora's world, she had taken for granted how breathtaking it really was. The two girls were transfixed by the dark dome of stars, and Henry watched them watch the sky.

Nellie eye's climbed down the curve of the atmosphere, back to the horizon, and surveyed the far-reaching field before them. "Look at all this space," she said, stretching her arms out to her sides. She carefully laid the cotton sack in the grass, and began to run. Her arms still outstretched, her dress swinging back and forth behind her, Nellie ran forward, around, ran great circles on the grass. Cora picked up Nellie's bag, gripping it gently, and began to chase her. Henry just stared. Finally, smiling and breathless, Nellie ran back to where the boy stood.

"Isn't it just wonderful?" she said. "Don't you ever feel like running, sometimes?"

Henry grimaced. "Yup. I guess I do."

Cora scurried to Nellie's side, still holding the bag. "Well thanks," Nellie said, and took the bag from Cora's hands. "That is just great. I probably won't be able to do it again for a while, will I?" she looked at Henry.

"Oh," he nodded and rubbed the back of his neck. "Oh, I get it. No. Sorry."

"It can't be helped," Nellie began walking down the road, but she looked back at them and smiled. "And there's no need for you to be sorry. No need at all."

Cora and Henry watched Nellie's back, and the three of them moved across the moonlit flatlands, to the grain farm.

The rabbit Artulyn woke and turned to face his mate. Lying on her side, the doe shifted a little, dreaming, when Artulyn sat up in the burrow and shook out his body like he always did when he wanted to wake himself quickly. As a soldier promoted months ago to head footman, he now enjoyed one of the best burrows in the warren, so large that he could sit straight up, and his ears didn't even touch the earth above him. As Artulyn began to clean his fur, the female rabbit woke up.

"Wha—what time is it?" Boxy murmured, and lifted herself up on her front paws.

"Nearly six," the male rabbit replied as he twisted his head to one side and cleaned his shoulder.

"Are you asking him today?" Boxy sat up and began grooming her mate's back.

"Yes."

"I wish you'd wait," the young doe said. "You have such a good position, why jeopardize it by alienating the Chief?"

"I'm just going to speak to him about it. Speaking to

someone is not the same as alienating them, Boxy."

"But that's what you'll do. I know you. And if he doesn't react how you want, you'll say something that will make him look down on you. He's not like the other Chiefs, you know that. And bending him to your own intention, especially an intention like you have, is like walking a fence—delicate."

"You think it's too delicate a job for me, I suppose?" Artulyn snarled.

Boxy put her chin on the ground. "I know you, Artulyn. I just wish you'd wait."

"Until when? Until it's too late for me to be considered an option at all?"

"All right, I wish you wouldn't ask him at all. I wish you'd be happy with what you have," the rabbit kept her head down, but spoke sternly.

"Yes, well, you're just too easily impressed. Just because you grew up in a run, you think having your own burrow is the height of luxury," Artulyn growled again.

Boxy sat up, and frowned. "I'm happy with you. Aren't you happy with me?"

"I have to go," Artulyn mumbled.

"I thought you'd be pleased that I'm not like those other does who push and push their mates to get the highest rank, the biggest burrow—"

Artulyn turned back to his mate, and saw how sad she looked. The rabbit nudged her shoulder with the top of his head. "Oh, you know I'm happy with you, little feral Boxy. I sought you, didn't I? Out of all the smooth, well-bred does, I said, 'Who is that one? The one with the big eyes?'"

Boxy smiled.

"And the commander said, 'that is one of the new immigrants, solitary lived. One of the footmen saw her and invited her in. But really, Artulyn, he only did so to pad out our number of available females. She's low-end,'" Boxy flinched a little at this, but Artulyn didn't notice; he went on quoting the commander. "'I mean, many of the civilians would be happy to have her, I'm sure, but with your new position you could likely catch the eye of one from one of the old families. Or, you know, any that you would chose.' But I said to him, 'I want that one. Solitary lived means she is strong, experienced and clever. And that she'll be grateful for company, even if it's only a brash, difficult, war-hand like me."

Boxy leaned her body against her mate's, and rested her chin on his shoulder. "Do what you have to do," she said, "just don't forget the things that matter."

Artulyn hopped out of the burrow. He was aware of how tall and serious he appeared as the rabbits of lesser rank rushed about, lining up to give him the morning's report. It was still dim in the brush and Artulyn looked at the unfamiliar surroundings. Tall shrubs climbed up the sides of the open grass clearing, arcing inward where they touched the skyline. When the sun was directly overhead, it bathed the ground in a golden glow, and as it moved back across the sky, the circle of gold grew smaller and smaller until it was just a pinpoint, and then nothing at all. On a handful of occasions, Artulyn had noticed Boxy laying a front foot atop the circle of light, and holding it there for the few moments where the circumference of the beam matched the size of her paw exactly. She would watch the light lay across her paw and turn it shining gold, then pull her paw away as soon as the light began to shrink and darken around the edges of her fur.

Since the beginning of the onslaught, the rabbit Chief had been organizing new living areas for the whole populous—those who would move. The new headquarters was small and a bit cramped, although as a point of respect the high ranks like Artulyn were still given the option of a larger space, so that their does could dig a larger, more comfortable burrow. This rule of wartime or non-war relocation was an old one, mentioned only in passing when it even came to be considered at all. Over the years it had grown to serve as a mark of martyrdom and camaraderie, an opportunity for those in command to prove their loyalty to the warren by turning away any additional luxuries they might have demanded, and living the same as the rabbit civilians. Artulyn didn't know this. He also didn't know that the rabbit Chief used it not only as a way for the soldiers to show their solidarity with the causes of the warren, but also as a test, to see who might take more when it was offered, and who would turn it away.

"Good morning sir," one of the small footmen stepped out to address Artulyn first. Artulyn nodded at him. "I've come to tell you that the night spy, the dirt-carver, has come out of his silence and rendered a picture of what he saw. Of—the tragedy, sir."

"Then I must bring the Chief immediately," Artulyn said. "Does anyone have more pressing news than this?" he cast an eye down the line of rabbits. They shook their heads. "Then I will get him now. Have you seen it?" he said to the young rabbit who'd made the report.

"No, sir. I thought it best to alert you, first."

"Quite right. Good job. You wait here. I will get the Chief."

The rabbit Chief, Basajaun's father, was silent as Artulyn led him back to the waiting soldiers, where the young footman took the lead. The Chief moved to Artulyn's side as the three rabbits approached the thick oak tree, whose shade kept the grasses from growing beneath its branches. The ring of dirt extended four feet out from the tree, all around its trunk. The rabbit Chief had previously used his claws on this blank, earth canvas, carving out maps and plans, and showing locations to his ranks. Now a mottled, wiry rabbit with wild eyes waited alongside the trunk, sitting behind a large image he had drawn in the dirt.

They wiry rabbit bowed to the Chief and to Artulyn, and watched the old rabbit's eyes move over the lines in the earth. "I'm sorry, sir," he said.

"Oh my God," the rabbit Chief didn't look up, and he stared at the picture for a long, long time. He even thought that he recognized some of his individual subjects in the carving, though many were rendered faceless, a mass, piled on one another, over and over and over.

The wiry rabbit looked back and forth between the Chief and Artulyn. Artulyn shrugged. "I'm sorry, sir, that I didn't finish it sooner," the wiry rabbit said. "When I returned from seeing the tragedy I fell down and couldn't

94

get up again until the next afternoon," he shifted on his haunches. "I wept, sir. I am not a soldier, I am only a carver and storyteller. And in all my stories and imaginings I would never have imagined something like this, even if it had been told to me."

The Chief didn't reply.

The Carver looked at Artulyn again. Artulyn was also quiet.

"I'm so very sorry, sir," the Carver rabbit said again, but still the Chief wouldn't respond. The wiry rabbit looked to Artulyn.

Artulyn leaned closer to the Chief. "Would you like me to have it rubbed over, sir?"

The Chief looked up, his eyes glassy at first before they settled on Artulyn. "No! By no means! No one must touch it," the Chief sat up straight and pointed to the carving with his paw. "Everyone must see it. Every rabbit in our warren, the ones that still live, must see this."

"But we cannot bring them all here, sir," Artulyn said. "Even if we were able, it would arouse suspicion."

"Then you must bring it to them. Carver," the Chief turned to the wiry rabbit, "I am quite sorry to ask this of you, but do you think you could reproduce this several times over? In all the new, subsections of the warren? Artulyn is right, we cannot bring all the civilians marching through here. But you could bring it to them, if you are able. Will it tax you too much?"

"No sir," the Carver said. "I am able, now. It would be an honor."

"Go then," the Chief turned to leave, "go now. Artulyn

will instruct you on safely moving between all the new locales, and how to find them. And perhaps, Artulyn," the rabbit turned to his first-in-command, "you can assign him a guide. Someone to keep him from getting lost, or too tired. Go."

"But," Artulyn glanced at the Chief's back. "Sir, can I talk to you? In private? I must talk to you."

The Chief stopped. "You have something more important than this?"

"Sir, it cannot wait."

"Get him started," the Chief harrumphed toward the Carver. "Get him to his first destination, get him a guide and then come see me."

"Yes sir," Artulyn bowed.

"This better be important, Artulyn," the Chief said as he hopped away.

At the mouth of the Chief's burrow, Artulyn smoothed the white fur at his chest. He was putting his head inside the hole when a voice behind him made him jump.

"You are looking for me, Artulyn?" the Chief rabbit said. He had come up so quietly, Artulyn hadn't even heard him.

"Oh! Yes sir. I'm sorry, I thought you would be in your burrow."

"Too much to do," the old rabbit shambled past him. "Follow me. We can talk." The rabbit Chief led Artulyn to a small cluster of bushes behind his burrow. He pressed himself between them and motioned for Artulyn to do the same, then stood so large and square, with his thick, loose neck rolled out like a scarf, that Artulyn remembered how intimidated he used to feel by the Chief. And still did.

Artulyn cleared his throat. "This plan, sir, do you think it will help?"

The rabbit Chief blinked, and didn't move. "I would not have formulated it otherwise."

"Of course not sir," Artulyn bowed a little. "It's not you I doubt, but the populous. They are so complacent, and so weak. They don't believe the danger, or I dare say they are too thick-headed to know what to do about it."

"Change is difficult," the Chief said, "and large-scope menace is hard to believe. Such is my reasoning for the carvings. Scare tactics are an unkind motivator, but a powerful one. It is not condemnable to scare someone into better action and safety."

"No, of course not. I just worry that it won't help. That they will be too stupid to see the truth."

"That part, I cannot control," the Chief said. "But do not think so ill of your own kind, Artulyn. Complacency can make one soft and slow, but all the capabilities to be otherwise are still there. Have a little faith that when pushed, our rabbits will move with faster motion, and better thought."

"Yes sir," Artulyn bowed again.

The Chief squinted one eye at his head footman. "But I haven't known an experienced soldier like yourself to trouble a Chief with premature worry by calling it urgent. Artulyn, what did you really want to speak to me about?"

Artulyn took a deep breath. "Well sir, with all due respect, I want to talk to you about Basajaun."

"Basajaun?"

"Yes. Well, I must know, what is your intent for his involvement in our cause?"

The Chief peered at the young rabbit. "Were you not with me the day he relayed his own plans?"

"Yes sir, but, the girl. I beg your pardon sir, but he was sent for the man, and all he could get was a very small girl. If he can't even do that, how are we to expect him to carry out anything else? Especially something as direly important as what you expect of him."

"Basajaun is working on the inside," the Chief said. "We need someone on the inside. We need any human consort we can sway, girl or man."

Artulyn leaned forward. "But what is he doing? It's been a day and we've heard nothing of this supposed plan of his to murder the enemy. How is he to do it? I'm sorry sir, my faith—"

"What would you do?" the Chief cut in.

"What?"

"What would you do? You say his plan has not moved forward enough since the meeting. How would you have moved it forward in that time?"

"Well I," Artulyn fumbled, "I didn't mean that. I just mean, perhaps your view of him is clouded. He is your son, it is understandable. I just don't want it to jeopardize—"

"Speak plainly, Artulyn," the rabbit Chief said.

"What is Basajaun doing out there?" Artulyn's fear of his superior fell away. "Nothing! He is cavorting with some human girl, right under the nose of the supposed savior, and he has done nothing for the cause while we wait and worry and die!"

"We are none of us well-informed on how to deal with this," the Chief growled. "Basajaun has been thrown into a completely different world, one that you have no idea about. It is difficult, it is strange, and he is reliant on the human help. That is what it is to be an insider, an infiltrator, on the human side. What he is not able to do, she must. His task is to move her to help, and that is the most difficult task of all."

"Basajaun is a coward!" Artulyn yelled.

"Maybe so, but he is alive," the Chief said, and eased himself down a little, as he always did when he was about to make an address. "All my other children were brave and headstrong, and they are all dead, at the hand of my teaching. I taught them to be brave, vicious, ferocious, because in my younger manhood that was what I thought most important. And even as I watched them die one after the other, I still felt myself justified in preserving their honor and thusly mine. Because how could the Chief of the rabbits spawn cowards? What would rabbits think?

"But as I grew older, I realized I was alone. I didn't like being alone in my legacy, the taste was bitter. I had made my opinion of honor so narrow, no one could fill it. I thought I would prefer to be alone than to be in the company of less-than-brave offspring, but I was wrong. I wanted a child of my own, to live. I wanted a son. Someone who would stay around, and who I could teach in a way I hadn't before. Or, just to talk to. And just—to be. I wanted something of mine to survive when I depart from this world, so I don't just leave behind a smattering of dictation, posturing, and pressured decisions; sometimes well-decided and sometimes not. Honor may be honorable, but permanence, and the ability to continue influencing things that change, is found only in things that live."

"So let him live," Artulyn said. "Keep him if you like but don't hand him over to the most important task of our survival! What is the infiltration? A way to preserve our lives, or a way for you to hide your only child until the danger is over? Well, I tell you, at this rate the danger won't be over until we're all dead. And your precious son will be Chief of nothing, save the idiotic human girl who has bewitched him!"

The Chief leaned forward now, and his voice rumbled. "The task is the task, and there are variables within, and more than one possible outcome."

Artulyn rushed at his Chief. "So you would gamble all our lives for an opportunity to test your runt? You—"

"No!" the old rabbit yelled, and let out a growl that rendered Artulyn deathly silent. "The task is the task, and only one of my blood has any chance to complete it at all. You think the infiltration is easy? Or even attemptable by just *anyone*? You think any rabbit can just hop up to any human and say, 'Please stop slaughtering my kind?' Do you know nothing?" Artulyn flinched and squeezed his head down into his shoulders at the large rabbit's roar. "The opportunity to infiltrate comes once in a lifetime, and it began with mine. The chance was so slim it was no chance at all, but we fell into it, the man and me. I sent Basajaun to the father for he was the infiltration I knew, but I didn't see it clear, I didn't see the full circle. The father to the father, and the child to the child. Basajaun could not reach the father for the father was mine. But the child—my blood in my son and the human man's blood in his daughter—that is the full circle. Basajaun's infiltration to the girl was the only possibility there ever was, and as a possibility it was almost nothing. The fact that it happened at all was a miracle. And what Basajaun decides to do with it, is the task."

"And what if he abandons us?" Artulyn said. "What then?"

"Then, he will live."

Artulyn sneered. "You have grown fanciful in your late years, sir. And reckless. In grooming your successor, you are creating a deserter. So be it. He is no Chief."

The rabbit Chief lunged at the footman, and pushed the younger rabbit's head against the dirt, holding it there with his front paws and the weight of his broad body. "You are out of line, Artulyn," he leaned close to his junior's face. "And remember this: Even if Basajaun is not yet Chief, he will be. And if the immediate is your only concern, remember that *I* am still Chief, here and now, and Basajaun is *my* son. You have given me your opinion, which I respect and will take under consideration, but henceforth I will not hear another word from you spoken against my child. Is that clear?"

Artulyn tried to nod, but large rabbit held his head still. "Yes sir."

"And don't think I didn't notice your other opinions woven into the worries you voiced here. 'Supposed savior.' I am not so old that you can hide disrespectful insults in your veiled complaints."

Artulyn's breathing quickened. "I understand, sir. I am sorry. I was out of line."

The old rabbit was quiet a moment. He still held Artulyn's head against the dirt. He leaned close to it and screamed, "I am still Chief!" and let the younger rabbit go. Artulyn jumped up and held his paws in front of his chest. "And you, Artulyn," the Chief said, "will never be."

Artulyn turned, and ran out of the bushes. He ran and ran. He kept running until he reached his own, big burrow, and flew inside. Boxy was there waiting for him, and watched her mate lay down in their run. She put her body against his side.

"What happened?" she whispered.

"He made a fool of me!" Artulyn cried. "He made me a fool. But *he* is the fool. A superstitious, sentimental, bitter old fool. He will be the death of us!"

"No," Boxy said. "It is the enemy that will be that. The Chief is a good Chief, he cares for all his subjects. But you cannot blame him for loving his son more than he loves you."

"I don't want his love," Artulyn growled, "I want his power."

Boxy laid her chin against her mate's back. "And that is why you will never have either."

The old Chief rabbit came out of the bushes. He looked at the hole to his burrow, and sighed. Then he looked at the sky. He looked at it for a long, long time. Finally, he turned away from the headquarters, and began to hop slowly toward the clearing that led to the road on the outskirts of the town, and the old dairy farm.

CHAPTER SIX

FRIENDS

Cora moved across the golden-brown field. The rising sun made the grain twinkle as it shifted in the breeze. The two pails Cora carried swung next to her calves and she smiled to herself, squinting into the light as she tried to see past the edge of the field, where the box-like squares peeked above the grass.

At the side of the field, a huge man was bending and throwing a pickax into a crunchy flat of dirt, over and over. Cora could see wetness in the center of his back that made his heavy cotton shirt stick to his skin. He turned and Cora shrunk back a little at the size of his arms. They were huge. He threw the point of the pickax down again, grunting and grimacing as he did so. His flat, square teeth clamped together and severed the stalk of grain between them. The man didn't see the flanged sliver of grain fluttering to the ground, but noticed the free half moving loosely around in his mouth. He rubbed his tongue between his teeth and cheek, and spat out the stem. His eyes rested on Cora.

"Oh, hello there," the man said, wiping the back of his hand across his forehead.

"Um, hello," Cora nodded.

"You're that little friend of Henry's, aren't you?" the man smiled. He spit again. His curly black hair was wild and damp with sweat. Cora tried to get a look at his features but all she could really take in was his thick, wiry black beard. He squinted and scratched his broad jaw through the dense hair.

"Yes," Cora said. "He said I could come by today."

"Sure," the man crouched closer to Cora and put his hands on his knees. Cora could see his cheeks and forehead were splattered with freckles from the sun, like Henry's. "You sure are a nice little thing!"

"Oh, thanks," Cora twisted her buckets from side to side.

"Well, you go on now," the man stood. He towered over Cora. "I think Henry is workin' puttin' some things into storage today, over there," he pointed toward the rectangular lids in the distance. "You go find him."

"Oh!" Cora pantomimed looking in the direction the man pointed. "Oh, thanks," she nodded, smiled, bowed a little bit, and hurried away. The man laughed.

"You two have a good time!" he called after her.

The pails rattled and clanked as Cora rushed toward the grass. Her eyes were fixed on the grain shed Henry had showed her the day before, but when she got closer she crossed the edge of the field to the lid that was nearest to her path. It occurred to Cora that if the man were watching her search for the farm boy, it would look suspicious if she somehow knew exactly which cellar to find Henry in. So she hunched and studied the shed in front of her, lifted the lid to peek in, and called Henry's name. Staring into the dark, empty cellar, she counted to five before laying the wooden top back down. She repeated this two more times along the empty cellars on the way to the one where her friends hid. When Cora finally disappeared into the fourth cellar, the big, black-haired man turned back to his work.

"Were you calling me out there?" Henry said.

Cora grabbed the rail, and her feet searched for the next wooden stair. She followed the sound of Henry's voice. "Yup, I—" but she stopped.

Henry sat on an overturned fruit crate. Nellie sat on a stool. On the floor beside the girl lay one of her little, brown slippers. Her stocking foot rested in Henry's lap, and Henry sat, bent forward, with his nose almost touching Nellie's knee. One of the boy's hands was wrapped around the pregnant girl's ankle, and the other cupped the inside of her calf, under her dress.

"My ankles are really swollen," Nellie smiled at Cora. "Henry is rubbing them for me. Isn't that nice of him?"

Cora looked at Nellie, and at her ankle. She looked at Henry, and ran back up the cellar stairs, her pails rattling at her sides.

"Wait," Cora heard Henry's voice coming up out of the ground behind her. She stopped and stared down at her feet, in the bright grass. "Wait," Henry said again. Cora turned around.

"What?"

"You know," Henry thumbed behind him, in the direction of the grain cellar, "I was just helping her out."

"Sure," Cora said.

"There's nothing wrong with that," Henry said.

"Nope," Cora said.

The two children stood silently for a moment, staring at each other. Henry kicked at a dandelion in the grass. "Okay, well," he said, "I thought she, I thought she would, you know," he shrugged. "Since she was already pregnant, I mean. I thought she would, 'cause it wouldn't matter."

Cora's eyes widened and her mouth hung open.

"No!" Henry waved his hands in front of him. "Don't get me wrong, I like her! I think she's nice! I wasn't trying to be a cad or anything!"

Cora laid her buckets down.

"I thought she and I could be friends, too. It would be friendly-like. I only thought if she didn't mind!"

"No!" Cora ran at Henry and shoved him. He stumbled backward. "What's wrong with you? That's bad! That's mean! That's—*bad*!"

Henry stepped toward Cora. "I wouldn't *tell* anyone!"

"She's special," Cora's pointed finger landed in the middle of the boy's chest, jabbing his sternum. "And even if she isn't special to the father of her child, she's special to me. She should be special to *someone*."

"I don't think that she isn't special!" Henry yelled back. "I don't *mean* it like that! You don't understand!"

"Well *why*, then?" Cora put her hands on her hips. "You tell me why."

"Because I've never," Henry said quietly, "and I just think she's really pretty."

Cora scowled.

"I would do whatever she wanted in exchange," Henry said. "I could get her food, whatever. I would be nice to her. I would be her friend."

"Nellie doesn't need a friend," Cora said, "she needs someone to marry. Or a miracle."

"You're wrong," Henry said. "Everybody needs friends."

"Sure, at what cost?"

"I didn't *mean* it like that. I only thought if she didn't mind. I didn't know—"

"Just because she's pregnant doesn't mean she's up for grabs."

Henry bit his lip. "All the other workers, they all talk about it. All the time. I just thought with her, if she didn't mind, with her it could be nice. Nice for both of us. Not like how the men say it is. Not like how the men are with theirs. I don't think I'd want to do that with someone I couldn't be friendly with. But I could picture being friendly with her." Henry's face flushed. "I don't want to be like them. I don't ever want to be like them. You don't know what it's like."

Cora looked up from her folded arms.

"I'm afraid that if I get old I'll be like them," Henry said. "I don't want something to happen to me that makes me like that, or, what if it just happens by itself? What if that's just the natural order of things and I can't stop it?"

"You don't have to be like them, if you don't want to," Cora said.

"I thought if I did it different, I would be different. If it started out different for me, then I could always stay the person I am."

"One thing doesn't make you who you are," Cora said. "It's lots and lots of little things," she turned away.

Henry studied Cora's back. "Don't be mad at me, Cora. I didn't mean any harm."

"It's fine," Cora turned around. She picked up the two pails and handed them to Henry. "Here, give these to Nellie. They're for her." She began to walk away.

"Wait. Where are you going?"

"Home. I have work to do. I was just dropping some food off for Nellie."

"Come back soon, ok?" Henry called after her. Cora walked away, through the empty field.

Cora opened Basajaun's cage. He hopped out onto her bedroom floor and looked at her, waiting for the newest report. But Cora turned her back to him and quietly pulled on the cable-knit sweater.

"Is everything ok?" Basajaun said.

"Yes," Cora reached under the bed and pulled out a gingham cheesecloth—and a pail.

"Are we going somewhere?" Basajaun said.

"Yes. I have a plan."

"Is Nellie coming?"

"Nope."

"Oh," Basajaun said. "Will Henry be helping you,

then?"

"No," Cora unfolded the cheesecloth. "It's just you and me."

"Ok," Basajaun jumped into the pail. Cora laid the cloth over the tin opening, and Basajaun smiled to himself.

Cora's rapid breath huffed in her ears against the silence of the woods. She found that if she walked almost tiptoeing, up on the balls of her feet, it minimized the crunching of the sticks and debris she passed over. The trees were getting thinner, and closer together.

"Are we almost there?" Basajaun's little voice floated up from below. Cora lifted the pail to her face and whispered into the gingham.

"If I'm right, we are." She turned sideways to slide between two slender birch trees. Wrapping her palm around one of the papery trunks, Cora stretched her leg toward the smooth spot of dirt she could see on the other side. But when she laid her foot down, it crinkled against the ground. The girl stopped. She lifted her foot, and she heard the crunch again. And again. Footsteps, in the distance.

"Oh God," Cora breathed. She thrust her body through the trees, and her heart pounded. As her eyes darted over her surroundings, the pail trembled in her hands.

"Cora, is everything ok?"

"You must watch me," Cora whispered. "Follow my lead. Do exactly as I say."

"Yes," Basajaun said.

Cora ran around the back of a fallen tree that lay half-covered by earth. Kneeling down, she braced the heels of her hands against the bark and pushed. It didn't budge. Cora scooped Basajaun up out of the pail, cheesecloth and all, and sat him at her side. She replaced her hands on the tree and looked at him.

"Help me."

Basajaun moved up against the tree trunk and braced his back under its curve. Cora nodded. They pushed, and the tree didn't move. The footsteps rustled, moving closer. Cora turned to Basajaun, and the rabbit saw the fear in her eyes.

"Please," she said.

They pushed again. Basajaun strained with all his strength and the rough tree bark pressed into his skin as the trunk began to move. He watched Cora grimace through her squeezed-shut eyes, and the trunk rolled up onto the flat ground in front of it.

On the underside of the fallen tree, small worms, little grubs and pill bugs flopped and twisted, falling onto the dirt below where panicked insects burrowed back into the ground. Cora grabbed Basajaun and placed him in the concave dirt hollow. She pulled up some dirt, leaves and twigs, and used them to cover him up. Then she raked her hands all over the forest floor until she'd amassed a small pile of debris. Cora made her body as narrow as possible as she lay down in the slim trench, and dragged the dirt, leaves and sticks on top of her. Basajaun, who lay at her head, moved smoothly beneath the leaves as he crawled down her cheek, past her neck, to stretch out at her chest.

The footsteps were loud now, and Cora felt the little

'thumps' in the ground as they approached. She was trying to hold her breath when she gasped.

"Oh no." Cora poked her index finger out of her covering and pushed a single leaf aside. There, lying on its side in plain sight, was the pail.

The thumps reverberated through the tightly packed earth, into Cora's ear. The footsteps were almost upon them. Basajaun whispered so quietly, Cora had to strain to hear. "Now you listen," he said, "don't come out of hiding, no matter what I do. Don't follow me."

"No," Cora grabbed hold of Basajaun's hind leg, "don't you dare."

The footsteps stopped on the other side of the log. Both Cora and Basajaun lay deathly still. Cora felt the tiny worms and insects crawling on her hands and face, and felt Basajaun's ears twitch. The feet walked around the side of the log and the rabbit's body tensed. Through her peephole, Cora saw a big, black shoe roll the tin pail to one side.

Basajaun shot out of the leaf pile. He had broken free from Cora's grasp easily, and a man's voice gasped and stumbled backward.

"No!" Cora bolted up and a shower of dirt and twigs fell around her. The Pastor was running away, his wide, stomping strides banging the ground with each impact. "No!" Cora ran after the man. She could see Basajaun ahead, racing and weaving like a streak. His agility as he darted through the woods was so precise, his body didn't even brush against the trees he raced between.

"Get back here!" the Pastor growled at the rabbit. The

man flew between steps now. A small tree snapped under his weight before a final leap landed him, hunched and reaching, for Basajaun's ears. But by the time the man's grappling hand reached where Basajaun had been, the rabbit was two feet away and the Pastor's fingers swiped the empty air.

"No!" Cora grabbed the man's elbow, and Basajaun disappeared into a cluster of bushes. Cora winced as the Pastor turned to face her.

But it wasn't the Pastor. For a moment Cora didn't recognize the Constable, it had been so long since she'd seen him. No, not so long, but he looked—different. His face was terribly thin.

"Cora," he said. "Oh, I'm sorry, honey. Was that your rabbit?"

Cora panted and stared. She didn't say anything.

"Don't be upset with me. I would've let you have him, I swear." The Constable took his hand out of his coat pocket and flipped open a jackknife splattered with dark, old blood. The man spit on the knife and rubbed it on the ground. "Would've even skinned him for you too." He looked up at Cora and smiled. "Tracking him long, were you?" the man's eyes drifted to the dirt and bugs in Cora's hair.

"Yes," Cora's voice shook. "I—I followed him here. I've never been here before," she feigned looking around at the trees.

The Constable leaned down to glance under the bushes. "Well, fat chance of either of us catching him now. You want me to walk you home?"

"No, I'll just go back the way I came," Cora tried to smile. "I left my cart a ways back."

"Yup, your pail's back there," the Constable pointed.

"Oh! Thanks," Cora turned toward the log. "I'll see you later, sir."

"Cora?"

"Yes?"

"You and Wayne—I mean your father—you two okay? You have enough to eat?"

"We're okay, yes," Cora said.

"Good," the man nodded. He got down on his hands and knees and stuck his head under the branches where Basajaun had disappeared. "Good," he sighed as he stood up, and didn't look at Cora again before he walked away.

Cora walked back to the fallen tree trunk and picked up her pail. She lifted the cheesecloth out of the dirt and shook the bugs off of it, stuffing it into the bucket. She took a deep breath before she turned around. The Constable was gone.

She ran back to the bush where the man had been kneeling. She looked left, looked right, then bent down and whispered into the leaves.

"Basajaun?" she pulled a branch aside. "Basajaun?"

"I'm here."

Cora jumped. She turned and saw the rabbit sitting behind her. "How did you get there?" she looked past him. "And why did you do that? I told you not to."

"It was my decision. It was the best choice."

"No, it was not," Cora said. "You put yourself in danger."

113

"I knew what I was doing. You need to have confidence in me."

"But I told you not to!"

"Just because you're bigger than me doesn't mean you get to tell me what to do!" Basajaun said.

"Your father wants me to protect you, and I mean to!"

"My father doesn't know everything!" Basajaun yelled. "What would you have done if the Pastor had caught you, hm? My father also wants you to take action for us. How would you do that if you are dead?"

"It wasn't the Pastor, anyway!" Cora yelled.

"But you thought it was," Basajaun said.

"Who it was doesn't matter because *you* were still in danger. He was going to eat you!"

"Look at these woods," the rabbit said. "Look at how narrow the passages are between the trees. I can zip through this maze like a fish in water. A grown man can't move among the trees like that, even you can't. Yes, there was danger, but it was not so great as you think. And what good is my risk if you don't stay in hiding, *like I told you to!*"

"I don't want anything to happen to you!" Cora yelled.

"And I don't want anything to happen to you! That's why I did it!" Basajaun yelled back.

The girl and the rabbit were quiet. Cora fiddled with her hands in her lap, waiting for Basajaun to speak.

"Who was that man?" he said finally.

"The Constable," Cora said. "He's like, the Chief of our town."

"But you thought it was Pastor. Do they look alike?"

"No but—and this is the strangest thing—he was wearing the Pastor's coat. I swear he was. Why would he do that?"

"Are they friends?" Basajaun said.

"I suppose. I don't know," Cora said. "Maybe the Pastor gave it to him?"

"Or maybe he wanted someone to think he was the Pastor."

"What?"

"If they saw him from the back, or far away. Maybe he wanted it to appear he was the Pastor."

"But, appear to who? Who was he trying to fool?"

"Not someone in particular," Basajaun said, "but anyone. Anyone who might see him doing whatever it was he came out to do. Because he was somewhere he didn't belong."

Cora stared deeper into the trees. "That's where we're going."

"Should I get back in the bucket?" Basajaun said.

"No. If anyone sees me out here, it's trouble. Having you with me isn't going to make any difference then. Besides, I think you're safer if you can run." Cora carried the bucket, and Basajaun hopped beside her.

Soon they were approaching a dark, wood shack; unpainted but gray and moist from years of continuous weather. A few shingles were loose on the roof, lying angled so they looked the shape of diamonds atop the overlapping squares. The door was old too, but the handle and lock glinted with shiny, new brass.

"I think this is it," Cora said.

"There's a smell," Basajaun stopped in front of the decrepit building. "It's a bad smell. It's danger. It will hurt you."

"Only if you eat it," Cora pressed her face up to one of the cloudy, gray windows. "At least, that's what I think. Bags!" she said, "Woven, cloth bags. I think this is it! We can destroy it! We can do it!"

"What's this?" Basajaun said. "Look, there's another shed, back there."

"Another one?" Cora said. She walked past the windowed shack she'd been peering in to a small, similar building that stood a few feet away. The same dilapidated wood, the same shiny brass padlock. Cora looked in. "There's more bags," she said, "but maybe we—oh no." A third building was visible now, behind the second. The shacks were built in a row, but yards apart. Cora stepped back several feet to survey them all at once, all four of them.

"How many are there?" Basajaun hopped to her side.

"Too many for us to empty on our own. We need help."

"Nellie?" Basajaun said. "And the boy?"

Cora frowned, and crouched to face Basajaun. "No," she said. "The rabbits. Your rabbits."

It was a long climb up the back hill beside the cow pasture. The Chief rabbit breathed slow and steady as he rounded the top of the horizon and saw the house next to the dairy farm. As he passed the wooden fence between the house and the barn, he stopped to peer through. The ax that stood handle up, suspended in mid-air, was rusted along the wedge and spilt up the wood of the handle. The top point of the steel lay buried in its soft, weather beaten platform: an old stump. The grass around the stump was sparse and the air over the yard was crisp and still. The Chief rabbit bumped his nose against a plank in the fence, and moved on.

He crossed the yard to the barn, moving in a zigzag pattern from bush to shrub, from shrub to tall grass. Finally he reached the wide barn door with the 'x'-shaped brace, left open just a crack. The entryway appeared a tall, slim shadow against the gray wood.

The barn was soft and dim. Cobwebs weighted in layers of dust hung in the corners along the awnings. Only one cow stood in the center of the barn, illuminated by a single lamp. And there, on the low stool, sat the man.

The fabric over his back and the taut skin on his arms were all the rabbit could see, but it was exactly as he remembered. The rabbit's feet made no noise on the dry, sawdust floor as he hopped toward the center of the barn. There was a steady 'swoosh, swoosh' sound as streams of milk hit the bottom of the tin bucket. The rabbit stopped next to the man's boot and looked up at him, waiting. The man's concentrated face watched his own hands at work, staring forward but seeing nothing, his thoughts beyond the scene before him to somewhere far away. The rabbit nudged the man's leg with his nose.

"Oh," Wayne said, "Wha—" he turned down toward his feet, and saw an old rabbit looking up at him.

The man breathed in, and didn't move. The barn was quiet now that the 'swoosh, swoosh' of the milk had stopped hitting the pail.

"Hello?" Wayne said. He looked around the barn to be sure he was alone. "Do—do you want something?" he whispered. The rabbit just sat there. The man looked from the door to the rabbit, looked at his own hands, and said, "I can take care of you." He reached down to pick up the rabbit as he had seen Cora do to Basajaun so many times, but the old rabbit kicked and scrambled against the man's grasp. His thick claws scraped Wayne's skin when he used his strong hind legs to launch himself off the man's forearms. The rabbit landed in the sawdust a foot and a half away while Wayne's empty hands grappled in the air. The rabbit hopped back to the barn door but when he reached the cracked opening he paused, and turned to face the man. And at this distance he stared, looking at the man, and allowing the man to look at him.

"Please," the Chief rabbit said, "please help." Then he turned and disappeared through the slender gap in the old, wood door.

Wayne sat, barely breathing, with his upturned hands on his knees. He raced to the barn door, braced his shoulder against it and shoved it open, and ran out onto the grass. The canopy of the sky was high and bright as he spun around, running from shrub to bush, from bush to fence, and down the wide aisle between the fence and the farmhouse. The rabbit was gone. The man hadn't heard the rabbit's words, but still tears streamed down his face.

CHAPTER SEVEN

POISON

Cora crawled on her hands and knees through a low, dense tunnel of bushes. She could see Basajaun's white tail bobbing ahead of her, but it was shrinking fast.

"Wait!" Cora called. "Don't lose me!" The rabbit's tail disappeared around a tight left bend. Cora scrambled along like an infant, her knees banging against the tightly-packed dirt as she tried to pick up speed. "Basajaun!"

The rabbit sat at the end of the branchy tunnel twenty feet away, and watched Cora struggle to reach him. Finally she sat, winded, next to him, and rubbed her raw palms together.

"You wait here," Basajaun said.

"What?"

"You wait here."

"You mean, this is it?" Cora said.

"No, through there," Basajaun nodded behind him. "But don't let yourself be seen until I come for you. Stay here. I'll be back."

"Ok."

Basajaun slipped through the center of the plants. Cora tapped her fingers on her knees and waited. She listened carefully, but could hear no noise through the dark undergrowth. Cora leaned forward, and worked her hand between the winding branches. By spreading her fingers apart, she created a small peephole, just big enough to see through.

The golden sun laid a blanketed haze over the wide, round clearing. Blades of tall grass shimmered between blonde and green in the light, reflecting their color into the tree trunks encasing the small valley. All those trees—tall and squat, slender and bunchy—turned a slight bluish hue where their tops touched the light sky, and all were so dense Cora couldn't see past them to what lay beyond.

Over fifty rabbits moved about in the clearing. Cora had to press her face into the branches to see them all. Some sat quietly eating, some leaned close to one another in groups of two or more, and others sat tall and still in a way that seemed, to Cora, like standing guard. Cora blinked in wonder. She felt strange, both guilty and privileged to be audience to the private world before her eyes. She took a slow breath, realizing that she hadn't inhaled for several moments. She thought she felt a prickling in her eyes, but she blinked it away.

Two rabbits hopped out of a cluster of bushes. They moved in circles around each other, raising and lowering their heads. Finally they stopped this and moved close together. They stayed that way for several minutes. When one of the rabbits began hopping across the grass, the other began moving quickly among the large group, addressing them and appearing to nudge and place them around the clearing. Cora could see the first rabbit coming her way. It was Basajaun.

Cora jumped back from her peephole and sat in the dirt. She crossed her legs. She picked at a spot on her hand and pretended to be quite intent on rubbing it and looking at it.

"Okay," Basajaun emerged through the bushes, breathless. "I think it's all pretty much ready."

"What did you tell them?" Cora said.

"Just the basics of why you're here. And that you're a friend. Right now, you are to make your entrance and receive the troops. Then I will talk to you about the address."

"Address?"

"Yes. How did you think you were going to rally all the rabbits to your side?" Basajaun said. Cora stared into the winding twist of leaves. Basajaun bumped his nose against her leg. "Come on now, this is the easy part. You go first, and I'll follow." Cora ran her hand over Basajaun's back, pushed her way through the branches, and stepped onto the warm, green-blonde clearing.

Two rows of rabbits, extending yards back into the grass, stared up at the girl with round, dark eyes. The clearing had looked so vast when Cora spied on it through the bushes, but now as she stepped onto the lush grass she saw how small it was for a human girl. She towered over the rows of rabbits on either side of her ankles, and they lowered their chins to the ground and their eyes as well, blinking for a moment before they looked back up at her. Two rabbits a few feet ahead, one across from the other, hopped into the center of the aisle, and down the path to Cora's feet. One carried a large clover in its mouth, and that rabbit stood on its hind legs, nose up, to offer this to Cora. Cora reached down and took the little plant.

"Thank you," Cora said.

"We wish to welcome you," the other rabbit said, "and thank you for coming to our aid."

"Oh, you're welcome," Cora said. "Um, thank you for having me."

The rabbit who'd spoken bowed and moved to the right. The other rabbit blinked at Cora for a minute before hopping back to the other side. Cora fingered the clover in her hands.

"Walk, now," Basajaun whispered behind her. He hopped next to Cora as she hurried down the center of the aisle of rabbits. "Not so fast," Basajaun whispered. "Take your time. Don't look at them, keep your eyes ahead, on that big willow, just there. Watch it. But approach it slowly. When you arrive, sit under it."

Cora slowed her stride to what felt like a crawl. Even concentrating she could only lessen her pace so much, so she counted to two between each step. She could feel the stares of every rabbit in the clearing, but fixed her gaze on the willow. It was beautiful. It grew larger with each step Cora took, and from the lush mass of its foliage, Cora began to see the outlines of the tree's small, slender leaves. They were pale, almost white on the tops facing the sky, and dark green on the undersides where the stems connected to the tree's green-brown branches. Like Cora's wavy mass of dark hair, these soft branches grew up and out, finally arcing toward the earth where schools of tiny leaves weighted down the branches' narrow tips. Cora used a hand to pull aside a curtain of leaves, and sat beneath the umbrella of the weeping willow.

"The human must arrange her thoughts before the address," Basajaun announced to the field of rabbits. Cora noticed how deep and clear his voice sounded. "Group by the west bushes and wait." The rabbits began to shuffle away from the center of the clearing. Basajaun ducked under the willow tree's branches and hopped close to Cora. "It's all set now. You will stand before them at the west bushes," Basajaun nodded to his left and Cora peeked through the leaves, "and make your address."

Cora saw the throng of rabbits from the side as they made their way across the grass. One by one they began to sit before the squat, dense shrubs Cora had seen from her far-away peephole back up the slope. And they stared ahead, patient, poised, and completely unquestioning.

"What am I to say?" Cora said against the willow's leaves.

"Tell them what you found. Tell them what you need. Be honest, and direct."

"Ok."

"Just explain it to them like you would to me."

Cora smoothed the front of her shirt. "I'm nervous. Maybe you should do it."

"No," Basajaun said, "you're a human. You're foreboding, and big. They'll listen to you."

"But you're the Chief's son, they have reason to listen to you."

"Yes, I am the Chief's son. And I was not well thought of at the time of my departure."

"Oh."

"Besides, you're a novelty. A word from you inspires change."

"A novelty?" Cora said. She put one hand on the ground and pulled aside the willow branch that separated her from the warren of rabbits. "Will your father be listening to the address?"

"No."

A sea of rabbit faces turned when Cora stepped out from under the tree. They watched her walk to the head of the group, and turn to face them. Cora noticed how they all resembled Basajaun, yet they all looked different. And they sat in silent, regal respect as though, Cora thought, they believed she were some great soldier, leader or wise woman. Then she realized that, likely, none of these rabbits had ever interacted with a human, and thus had no frame of reference for the seniority of age in people, of adults over children. For the rabbits looked at Cora now in expectation of her wisdom and plan of action, like children watching a parent whom they thought had the answers to everything. Cora only hoped she didn't disappoint them.

"Uh, hello," Cora said. "I want to thank you for gathering to listen to me today. I know that it's, well, probably never been done before. I know how strange it is to have a human here with you on your territory, and I want to thank you for putting your trust in me. I know that almost all humans are your enemy, but I want you to know that I am your friend. And I am on your side." Cora waited for a response, but the rabbits were quiet. "There's a bad man who's trying to kill you all. You probably know that. What he has is some poison," Cora paused. "Do you know what poison is?"

The rabbits were still quiet.

"It's a powder, or dust, and the bad man puts it on food that he knows you will eat, so when you eat that food, it kills you."

The rabbits gasped. Cora could hear the low sound of them whispering to each other. One rabbit put a paw up.

"We knew, or thought, it was something like that," the rabbit said. "In the north field, there were suddenly some roots there that were never there before. And they weren't growing there, they were just lying on the grass. Some of us thought a crop cart had spilled. Others thought it was a blessing. But when the rabbits ate them, they fell down and began shaking. Hundreds of them, shaking faster and faster until you could hardly tell who was who. They were all distorted. The roots and the rabbits' insides came back out through their mouths, and then—" the rabbit sitting next to the one who spoke gave the speaker a little nip, and looked at him very crossly. Half the rabbits in the room were gaping at the rabbit who spoke with stark horror.

"What I mean is," the rabbit began again, "what are we to do if we can't eat food?"

"That's the thing," Cora said. "What we must do is destroy the poison. Get rid of it. If the bad man has no poison to put on your food, then the food won't be a danger to eat."

"And then we'll be safe?" a rabbit asked.

"For a time," Cora said. "I'm sorry, but it will probably not mean that you'll be safe forever. You may only be safe for a little while. You see, the bad man might get more poison, or he might find another way to hurt you. I'm sorry."

"What happens if we destroy the poison, like you said?" a rabbit asked.

"You will be safe for a while, I don't know how long. But you will be able to eat without worrying, and during that time, no one will die. And during that time, I will try to think of a way to make you safe, permanently."

A new rabbit's voice piped up from the back of the crowd. "What happened to Basajaun's plan of killing 'the bad man'?"

Cora scanned the rabbits. "What?" She felt a sickness in the pit of her stomach.

"The last I heard, Basajaun had a plan to kill the enemy."

"That plan," Cora said, "is still in question."

"It was in question days ago, if I remember," the rabbit began moving to the front. Cora recognized him as soldier rabbit who had accompanied the Chief the day she met him under the big pine. "Surely you've had time to question it at great length. What have you been doing? Or, rather, what has *Basajaun* been doing?"

Cora's mouth hung open. She blinked, pressed her lips tight together, and took a deep breath through her nose. "He's just been saving my life, that's all," she said. "Do you know how hard it is for a rabbit to save the life of a human? How rare?" Cora could see she'd piqued the crowd's interest, and she leaned forward with open hands to address them.

"When Basajaun and I were searching for where the poison was kept, we suddenly found ourselves in great danger. The bad man, the very man who's trying to kill you all, was coming our way! I tried to roll up a fallen tree trunk for us to hide behind, but even though I am big, I was not strong enough. Without Basajaun's strength, I never would've been able to move it. He pushed and pushed until we rolled it up out of the earth. We laid in the ground behind the tree trunk and covered ourselves with leaves, but I didn't hide us well enough. Just as the evil man was about to pull the leaves aside and expose my hiding place, Basajaun jumped out of hiding and went running through the woods like a streak! Zigzagging this way and that to distract the man and get his attention, and it worked! The man forgot all about looking for me in the leaf pile and took off after Basajaun. But now Basajaun was in real danger because that man wants him dead! Wants him dead so much he's letting all the trees and branches hit him in the face while he chases him. Basajaun is running for his life. And just as the man reaches down to grab Basajaun's ears, Basajaun shoots under a bush, and disappears! If that man had found me, he would have surely killed me, but he hates rabbits more. Much more. Basajaun was in real, terrible danger, and he put himself in it to save my life."

The crowd of rabbits stared at Cora, agog, then exploded into noisy approval. They were talking excitedly to one another when Artulyn pushed his way to the head of the clearing, where Cora stood. He hopped right up to her face, which was strange for Cora, for she'd never been that close to any rabbit other than Basajaun.

"That's all very sweet," Artulyn said, "but what about us? Why is Basajaun risking life and limb for you when hundreds of his kind die? You'll pardon me, miss, but you are just a human. And a young one, at that."

The crowd of rabbits fell silent and all eyes were on Cora. She bit her lip.

"There was nothing Basajaun could do to save those rabbits, as I think you know. Because if there were, why didn't you do it?" Cora said to the rabbit. "And, as for me, my life is precious to you, only because you need me. Why do you think Basajaun brought me here? To help your cause. That is the same reason he kept me alive. Your kinsfolk are floundering, and you need the help of a human. How can I help you if I am dead?"

"Where is the great Basajaun now? Why isn't he telling us this himself?"

"Because he is too modest to sing his own praises. Great rabbits never do. They don't need to, because their good actions speak for them."

The crowd of rabbits seemed particularly struck by this, and they were quiet. And Artulyn, for the first time, seemed at a loss of anything to say. A soft, female voice came up from the middle of the crowd.

"How do we destroy the poison?"

"That is where I need your help," Cora said. "Here is what we need to do."

Cora led a hundred rabbits through the dark woods. They moved more easily than she did between the close trees, and Cora put her hands in front of her to keep the thin, sharp branches that she couldn't see from hitting her in the face. The girl and the mass of rabbits made a rustling noise fifteen feet around that moved through the night like a wide, low animal. When they reached the first shed, Cora stopped in front of it to let her eyes adjust to the dark. But the moon was still low and one shadow looked very much like another in the dark woods before her. She turned and all she could see was the glint of two hundred little eyes looking at her.

"Ok," Cora began. "You all can see in the dark better than I can, so I am counting on your eyes to help me when mine aren't good enough. So if I have a question about something I can't see, I will ask whoever's closest to help me. Okay?"

"Yes," the rabbits replied.

"Now there are four sheds, all with poison. At least, I think. You must separate into—" she scanned pack of animals, "three groups. Now, who are the strongest rabbits?" First, no one moved. Then, one rabbit raised a paw. Then another. Soon over a third of the rabbits had a paw in the air. Cora separated these rabbits into groups of three. "There, now each group has some strong rabbits. Everyone else pick a group." Some of the rabbits hopped quickly to the group of their choice, but others shifted back and forth or just sat there. Cora walked into the soft, furry crowd and nudged rabbits this way and that until they had three reasonably sized groupings.

"Each group will work on one of the three sheds, and Basajaun and I will work on the fourth. When the first group finishes, could you come to the fourth shed and help Basajaun and I with whatever we haven't finished?" The first group, the largest, nodded.

Cora motioned for all the rabbits to follow her to the first shed. She grabbed the shiny padlock and rattled it. Then she pulled. The lock was steadfast, but Cora could hear the crackling of the old wood as it began to splinter. She leaned closer to the lock and saw a dark shadow forming between the flat metal base and the gray wood. She pulled some more, and the shadow became a space as the metal bent forward. Cora put a foot against the side of the shack, yanked the lock, and the door flew open, and Cora fell backwards onto the ground. The open door banged against the shed's outer wall while the brass padlock, still locked, swayed back and forth on its hinge.

Cora ran a hand over the light, broken wood where the lock's back had pulled away. Once inside the shed, she smelled the odor Basajaun had noticed when they'd been there in the morning—acrid and sweet. Cora turned to the rabbits.

"Now, I don't want you to be afraid, but this is death," she pointed to one of the cloth bags. "If you get any of it in your mouth, even the smallest amount, it will kill you. And if you touch it with your paws, and then you lick your paws, it will kill you. This is so important. After you touch the bags or anything in any of these sheds, *do not* lick your paws or try to clean any part of your body or fur until I say it's okay. Don't try to clean each other either. Don't do it

130

until *I* say it's okay. Do you understand?"

The rabbits nodded.

"I don't want any of you to die." Cora walked into the shed. "Now, let's see how to do this." She regretted not having the foresight to bring some tools, or a lamp, or anything along with her that night. She had avoided going home at all because despite her agility in timing her excursions with her father's work schedule, she didn't know how long she could keep slipping in and out of the house without telling him anything about where she was going. The rabbits watched Cora rummage around the shed. She had half-planned that the rabbits would use their mouths to grab the edges of the bags and drag them out into the woods, but she couldn't imagine even the outsides of the bags not having some residual poison. No, whatever method she instructed the rabbits to use, she had to be sure it was safe.

"Wait a minute!" Cora grabbed one of the bags and laid it flat, turning it clockwise until the tied opening faced the shed door. She pulled the cheese knife, which she'd taken to carrying at all times, out of her pocket. Cora made a slit in the bag's loose top, above the gathered tie, and spread it out like a fan. "How many of you do you think it would take to pull this?"

"Twelve. Maybe ten?" one of the strong rabbits said.

Cora tapped her finger along the flanged top of the bag, counting, then did the same thing along the bag's stuffed bottom. "Do you think you could do it with nine if four of you pull and five push?"

"We can try," the same rabbit said.

Cora used her knife to make eight small holes across the bag's flat top. "Who are four of the strong rabbits from the first group?" she said. Four rabbits hopped forward. Cora ushered them near. "I'm going to put your back legs through these holes in the mesh. Is that okay?" The rabbits nodded, but none of them had ever been touched by human hands, and doing so went against everything they had learned through survival and instinct. They wanted to hold still, and they tried to stay composed, but they couldn't help it—they twitched and flinched when Cora reached for their legs. Two of them kicked her. Cora was used to the jumpiness of Basajaun, but hadn't thought about how much stronger the strong rabbits were. Their hind legs could really do some damage, if they'd wanted. Cora began cooing at them in a soft voice and stroking their fur. She could feel the rigid muscles on the rabbits' backs, tense and ready to spring, but finally the rabbits stopped kicking long enough for Cora to slip their legs into the holes she'd made.

Cora waved five more rabbits to her, and laid her hands on the butt of the full bag. "Now, I don't care how you push it—use your side, your paws, turn around and move backwards pushing it with your bottom if you like. But don't ever, ever let it touch your face or mouth. Can you do that?" The rabbits positioned themselves against the bag of powdered poison. "All right," Cora said. "On the count of three. One, two—three!"

The rabbits began. Cora was surprised by how formidable they were—grunting and straining, eyes squeezed shut, feet sliding on the dry dirt. They looked like a team of horses hitched up to the big bag between them. In moments they settled into the rhythm of one other, and began pushing and pulling in unison. And slowly, the bag began to move. Cora squeezed her hands together hopefully.

For almost two hours, Cora moved back and forth between the three shacks, harnessing the rabbits to the bags, directing them where to take the poison. She assigned each group one lookout rabbit to keep watch, and one to move between the sheds to keep the entire crowd in communication. When all the bags were prepared for relocation and all the rabbits were working in unison, Cora and Basajaun went to the fourth shack at the end of the row to begin their work.

"You're not as strong as thirty rabbits, you know," Basajaun said and bumped his friend, good-naturedly.

"I know, but we'll have the help of the first group soon enough," Cora said. The moon climbed slowly up the sky, and Cora could see this final shed better than the rest. She noticed that although the glass in the windows was intact, there were boards on the inside, making it impossible for her to see in. "That's strange," Cora said. Then she saw that unlike the shiny, new brass locks on the first three sheds, the lock on this one was old. Very old. Silver tarnished with rusty blocks of pink and orange, and completely flat like a sheet of thick paper. It was oblong and edged in an uneven, embellished cut, but that rough scalloping was the only detail that appeared on the lock, save the narrow keyhole.

"This one is different," Cora touched the lock. The

metal was prickly and rough.

"Must be the original lock for the building," Basajaun said. "Well, it's old. It should be even easier to break."

Cora wrapped her fingernails over the edges of the lock and pulled, but it didn't move. "It's so flat, I can't get a grip," she said, and pulled her knife out of her sweater pocket. Jamming the tip of the knife under the metal she wrenched it forward, but the lock didn't give at all.

"Try again," Basajaun said.

Cora pressed her knife long-ways between the lock and the wood, holding it by the handle and the end of the blade, and pulled. The blade cracked in half. Cora huffed and kicked the door, and still it didn't move. It didn't even rattle. She scrutinized the lock again. "It's old, but it's not the original lock for the building. Look," she ran her fingertip around the base, "the original lock was shorter and wider. You can see the shape of it still, where the wood is lighter in color," she pointed. "This lock is old, but it hasn't been on the shed very long."

"What do you think is in there?" Basajaun said.

"More poison," Cora said. "You know, this lock looks really, really old—"

"What if," Basajaun paused, "it's the stolen money."

"What?"

"This could be the Pastor's secret place to hide the stolen money. That would explain why the windows are covered here, but nowhere else. That man, that man who chased me—"

"The Constable?"

"Yes, maybe *this* is what he was looking for," Basajaun

pointed a paw at the shack. "He wouldn't be out here looking for poison; he was trying to hunt me, eat me! Maybe he was trying to get in *here*. Maybe *that's* why he was in disguise as Pastor." The rabbit began hopping excitedly around the sides of the building. "If this is someplace everyone knows only the Pastor has secret access to, all we have to do is show them the stolen money is inside. That will prove his guilt! Everyone will see! Cora, we *have* to get inside there! Open it! Open it now!"

Cora pulled on the edges of the door and kicked at it again. She ran around the side of the shed, grabbed a rock, and hurled it at the window. The rock bounced off without making even a scratch. Cora blinked. She picked up the rock, and threw it again. It rolled back onto the ground and the window stood, unscathed. Cora walked back to the front of the shed, where Basajaun was digging furiously at the earth next to the door. He stopped.

"Look!" he exclaimed. "It won't—it doesn't— I can't—" he began digging again, and Cora saw a dust cloud of dirt flying over the rabbit's legs, and nothing else. It was the same dirt Basajaun had already turned up, the same dirt over and over. And on the flat ground where there should've been a hole a foot deep, there were only a few claw marks.

"There's something strange here," Basajaun grazed his paw over the dirt, "something I can't explain."

Cora shrugged. "Maybe, it's a spell?"

"A spell?" Basajaun laughed. "Don't be daft, that's not possible. The—" he stopped, because he saw Cora feeling the outline of the brown stone hanging under her shirt.

135

Cora crouched down, and looked into the keyhole. "You know, usually if there's no padlock, there's a knob. This lock doesn't have either. How do you think it opens?"

"With a key."

"I know, but—" Cora pressed the tip of her pinky against the keyhole, and felt the outline of the keyhole-shaped notch cut into the wood, behind the flat piece of metal. "Why do you think this is so hard to open?"

"That man, that Constable, is he as smart as you?" Basajaun said.

"What do you mean?"

"At finding places, getting into things. Is he as smart as you?"

"He's an adult. Of course he's smarter," Cora said.

"And stronger?"

"Yes. He's much bigger. What are you talking about?"

Basajaun put an ear up to the shed door. "He couldn't get in here either. I'll bet he tried as hard as we have. If he can't, and you can't, there isn't a way in without the key. We need the key."

Suddenly, Cora began to notice a chattering of voices. She didn't know how long the sound had been carrying up the hill, but she paused to listen. "What's that?"

Basajaun's ears shot up. He began hopping toward the sound and Cora followed. Coming toward them with a happy bounce was the go-between from the second shed. He began calling to them.

"Haanlea Found food! Roots, and a whole little pile of plants! Come see!"

"Food?" Cora said. She ran after the rabbit. When she

got closer she could see all the rabbits filing in to the second shed. She pushed her way past them to get inside.

"It's really quite good," the large rabbit said to the group of rabbits in front of him, and went back to munching the thick root he'd rolled into the middle of the floor.

"No!" Cora screamed and kicked the carrot toward the other side of the shed. It bounced off the wall and hit the floor in front on the vegetable pile under the old sawhorse. It rolled back toward the group. "What are you doing? You can't eat anything in here! You can't! It's—" Cora stopped herself.

The rabbit laid his ears back. "What do you think you're doing?" he leapt forward and grunted at Cora, then his eyes grew huge.

"No," Cora said. "You mustn't eat anything you find here! Not anything!" she began to cry.

All four of the rabbit's legs stiffened and buckled. His body hit the floor. Mouth open, eyes bulging until Cora could see the whites under his lids, the rabbit began shaking. A stream of white fluid drained out of his mouth.

"Oh no, it's happening again!" one of the rabbits yelled.

"Do something! Can't you help him?" another screamed at her.

Sobbing, Cora picked up the rabbit's convulsing body. Using her arms to try and hold him still, she hugged the rabbit close, cradled his body into hers, and closed her eyes until she felt him stop thrashing. "I'm sorry," she cried.

"This is all of them," one of the rabbits patted a taut, overstuffed sack. Cora stood quietly and stared at the bundled sweater in her arms.

"Ok," Cora didn't look up. "You all can go now. I will dispose of them."

The rabbits waited, and watched her. They didn't reply, and they didn't move.

"Thank you all so, so much," Cora murmured into her arms. "I couldn't have done it without you. You are all very strong."

"What now?" another of the rabbits said.

"What?" Cora said.

"Where are you bringing them now? How are you getting rid of them?"

Cora looked up to see all the rabbits sitting around the pile of mesh bags, watching her. "I'm taking them out of the woods, through there," she tipped her head toward a path in the trees where the low brush was already trampled to the ground.

"We can help you," the rabbit said.

"No, I can do this myself," Cora replied. "You all have done more than enough already."

"We want to help. We want to help more," the rabbit said. The animals around him all nodded.

Cora laid the wrapped body next to her on the ground, and crouched down to face the rabbits. "The place I am disposing of them, it is not a nice place to go. It—it is not somewhere you want to see."

"We know what it is," a rabbit from the back of the group said and moved forward. "We have heard."

Cora frowned. "Hearing and seeing are not the same thing. It is not somewhere I want you to see."

"You are doing this for us, for all of us," the first rabbit gestured at his sides. "You can't decide when or how much we help now. This is for us."

"If you see it, afterward, you won't be the same," Cora said.

"Then it is right for us not to be the same," the rabbit said.

Cora sighed and turned to Basajaun, who had been silent at her side. He nodded. Cora picked her rolled sweater back up and led the mass of rabbits through the brush to another mass. By the time she and the rabbits had finished emptying the bags of poison deep into the center of the decaying carcasses, it was almost light.

CHAPTER EIGHT

BOXY

Cora woke under the big willow tree. The bright morning set her mind sorting through her usual roster of farm chores, until she opened her eyes and remembered where she was, and what she had done the night before. Through the leaves she could make out the backs of two rabbits sitting erect, at her head and feet.

"She's waking up." A rabbit face appeared close to Cora's. "Good morning your Majesty, did you sleep well?" he said. Cora struggled to focus.

"Yes, thank you," Cora propped herself up on an elbow and rubbed her eyes with the back of her hand. "But don't call me your Majesty, please. Just call me Cora."

"Very well, Cora," the rabbit smiled. "Can I get you anything?"

"Where's Basajaun?" Cora sat and folded her legs.

"He's in a meeting, miss. But I will fetch him for you as soon as he's available."

Cora parted the dangling branches peered between them. "Is it all right if I get up and look around?"

"Yes, of course," the guard rabbit hopped to one side. "Please do. If you need anything, don't hesitate to ask one of the guards."

"Thank you." The willow branches brushed Cora's arms as she stepped into the clearing. The bright sun warmed her almost instantly, and she squinted into the sky. Fewer rabbits dotted the grassy expanse today compared to yesterday, and Cora walked around, taking in the myriad of plants and trees that surrounded her.

"Hi," a little voice said behind Cora.

Cora turned around, and squatted. "Oh, hi."

"I'm Boxy," the rabbit put out a paw.

Cora touched the animals little paw. "I'm Cora."

"Yes, I know," the rabbit paused. "I wanted to apologize for not coming along on the mission yesterday."

"Oh, that's ok," Cora said, "no need to apologize. We had plenty of help."

"You see, Artulyn didn't want me to go."

"Artulyn?" Cora said. Then she frowned. "Oh."

"Artulyn isn't a bad rabbit. He is just misguided. I want you to know that. He really does have good intentions for the cause; for everyone."

"You don't have to apologize for him," Cora said. "And you don't have to answer to me. I'm just a stranger here."

The little rabbit blinked her big, clear eyes at Cora. "It's not that. I just want you to know there's a side to Artulyn you haven't seen. I know how he acted toward you yesterday was very unpleasant. I don't want you to think that's all there is to him."

"What I think doesn't matter," Cora folded her arms over her chest. "Is he your—?"

"Yes, he's my mate. I was all alone in the world before I met him. He has given me everything I have, but others here don't like me because of him." Boxy sat down next to Cora, but didn't look at the girl. She just stared straight ahead, into the grass.

"I'm sorry," Cora said.

"No, I'm sorry," Boxy said.

Cora pulled her knees up to her chest and curled her lips inside her mouth, biting them. "A rabbit died yesterday, because of me. It was my fault."

Boxy turned to her. "He died for the good of the cause. It wasn't your fault."

"Yes it was. I didn't warn them enough. I never even imagined there'd be poisoned food in there, I didn't think to tell them. If only I'd said not to eat anything, they couldn't have known—"

"You have given us all a second chance. The casualty was very, very sad, but in doing what you did, you made it so no one else will be poisoned. We never thought that possible. It is an amazing feat."

"His death wasn't a casualty, it was a mistake. And it could've been avoided if only I'd been more careful."

The rabbit leaned close to Cora, "Then, be more careful next time."

"But when he died, it's like no one cared," Cora whispered. "Don't you care?"

"Of course we do. And those who were closest to him, more than anything. We all cry. Inside." Boxy's paw edged closer to Cora's hand. "We are so many, and we die every day. If we mourned each and every passing to our fullest grief, we would never stop crying. Our world would halt, and we'd all forget ourselves until we, too, were dead."

"What are you doing, Boxy?" a gruff voice clapped behind Cora and the rabbit. Cora startled. "I hope you aren't upsetting our new commander," Artulyn said.

"The lady is upset by the passing of Haanlea," Boxy said to Artulyn. "She will need a moment to compose herself."

"I'm sure she is," Artulyn narrowed his eyes, "since he was killed by the very thing she went to destroy."

"I want to talk to Basajaun," Cora wiped at her tears with her fist.

"He's on his way," Artulyn said. "And listen, *girl*, things die every day. That's just the way it is. So if something is special to you, you'd better make damn sure you give it the utmost protection and care. Watch it. Worry about it. Treat it better than all else because if you don't, and it dies, you have no one to blame but yourself. And your tears will mean nothing, for they are impotent, self-pitying, and false." The rabbit stood up on his hind legs. "When you are ready, we will be expecting another address."

"Take your time," Boxy said, and turned to follow her mate as he hopped away.

Basajaun found Cora back under the willow tree, alone. "Are you all right?" he said.

"I'm fine."

"I want to talk to you about what we're planning to do now."

"I don't know," Cora said. "Artulyn says I have to make another speech, and—"

"No, I don't mean about that," Basajaun said. "I mean, are we going to go back home, to the farm house?"

"I don't know about that either," Cora sighed. "You can stay here, but if I return to the town I'll be lynched, probably. I don't think even my father could protect me now that I'm in this deep. I can't go home, at least not until it's over."

"Then, what about hiding with Nellie?"

"*No.*"

"I know it's still in the town, but Henry—"

"No. I'm not going back there."

"You have to be safe, I—"

"No!" Cora yelled.

"You have to be safe! Henry can give you food, and you'd be with Nellie. Why are you being so difficult?"

"I don't want to talk about it," Cora mumbled, and pulled her knees back up to her chest. Looking down, she let her hair cover her face as she pressed a small stone into the dirt. And another. She pulled them out again. "I don't think anyone ever thought I was pretty," she said. "Or special. That must be the reason why I never had any friends."

Basajaun looked at her. Cora kept her eyes on her thumb as it flattened out against the dirt. "Come on," he said.

"What?"

"Come with me. I want to show you something."

The grazing rabbits watched Basajaun lead Cora through the clearing, into the blue-green tress, and out of sight. Cora followed Basajaun and said nothing. She kept her eyes on the ground until she noticed the thick, green grass getting higher and higher. It covered her feet, then her ankles, then grew up to her knees.

"Basajaun?" Cora looked in front of her, but the rabbit had disappeared. She quickened her pace, following the shifting grasses that rustled ahead.

"Yes?" Basajaun's voice came out of the grass.

"Where are we going?"

"You'll see."

For the first time, Cora looked around at the land on her sides. She turned it over in her brain, rotating it this way and that, trying to find where it fit into the sprawling country map she'd been charting in her mind since she was five years old. "I've never been here before," she said.

"Neither have I," Basajaun said.

"Are we going to those trees?" Cora squinted into the light ahead.

Basajaun's rustling form stopped. "Boxy?" he said.

"Right here," the female rabbit's voice rose out of the grass—no—out of the ground.

Basajaun stood on his hind legs so Cora could see his ears peeking out of the grass. "Here," he said. "Follow me down." He disappeared.

Cora kneeled with one hand on the ground and parted the grass where Basajaun had disappeared. All she saw was earth. She moved forward and parted the grass again. And again. There she saw a hole, a big hole. Much bigger than the ones the warren rabbits used.

"Basajaun?" Cora called into the hole. "Are you in there?"

"Yes. Come down."

First, Cora stuck her head into the hole. But this turned her almost completely upside down, so she pulled it out again. Instead she put her feet in, followed by her legs, and gradually her body slipped into the ground.

Cora scooted along the length of the dirt passageway. She moved in a seated position, but the tunnel was tall enough for her to straighten out her arms and put her palms against the ground above her. When she did this, a powdery dusting of dirt fell onto her hair and shoulders. Finally, Cora felt her feet hit the free, open space at the end of the tunnel. She felt around with her legs, searching for a place to step, but fell out of the tunnel and landed on the small of her back.

Cora leaned forward and rubbed her tailbone. She stood up, all the way up, and even at her full height she still had three feet of open space above her. The space before her was bigger than her farmhouse kitchen and bedroom combined. Small, meaty roots reached down out of the ceiling, some dangling low enough for Cora to brush with the tips of her fingers. The winding cords of tree roots—thick and rope-like—extended from floor to ceiling in three places. These roots were so wide that when Cora wrapped her hands around them, her fingers didn't even touch. The passageway Cora had come down was three feet off the ground, but on the facing wall, far away, Cora saw a hole that even the smallest of rabbits could reach with a little jump. Smooth dirt walls curved to form the ground she stood on, making the whole enclosure the shape of an oval. And in the center of that oval, looking very, very small, sat Boxy and Basajaun.

"Hello Cora," Boxy said. "Welcome to the secret underground."

Cora sat devouring the berries and lettuce leaves the rabbits had brought for her. She hadn't even realized how hungry she was. "So, how did you find this place?" she said to Basajaun. "Did rabbits used to live here?"

"No," Basajaun said, "and I didn't find it. Boxy did."

"I used to hide out here," Boxy said. "But no real rabbit groups have ever lived here, at least not in my lifetime. What it was made for, I don't know. But I think it was abandoned long before I found it."

"Basajaun!" Cora said. "We could move some of the rabbits here, maybe even a whole field of them! It's so big, they could—"

"No," Basajaun said. "There's a reason it's empty. It's *too* big. It would fit a portion of warren, yes, but the size of it would leave us completely vulnerable. Badgers, foxes, even men could enter easily and pick us off one by one, like pups. The benefit of our underground warrens is that they fit us exactly. We bunch up together, inside, and there's just enough room for us to move around. Our tunnels are tight and winding so that even if a predator gets in, he won't be able to maneuver through as quickly as we can. Because then, especially then, our speed is our only chance for survival."

"When I stayed in here," Boxy said, "I lived in constant fear attack. I made myself a little hole over there, in the wall, to hide in," the rabbit nodded her head to the right. "It's filled itself in, now, but I used it when the foxes came; that was when there were more foxes than there are now. I had to watch and wait for them to reach the other end of the wall, and then I'd bolt out. This one fox almost caught me several times. I don't know how I survived. Living like that, it was exhausting," Boxy sighed, and looked to where her hiding hole used to be.

"I understand," Cora nodded. "It's just a shame for all this to go to waste." Cora looked above and all around her, taking it all in with a sort of reverence. "We must remember this place, and maybe sometime we can use it."

"We're going to use it now," Basajaun said, "for you."

"Me?"

"You need a place to stay. You're far too big to live in our underground tunnels, but not too big for this one."

Cora looked back and forth between the two rabbits.

"Not for good, of course. Just until you can go home."

"Ok," Cora said. "Yes."

"And if you like," Basajaun flipped his ears, "I'll stay here too."

"Oh, I don't want you in danger," Cora said. "After all you two just told me? No, it wouldn't be safe," Cora shook her head.

"I'll dig a hiding hole, just like Boxy did," Basajaun said. "And you'll protect me. I trust you."

"But what if something happens to me, and you're left alone?" Cora said. "I can't control what might happen out here. You can't trust that way, not completely."

"I do. Just like you trust me."

Cora was quiet.

"You have to trust me," Basajaun said. "I'm not leaving you alone, out in the world."

Boxy hopped to the back wall. At this end of the burrow she could no longer hear Basajaun and Cora, but could see their backs as the rabbit moved closer to his human friend. The little female rabbit emerged from the underground in a cluster of nettles, and she paused to pluck them out of her fur with her mouth. Daylight was almost over, and she zipped along the familiar path to her own underground home. She didn't see Artulyn out in the green-blonde clearing and he wasn't in their burrow either, so Boxy started digging up the earth where he slept with her claws, fluffing the dirt into a uniform pile the length of her mate's body.

"Getting my bed ready, I see."

Artulyn's low voice made Boxy jump. "Yes," she said as she turned around. "I didn't hear you come down."

Artulyn looked down his nose at the loose dirt. "Very thoughtful of you."

"I always do that, Artulyn," Boxy backed up a step. "Every night."

"I wasn't sure what to expect from you, henceforth," Artulyn said. "Now that you've turned to the other side."

"We are on the same side, Artulyn. We are all on the same side."

"Don't lie to me," Artulyn barked. "Don't lie to yourself. What made you switch favor, hmm? First you interrupt me during the address, now you go to *his* cause. What made you decide to help him instead of me?"

"He is doing good work, Artulyn. You must see that. He has the human help. Who would've ever thought we would have that luxury?"

"If it's luxury you're after, maybe you're just hoping to be taken into his burrow once he becomes Chief!"

"Artulyn!"

"I wouldn't bother," the soldier rabbit sneered, "he is perverted. He will follow that human girl above all else, and you will be left alone."

"I would never leave you," Boxy walked toward her mate. "And because I love you, I will tell you this—you are digging yourself deeper and deeper into a rift you cannot win. You are making an enemy of everyone left who is still on your side."

"You are a traitor!" Artulyn yelled.

"I am not a traitor!" Boxy yelled back. "I just don't want to die!"

The big rabbit growled and lunged at his mate. His teeth took hold of the skin around her neck and she let out a piercing screech. Artulyn lurched to one side, throwing Boxy down and rolling over her body, back to his feet. "You are a coward," he spit out a clump of fur. "And there are worse things than death."

Artulyn ran out into the dusk. Running and running and ignoring the stares of the rabbits outside who'd heard his mate's scream. Tall grass hit him in the face as the sun crept further down the skyline. Back in the burrow, Boxy lay on the freshly turned earth, and buried her face in the dirt.

When Artulyn stopped running, he was in the town. He looked up and down the loose stone street, and touched the gravel with his paw. It shifted, and his foot sunk down a little. He pulled it back. Then he tried again. The same thing happened, but his foot didn't sink any further the second time than it had the first, so Artulyn deemed that amount of shifting safe, and reasonable for his mobility. He hopped onto the road. There was a 'crunch' of stone on stone when Artulyn's feet dug into the gravel, and a lighter, 'swooshing' sound when he pushed off and landed a half-foot further on the path. Crunch, swoosh, crunch, swoosh, the rabbit moved slowly through the night, all the while whipping his head from side to side in the hope that no humans would venture out of their homes as he passed.

The gravel road ended. Three dirt paths veered off where Artulyn stood—one to the north, one to the west, in front of him, and one near that, just slightly southwest. Artulyn looked at them all. The southwest path had deep wheel grooves in the dirt, as did the west path, just not so many. The north path, to his left, had footprint marks, and no vehicle tracks of any kind. Artulyn took off running down the path in front of him, and hoped he'd have time to backtrack to another if he was wrong.

The houses on this path were varied, and far apart. Most of them were dark. Artulyn stood on his hind legs and arched his neck toward a few windows, but there was nothing to see even if they hadn't been almost completely black. Then the rabbit noticed a low light up ahead, on his right. He bobbed his head, scrutinizing the height of the brightness, and finally worked out the shape of the building that contained the glow. He snuck up on the window, the light itself making him all too aware of the threat of being seen. Ducking into a shadow on the grass, Artulyn stood as tall as he could. Through the glass he could see the top of a man's head, just the eyes and nose. The man was crying.

Artulyn hopped up to the front door. He looked around one last time, and started thumping his back foot on the dirt as hard as he could. When he heard footsteps, Artulyn ran around the side of the house and hid. The man opened the door and looked around. Artulyn's body was tense.

"Who's there?" the man breathed. He walked out onto the road. "Oh dear, is that you? Where are you, girl?"

"Hello," Artulyn said.

"What?" the man turned in fast circles. "Who's there?"

"I want to help you," Artulyn said. "I want to join your cause."

"Nellie," the man's voice choked, "where's Nellie?"

"I don't know who that is," Artulyn said.

The man dropped his hands at his sides. He sighed. "Where are you? I can't see you."

"That's because I want you to hear me out, regardless of what I look like."

"And what do you look like?"

"I am your enemy," Artulyn said. The man was quiet. Artulyn's ears bristled and he pressed his body up against the side of the cottage. "Promise that you will judge me on what I say and not who I am, and I will come out of hiding," he said.

"I promise," the man replied.

"You give me your word?"

"Yes."

The rabbit hopped over the grass, to the middle of the street, and sat in front of the Pastor. The man looked at him, and blinked.

"Come inside," the Pastor said as he turned and waved a hand toward the cottage front door. "We can talk." The rabbit nodded and followed the man inside the cottage.

The Pastor sat in a green, velvet armchair, and gestured to the hard-backed wooden chair opposite him. "Sit down."

"Really?" Artulyn said. He looked at the chair. "I mean, thanks." The rabbit jumped up onto the stiff cushion and placed his paws neatly in front of his stomach.

"Now," the Pastor folded his hands, "why would you come to me, when I am trying to kill out your species?"

Artulyn tried not to stumble over his carefully practiced speech. "I am mutinying, sir, against the new authority at my warren."

"You have a problem with authority?"

"None at all. I had served my previous Chief loyally since I was a pup. When I grew big enough, I became a soldier. Soon I was the youngest rabbit in our warren to reach the rank of footmen. This spring, I became head footman."

"And now you think you should be Chief."

"Oh no, I didn't mean—" Artulyn paused, "I was just explaining how well and how long I had served my Chief."

"I don't know why the thought didn't occur to you. Hearing your climb up the ranks, it seems the obvious next step to me." The Pastor tapped his foot. Artulyn shifted in his chair. "What else could make an animal so bitter he would sit politely with the man who has already killed a quarter of his kind?" the Pastor said.

"You think ill of me," Artulyn said.

"No, I think it's wonderful," the Pastor grinned, showing a row of narrow teeth. "Resourceful. Now," the man leaned forward in his chair, "you must have thought out some agenda, some way you think that we can work together. And you must have something to offer me, that you expect I will value, or else you would not have risked coming here at all."

Artulyn nodded.

"And what do you want from me, that you think I will be willing to give, in exchange for this great commodity you have in mind?"

"I want to live. Myself, and a small group of rabbits of my choosing."

"Ones that you're sure will be happy to serve you as Chief," the Pastor smiled. Artulyn turned an eye toward the closed door. The Pastor laughed. "Don't go just yet. What are you willing to offer me?"

"Aid, in effectively terminating the rabbits outside my chosen group, and information. Inside information."

The Pastor leaned back in his chair. "I'm listening."

"One of the rabbits has recruited a girl, a human girl, to lead us, and run with us as though she were one of our own. She led the rabbits in the mission to dispose of all the poison in the sheds."

The Pastor blinked twice and lurched forward. "A girl? What does she look like?"

"I don't know, just like a girl."

"Is she fair haired?" the Pastor's voice grew louder. "Is she with child? Her middle, is it big? Swollen?" he gestured at his own stomach.

"She's small," Artulyn said. "Very small, for a human; slight. Her hair is dark, and wild."

The Pastor began to laugh. He put his hands on his knees and looked into his lap. "Oh yes," he laughed. "Yes, I know her. Of course." He looked back up at Artulyn. "I accept. I accept your offer. So you've seen into the sheds, have you?"

"No, not me. I didn't go."

"But the other rabbits, they saw in them all?"

"Yes," Artulyn nodded. Then he squinted a little. "No, most of them. Most of the sheds. The girl couldn't open the last one. It was locked."

"They were all locked," the Pastor said.

"But this one was locked—better. They didn't get in."

"Well, as a show of good faith, I would like to show you what's in the final shed."

Artulyn's body stiffened. "I thought it was poison."

"Oh, I assure you, it is not poison," the Pastor stood and left the room. Artulyn heard a light clanking through the wall and the man returned. "Would you like to be the first to see?"

Artulyn followed the Pastor out of the cottage. The two of them didn't speak as they walked down the road, through the woods. Artulyn hoped there were no other rabbits out snooping by the old poison sheds, and he looked around at the trees, warily.

The man and the rabbit stood in front of the fourth shed. Artulyn looked it up and down, turning his head from side to side as his eyes moved all over the faded, gray wood. The Pastor looked down at the rabbit, watched him watch the shed, and pulled a big, clattering ring of keys out of his pocket. Some of the keys were old, some were shiny new brass. The key the Pastor selected was old silver, tarnished with pink and orange rust. It was the shape of a skeleton key, but flat like thin board, with no rounded or raised edges. On the tip of the key, there was only one notch.

The Pastor put the key in the lock, turned it, and a shimmery, gray light came out of the keyhole. When the key clicked in the lock, the light turned blue. And when the man pulled the key back out, the light turned to a puff of smoke that trailed out of the hole, and disappeared. The Pastor wrapped four knarled fingers around the side of the old door. The door creaked as the man opened it.

"You first," he gestured to Artulyn. The rabbit looked up at the man, and walked inside. A gold light hit Artulyn's face, and he squinted. Then he just stared, wide-eyed.

"Your Majesty!" Artulyn cried. "Oh, your Majesty!" he put his chin on the ground. The Pastor walked to Artulyn's side, and laid a hand on his back, stroking his fur.

"There, now you have seen something that no other rabbit here has seen," the Pastor said. Artulyn sobbed. The

Pastor rested his other hand over Artulyn's ears, and the room began to turn. Suddenly, Artulyn heard a loud 'crack'. He was looking up into the Pastor's face, even though his body was still against the earth. Artulyn screeched. Then he felt the pain. Then he felt nothing.

CHAPTER NINE

INTENTIONS

Wayne raised a hand and knocked on the door. He could hear shouts and laugher inside, the sounds of men trying to sing, and of someone trying to dance. Finally, heavy footsteps clomped closer, and the door swung open. A big-shouldered man with a thick, black beard was holding a short cigar and laughing to someone in the back of the room. He put the cigar stub in his mouth and leaned against the doorframe. His gray shirt was unbuttoned halfway down his chest, and a chunk of cigar ash fell on his bare skin. The man brushed it away.

"What you want?" he nodded at Wayne.

"I'm from across the way, from the dairy farm just there," Wayne pointed. "I—" a woman ran behind the big man, shrieking. Wayne jumped and the woman fell into a fit of guffaws, bending at the waist and slapping her leg.

"Get outta here, you," the man put the sole of his big work boot on the woman's hip, and gave her a little shove.

The woman fell to the side, giggling.

The man turned back to Wayne. "What can I do for you?" He smiled, closing one eye, his flat teeth sinking into the short cigar.

"I'm looking for my daughter. I wonder if she's here."

"Hey, now," the man put out his hands and backed up. "Lots of daughters are here. Everybody is somebody's daughter, you know? Nobody forces them to come our way. What are we supposed to do? Hunt down all their fathers and ask permission to—"

"No, I don't think you understand," Wayne said. "My daughter is—"

"Everybody's daughter is the same," the man nodded and stumbled.

Wayne could smell, now, the pungent odor of alcohol coming off the man's shiny skin. Wayne spoke louder. "My daughter is a friend of one of your farm boys. Henry. She's just a little girl!"

The man stared at Wayne, glassy eyed. He paused. "Oh! The little dark-haired girl?" he combed his fingers at his shoulder. Wayne nodded. "Yup, she was here yesterday. She sure is a nice little thing!" the man smiled.

"Is she here now?" Wayne took a step forward and began to duck inside the house.

"Not in here, she's not," the man stepped in front of Wayne, and laughed. "Left as soon as she came. Early in the morning."

"Can I talk to Henry?" Wayne said. "Where is he?"

"Still working in the old grain sheds, I expect. They're out in the grass, past the south pasture," the man pointed.

"I mean, go that way," the man extended his arm and pointed further, "past those small buildings, there, go around the big field next to them, then behind it. The old grain sheds are underground. Henry's been working out there."

"Thank you," Wayne hurried away.

"Come back here, when you're done!" the man called after him. "You can meet some of the other daughters!" He shook his head, laughing to himself, and slammed the door.

The field next to the aboveground grain sheds was golden. The serenity in the soft, lilting grain seemed almost impossible, and Wayne thought how peaceful it would be to lie down in its thin, reed-like cover. He imagined staying there, staring at the sky, until the seasons passed into years and no one could see him anymore, or remember who he was.

Wayne came upon the wooden doors in the grass, and rushed back and forth between them. Halfway down the line, he heard quiet voices rising up out of the ground, up out of one of the cellars; the second cellar from the last. A boy's and a girl's.

"Cora!" Wayne threw open the broken, slatted door and ran down the rickety steps. "Cora!"

"Sir?" Henry bolted up. He had been sitting on an overturned fruit crate, talking to a curled-up form under a dingy, gray sheet. Wayne looked at Henry, then at the huddled shape lying across a row of boxes.

"What's going on?" Wayne yelled, and yanked the sheet off the girl. Nellie, fists pressed up against her chin, blinked at him. "What?" Wayne looked at Henry again, then back at Nellie.

"You're not going to turn me in, are you?" Nellie said.

Wayne stood over the girl, holding the sheet in one hand. "What? Are you okay?" he said. "Why are you here?" Nellie stared at him.

"Please don't turn her in, sir!" Henry blurted out. "You don't know what, you don't know—Please don't make her go back!"

Wayne shook his head. "Where's Cora?"

"Sir?" Henry said.

"Where's Cora?" the man flung the sheet down. "My daughter! Remember? You two went on a picnic, and she came home hours later looking like she'd been dragged halfway across the world!"

Henry hunched his shoulders at the man. "She isn't home?"

Wayne frowned. He grabbed a stool, pulled it over next to the two teenagers, and sat down with his elbows on his knees. "Okay. What's going on?"

"Nellie's in hiding from the Pastor," Henry said. "He's—" Henry looked away. "He's mean to her."

"I don't doubt it," Wayne sighed. He turned to Nellie. "How long have you been here?"

"Couple days," Nellie said.

The man leaned closer to the pregnant girl. "You can't stay here. Live here. Where are you from? Do you have parents?" Nellie reached down and began playing with a piece of thick, dirty, light-brown hair lying across her shoulder.

"I'm taking care of her," Henry said.

161

"For how long?" Wayne said. "Until her baby's born? What then?" He looked around the dank cellar. "She can't stay here forever."

"She can't go back to that man," Henry said.

Wayne rubbed his forehead. "So, when did you last see Cora?"

"Yesterday morning. Sir, is she really missing?"

Wayne sighed. And even though the man was still sitting upright, it was as though all his muscles went limp, like the string that held him up had finally been cut. "I can't find her."

Henry swallowed. "Come outside," he said. "I want to talk to you."

The boy and the man stood next to the wide, golden field. A strong wind shifted the grain, and moved through their hair.

Henry put his hands in the pockets of his dirty, oversize overalls. "Cora came here yesterday morning. We had a fight." The boy cocked his head to the side. "At least, I think we did. It wasn't really a fight, but she went away," he looked into the man's eyes. "But I thought she was going back home, I swear! If I thought something would happen, I would've gone after her!"

"What did you fight about?" Wayne said.

"I don't know," Henry curled his lip a little and glanced at the grass.

Wayne folded his arms and sighed. "I know you're just a boy, and I see you already have your hands full," the man nodded back toward the old cellar, "but I feel like I'm going mad. I'm sorry, I honestly don't have anyone else to turn to. Will you help me find Cora?"

"Yes, sir. Of course. Let me just tell Nellie where I'm going."

"Be sure to tell your father, too."

Henry looked back. "I don't have a father, sir."

"Oh," Wayne said, "that man, with the dark beard—"

"Sam," Henry said.

"He's not your—"

"I am a foundling, sir. Sam is good enough to look after me."

"Oh," Wayne said. "He has your eyes."

Henry shrugged. "I never noticed."

Henry's footsteps receded into the earth. Wayne turned back to the grain field and watched it shimmer. When Henry returned, he came up close next to the man.

"Nellie wanted me to ask you if Cora has Basajaun with her," Henry said. "Who's Basajaun?"

Wayne blinked. "A friend of hers."

"Oh," Henry said. "I didn't think Cora had any friends—" he paused and gaped at Cora's father, "with such funny names, I mean."

Wayne didn't bat an eye. "What did Nellie say about Basajaun?" he asked.

"Well, she said as long as Cora has Basajaun with her, she'll be ok."

"And what we're going to do," Cora stood once again with the dark row of bushes at her back, and a sea of rabbit faces before her, "is sneak into the bad man's cottage, steal the key, and destroy the rest of the poison in the last shed."

The crowd of rabbits erupted into a torrent of cheers. Some of them jumped in the air, and hugged each other. Cora looked down at Basajaun for this time, he sat at her side during the address. He smiled at her. Then Cora noticed a lone voice in the clearing, getting louder and louder. She squinted into the crowd, and saw a thin, wiry rabbit pushing his way to the front.

"He's back!" the rabbit yelled. "He's returned!" the rabbit reached the front of the pack and bowed. "He's back miss—the Chief! Oh, he'll want to congratulate you! You must meet him!" the rabbit reached a paw toward Cora's hand.

"The Chief?" Cora said to Basajaun. "Was he gone?" Basajaun nodded. Of course he was gone. Cora hadn't even thought about it. Of course she'd have met with him already if he'd been there. Where had he been?

"Cora did meet with the Chief, before his departure," Basajaun said to the wiry rabbit, "so I'm sure he'll be anxious to hear how her plan progressed."

"Oh my," the wiry rabbit said. "It's all so official, isn't it? Well come on then, both of you. You are to be congratulated," the rabbit got behind Cora and nudged her heel with his forehead. The crowd of rabbits parted and Cora and Basajaun, with the other rabbit in front of them, walked down its center. All the rabbits smiled at Cora as she passed, and many of them smiled at Basajaun, too.

The wiry rabbit stopped at a cluster of miniature trees. They were as tall as Cora was, but for the types of trees they were, that size seemed to her absolutely miniscule. Three types of pines, some firs, something that looked like a maple, and a few birches, all in scale to the rabbits as the trees' full-size cousins were to Cora. Basajaun knew this place all too well, but Cora looked around in wonder.

"Come on in," the wiry rabbit smiled, and led Cora and Basajaun between the pines. Cora was accustomed, now, to the rabbits' tree-encased hiding places—foliage-lined clearings and pastures, always hidden, always secret. This one was no different, except when Cora and Basajaun entered, there the Chief sat, just as stoic and regal as the first time Cora had seen him. And just as old.

"The little girl, and my son," the Chief nodded a bow, ever so slightly. "I hear you are both to be congratulated."

"Hello sir," Cora bowed.

"I am so relieved to see you home safe, Father," Basajaun said.

"Not nearly as relieved as I am to see you," the Chief said. "So, the two of you rallied our entire troop to what many would say was an impossible task?"

"Almost the whole troop, sir," Basajaun said. "And yes, but it was Cora's doing. It was she who gained the support of the rabbits, who swayed them."

"It was I who spoke to the rabbits, sir," Cora said, "but that was at Basajaun's instruction. He said they would more readily believe me because I am bigger and a human, and therefore a novelty. And he was right."

"Both so eager to give credit to the other," the Chief smiled. "You certainly have the support of the warren now. What's next on the agenda?"

"Well sir, that's what we were just announcing to the group," Cora said. "There was a fourth shed we were unable to open the night of the poison heist, and Basajaun thinks it contains the town's missing money. If we expose the Pastor as a thief, he'll be run out of town for good."

"By your people," the Chief said.

"Yes sir," Cora replied.

"So this plan involves more humans like you," the Chief said. "Many humans; your whole town."

"Yes sir. But it is no additional danger to the rabbits. The townspeople will never know you were involved," Cora said.

"What do you think?" the Chief asked Cora.

"What do you mean?" Cora said.

The Chief shifted on his haunches, and sat up. "You said Basajaun thinks the fourth shed contains the missing money. I want to know what you think."

Basajaun looked at Cora.

"I don't know," Cora said. "But I can't think of any other plan. And I think it's worth the risk to try."

"What is the risk?" the Chief said.

"We must sneak into the Pastor's home," Cora said, "and steal the key."

The Chief rabbit sat up a little straighter. "I see. Well, I can think of no other plan either. You and Basajaun have proved yourselves proficient up to now. I suggest you go ahead with this plan. Now, if you don't mind, dear, I'd like to speak to my son alone."

"Oh, of course," Cora half bowed as she half-stood. "Thank you, sir." She pushed her way through the small trees, and was surprised to find Boxy waiting for her on the other side. The little rabbit spoke fast.

"Cora, you haven't seen Artulyn, have you?"

"No, Boxy. Not since we all spoke yesterday. What's wrong?"

"He's missing. We had a bit of a fight last night," Boxy parted a line in the grass with her paw. "He ran off. I thought he'd come back when he'd cooled down—he usually does—but he hasn't come home. I'm scared."

"I'll help you look for him," Cora kneeled in front of the little rabbit. "Are there any places he likes to go, to hide?"

"That's just it. I've checked all those places. I've looked for him all over the warren, and asked everyone. He's not here. I think he's gone—" Boxy leaned close to Cora and whispered, "outside."

"Don't worry," Cora put her hand on the rabbit's back. "Basajaun and I are going outside tonight, to the town. We can look for Artulyn."

The little rabbit's eyes brightened. "Can I come?"

"Oh, it's a mission too," Cora said. "One for just Basajaun and I. That's why we're going. No one else is—"

"But I could come; I could help! Not just help look for Artulyn, but help out with the mission too. I'd like to help!" Boxy sat up.

"No, it's too dangerous," Cora said. "This is different than the poison mission, it's—"

Boxy shook her head. "I don't care. Please let me go. I am so ashamed that I didn't go along on the poison mission. I wanted to. Please let me go on this one to make up for it. Besides, I am the one asking you to look for Artulyn; that's adding another objective to your mission.

Thus you should add the help of another body. Please, I need this."

"It's too dangerous," the rabbit Chief said to Basajaun. "This is a run and hope mission. You can't go."

"Like hell I can't!" Basajaun said. "The mission was my idea!"

"All the more reason for you to stay," the Chief raised his nose. "You've contributed the idea. You're the planner. That's enough."

Basajaun let out a little growl. "I will not send Cora out on this job by herself. She needs my help."

"Then I will go in your place," the Chief said. "I can help her. I can be the rabbit presence, if she needs one."

"No!" Basajaun yelled. "You send me out for the human help and I get it, bring it back, make it work, and now you want to step in and take over? No. No blessed way. I'm going."

"I am trying to keep you safe," the Chief said. "This mission is miles more dangerous than any you've taken on yet. To go into the home of the enemy? It's insane."

"More insane than infiltrating the human world and bringing one to our side?" Basajaun sneered.

"That objective was up to you."

"What do you mean?" Basajaun said.

"I mean—the help is wonderful. It may save us all. But it was not expected of you. Whatever you chose, would've been ok."

"What? I don't understand," Basajaun narrowed his eyes. "You sent me out to get the human help. I got it."

"But," the Chief breathed in, "you weren't really expected to get it." Basajaun's face dropped. "It was a one in a million chance. Almost impossible. The fact that you connected at all is a miracle. And even if you never returned, who could blame you? A safe life, with a kind and caring human? Always enough food to eat and a safe place to sleep? Who could turn that down?"

"But, you sent me out to get the human help," Basajaun said again. "I got it."

"I wanted you to live, so I sent you to the only place I knew you'd be safe: into the heart of the beast."

"You mean, I wasn't meant to succeed?"

"I just wanted you to survive the massacre."

Basajaun looked down, and whispered. "I thought you sent me on a mission."

"Now Basajaun," the Chief said, "you are different because I raised you different. You're not a warmonger like Artulyn. You're crafty, intelligent. I raised you to survive because you are my last. You are alive. It is a great thing, to be alive."

"But you checked in on me," Basajaun said. "You summoned me to check my progress."

"Oh, that was to appease Artulyn. He just needed to see that you were trying."

"Trying," Basajaun said. He felt tears beginning in his eyes, and pulled them back as hard as he could. "What if I had never come home? Who would've been the successor?"

The Chief breathed in deeply again. "In your absence, Artulyn would've been Chief, as all your brothers and sisters are dead."

Little teardrops fell onto the clover at Basajaun's feet.

"Don't worry," the Chief moved close to his son. "That is different now that you're back."

"It's not that," Basajaun said. "Never mind."

"I acted as I did because I value your life. You should value it too."

Basajaun stiffened. "I value many things, including my own free will, which I will use now. For I am going on the mission tonight."

"So be it," the Chief closed his eyes. "Report back to me as soon as you can." Basajaun turned to leave. "Basajaun?" the Chief said.

"Yes?"

"I ought to tell you, Artulyn has gone missing. In the event that he doesn't return, I would approach his mate Boxy if I were you. She's a great rabbit. I always thought she was wasted on him."

Basajaun didn't reply and didn't look back. On the other side of the trees Cora sat waiting for him, skimming her hand over a little white flower in the grass.

"What were you and your father talking about?" she said.

"Just warren politics," Basajaun said. "I guess Artulyn has gone missing."

"I know," Cora said. "Boxy was just telling me."

"Boxy was here?"

"Yes. I told here we would look for Artulyn tonight, and she wants to go with us, on the mission."

"She does?"

"I told her and told her it wasn't safe, but she insisted. Is that all right?"

"Yes," Basajaun said. "I suppose so."

CHAPTER TEN

THE KEY

"This is the living room," Cora peered over the cottage sill into the gold-red room. She noticed the straight backed, scratchy-wood chair with the burgundy cushion, the greenish tan velvet armchair, and the empty wine bottle with the half-empty glass beside it. Cora pushed on the pane of glass. "This window doesn't open. Come on."

Basajaun and Boxy followed Cora through the weedy flowerbed, to what used to be Nellie's window. Cora reached for the windowsill, but the tips of her fingers landed a full six inches below the ledge. Cora jumped, clamored toward the window, and missed. She jumped again, and again. Finally she caught hold of the cement edge and dangled off it, her arms stretched rigid, and tried to keep her swinging feet from hitting the side of the house. Straining, Cora wedged the toe of her shoe into the shallow dip between two stones, and pulled herself up as she had seen Henry do. She slapped one elbow onto the sill, then the other. Leaning up on one forearm, she felt all the way along the edge of the window with her other hand. It was completely smooth. 'Of course there's not latch,' she thought, 'these windows aren't meant to open from the outside.' Cora gripped the sill with one hand, fished in her pocket with the other, and pulled out the cheese knife.

The broken cheese knife. Cora had snapped the blade in two when she'd pitted it against the old shed's unbreakable lock, but the lower half of the blade, square-edged and half its former size, still stuck out of the knife handle. Cora buried this end of the blade between the window and the windowpane, and pushed the wood handle toward the house. The blade was less pliable now that it was short, but still it bent, bent and bent, and Cora pushed harder, until the blade was almost the shape of the letter 'c'. Suddenly, the handle of the knife snapped off. The blade flew out backwards into the night and Cora's hand—still holding the wooden handle—slammed against the side of the cottage. Boxy and Basajaun winced.

Cora released her footing, and the cement windowsill scraped her fingers as she dropped back onto the flowerbed. She crouched down to face the two rabbits. "What are we going to do?" she said. "How are we going to get in? I remembered that window opening, but that's because Nellie opened it from the inside. And the last time, she just let Henry and I in through the front door."

"Could we get in through the front door this time?" Basajaun said.

Cora blew on her raw fingertips. "Not without waking

the entire town."

Basajaun leaned closer to his two companions. "We need another way. Some opening into the house. Anything. Is there a window into the Pastor's room?"

"Probably, on the other side," Cora said. "But then he'd hear us for sure. Even if he is drunk."

"Drunk?" Boxy said.

"Alcohol," Cora said. "It's a drink. It does a lot of things to a man. One of those things is to make him sleep long through the night, without waking."

"Where did you learn that?" Basajaun said.

"Henry told me."

"What's that?" Boxy whispered. Cora and Basajaun stopped. There was a soft rustling moving around the back of the house, growing louder, then quieter. It was followed by a scraping sound, and more rustling. Basajaun walked toward the noise.

"Basajaun! Wait!" Cora whispered, but Basajaun didn't even pause. Cora rushed after him and Boxy followed, until the three of them stood at the back of the cottage. "There's nothing here," Cora whispered. Then, out of the darkness, they heard a grunt; low at first, then higher and louder. Cora jumped, and both rabbits stiffened. Cora thought how it sounded like a rabbit, but deeper, louder, and angrier. Two little eyes appeared in the dark and, down on the ground, where the cottage met the grass, a low, wide shape emerged from the shadow. Covered all over in coarse, brown fur, the animal was wider across than two full-grown rabbits. It bared its long front teeth, squealed, and hissed. It was the most enormous marmot Cora had ever seen.

"You are trespassing on my homeland. Get out!" the marmot growled.

"This isn't your home," Basajaun said, "you are a stowaway. You have no claim here!"

"*You* have no claim here," the marmot said. "I was here first."

"How do you know I don't live here? This could be my home," Cora said.

"If it were, you would not be sneaking around the back wall," the marmot sneered at Cora. "I know the humans who have passed through here. You are not one of them. You are a stranger, too. A stranger who runs with *rabbits*," the animal stretched its neck toward Cora and sniffed the air in front of her. "You are not even a proper human."

Cora paused, and flicked her fingers together. "You are right. We are strangers here, and we don't live here. But we're trying to get in. Do you know the way in?"

"I know *my* way in. It is not for anyone but me."

"Please, it's very important," Cora said. "We just need to pass through. Afterward we'll go away and leave you alone."

"I fought hard for this spot—it is mine! I'll not risk expulsion just because you want to break in where the humans sleep!"

"Then there is a way into the house through there," Basajaun nodded his ears at the big dirt hole against the foundation of the cottage.

"'Course there is," the marmot squinted angrily at Basajaun. "It goes to the dead tree room. The man keeps all the dead trees in there to keep them dry. Burnable." The animal huffed through his nose at Basajaun. "Everyone knows a dead tree room leads into a house. Everyone knows that."

Suddenly, Basajaun leapt through the air and landed on the marmot's back. Cora gasped. Before the animal could even turn to throw him off, Basajaun dug his teeth into the back of the marmot's neck. The marmot squealed and Basajaun, using his mouth to hold himself steady atop the big animal, started clawing his front paws over the marmot's head. Basajaun's thick, dark claws raked the thin skin on the marmot's skull and ears, making deeper and deeper gashes in his furry flesh. Still squealing with a terrible grunting sound, the marmot threw his body from side to side, slamming Basajaun against the ground with each roll. But Basajaun wrapped his long hind feet at the marmot's sides and held fast, clawing deeper at the animal's ears.

"Basajaun!" Cora ran toward the scene, but Boxy grabbed the ankle of Cora's sock with her teeth. Cora stopped.

"No," Boxy said. "Just wait."

Clasping her hands over her mouth, Cora tensed every muscle in her body and tried to hold still. Finally, the marmot just lay on his side and flailed his short legs, reaching for Basajaun. His claws didn't even come close.

"Stop! Stop! I surrender!" the marmot said.

Basajaun paused but didn't loosen his tooth hold on the rolls of the animal's neck. Basajaun spoke out of the sides of his mouth, through a mouthful of fur. "Are you sure?"

"Yes!"

"And you will let us pass through as we please, without objection?"

"Yes! Yes!"

Basajaun let go. "When we leave, everything will be like before. You will have your home back."

The marmot stood and shook out his head. Little droplets of blood flew in a circle around him. "You won't tell anyone?"

"What?" Basajaun said.

"Please don't tell anyone about this, about the fight. If other marmots knew—"

"We won't tell anyone," Cora said.

"I would lose my home," the marmot said.

Basajaun looked at the big, panting marmot, who lowered his head.

"You have my word," Basajaun said.

Cora, Boxy and Basajaun surrounded the marmot's hole. "I can't fit through there," Cora said.

"No," Basajaun said.

"I thought I would be the one to go in," Cora breathed. She crouched down next to the hole and put a hand inside, feeling all around the dirt walls.

"Let me go," Boxy hopped to Cora's side. "Just tell me what to do. I can do it."

"No," Basajaun ran to Cora's other side. "I'll do it."

"Please, I want to help," Boxy said to Cora.

"This was my plan. I'll go," Basajaun said.

"You agreed to let me come, let me do this for you," Boxy put a paw on Cora's arm.

"This is my mission, I will say who goes," Basajaun glared at Boxy.

"I just want to help," Boxy said to Basajaun.

"Help by taking over command?" Basajaun barked. Cora flinched. The marmot sat back on the grass, but his eyes moved back and forth between the two rabbits, before resting on Cora.

"I thought you could both work together," Cora said. "I think that will suit everyone?" The rabbits were silent in assent, and Cora turned to face them both. She used her finger to draw a map in the dirt of where she expected the Pastor's room to be, by way of their entry. "Now," she said, "the time I was in the house, I saw the keys on a bedside table, next to the Pastor, as he slept. The table was tall, with thin legs and open sides, and a square top," Cora gestured the shape up and down with her hands. "The keys were on a big ring, and it's probably pretty heavy. Also on the table there should be," Cora struggled to remember, "a handkerchief, and a bible." She crouched closer to the rabbits and frowned. "Now, the only way I can think of for one of you to climb to the table is by way of the Pastor's bed." Basajaun and Boxy hardly flinched. Cora swallowed hard. "You'll have to jump up onto his bed, and walk to the top, to where his head is. Then you'll have to put your front paws on the side table, and get the keys. But—and this is the most important—at no point can you wake him. You must be absolutely silent and stealth, otherwise, it's all over."

Cora swallowed hard. This scenario was not at all what she expected, and the words she spoke sounded mad and alien to her. She wished upon wish that she could go herself. That had been her plan. And Basajaun and Boxy looked at her now with such faith and trust, that Cora wanted to grab them both up and take them home. What was she thinking? This was far too dangerous.

"We can do it," Basajaun said. Boxy nodded.

"Wait, I have a certain way I think it ought be done," Cora said quickly. "Both of you can go into the lumber room," Cora paused, nodding, "and Basajaun, you wait at the point where the lumber room connects to the house, while Boxy gets the keys."

"Why her?" Basajaun said.

"Because—" Cora dragged out the word, "she is smaller, so the Pastor will be less likely to notice her weight when she walks across the bed. There is very little room next to him there, we need to send the smallest presence possible. Besides, Basajaun," Cora put her hand on Basajaun's back. "Boxy has more experience running from predators, and hiding in confined, unfamiliar places. Isn't that true?"

Basajaun was stony silent. He didn't face Cora, but he looked angry. Finally he harrumphed, "Well, why do I have to go at all then? Why don't I just stay out here?"

"Because that way Boxy can hand off the keys to you, and you can run them out to me. I think the whole thing will move quickest if we approach it that way. Don't you think that's true?"

"Yes," Basajaun still didn't look at Cora.

"Now Boxy," Cora said, "I want you to wrap the keys in this," Cora reached down to the bottom flaps of her shirt and tore a strip off the front, "and carry it like a little bag. If you just hold the ring in your mouth the keys will make a whole mess of noise. But if wrap this around it and hold the edges of the fabric in your mouth, and let the keys rest inside, I think you can get it out quietly."

"Oh, like carrying a pup?" Boxy said.

Cora paused. "Yes, like that. You pass it to Basajaun, who will be waiting for you. And he will bring it out to me, with you following. But neither of you can run while you're holding the keys. Or they will make noise, and wake the Pastor." The rabbits nodded. "I think that's it. Soon we'll all be out safe, and back together," Cora said. She felt ill.

"Are you ready?" Basajaun said to Boxy.

"Yes," Boxy nodded. "See you soon," she said to Cora, and hopped into the hole.

Cora leaned down over Basajaun, and hugged and kissed him. "Please be careful," she said.

"Don't worry, it's not even dangerous—what I have to do, anyway." Basajaun sounded cross, but he bumped Cora's forehead with his nose. Still he pulled away from her arms quicker than she wanted him to, and followed Boxy, disappearing down the marmot hole.

Cora stared into the hole, took a few steps back, and stood with her arms crossed. The marmot watched her for a moment before shambling over to stand beside her.

"So, you're the leader?" he said.

"I don't know," Cora said.

"Never saw a human working alongside rabbits, or any other animal for that matter."

"Me neither," Cora said.

The marmot stared into the black opening in the earth. "He's a bit of a rogue, isn't he?"

"What?" Cora glanced at the animal next to her feet.

"Your friend. He's a rough sort, a bruiser."

"That's just the thing—he's not usually," Cora said. She put her hands in her pockets and stared all around the back wall of the cottage, as though she could see through the brick. "I'm sorry. Did he hurt you?"

"Well, it's just pain. It's no worry," the marmot paused. "That's some plan."

"Yup."

"Didn't really make sense to me, though. I mean, he was right. Why did he have to go in at all?"

Cora was quiet.

"You're protecting him, aren't you?"

"It's none of your concern," Cora murmured.

"I suppose not," the marmot said. He began cleaning the wounds on his head. Then he stopped. Cora could hear him breathing next to her. "So what you're doing, it's important?"

"Yes. We think so. I hope so."

The marmot followed Cora's gaze, to his hole. "My name's Rutai."

"I'm Cora."

"And I'm an outcast. I didn't fight to win this as my home, I just took it because no one else will dare come within miles of this place." The marmot glanced sideways up at Cora, waiting for a response. "It may not be much of a home, but I still want to protect it, you know," he said.

181

"It's okay," Cora replied.

"I'm sorry for what I said about you."

Cora stared ahead. "That's all right. It's true."

Boxy's claws clicked on the hardwood as she hopped from the lumber room into the cottage hall. She stopped and tried to stand, but all four of her feet began sliding away from her in all directions. She jumped. She could hear Basajaun making a 'shh!' noise behind her, but she didn't turn around. In her mind's eye, Boxy brought up an image of the dirt map Cora had drawn out for her, and tried to lay it over the surroundings she saw before her. She hopped forward, and her claws clicked again. She found that if she hopped slower, letting her front paws rest a moment before she brought her back legs up to meet them, she moved less audibly.

Boxy hopped down the hall. On her left she saw a dim bedroom, but as she moved closer to look inside, she heard a low, relaxed breathing sound coming through the door behind her. She turned, but a hard-backed chair that stood in the living room at the other end of the hall caught her eye. Boxy stopped. Craning her neck toward the living room, she sniffed the air. Something smelled—no, that would be impossible.

Boxy approached the sliver of dark that showed through the narrow opening to the Pastor's bedroom. She put her head inside. She still carried the scrap of Cora's shirt in her mouth, and could hear the man louder now, snoring with rhythmic precision. She made her body as small as possible as she passed through the doorway, but her hindquarters bumped the door and it moved open another inch. The Pastor didn't stir. His bed was higher than Boxy had expected, with a dark green blanket that hung almost to the floor. Boxy stood on her hind legs and rubbed her front paws down the draped side of the blanket, smoothing it, then hunched down and kicked her back legs hard, propelling herself into the air.

She landed like a gentle puff next to the Pastor's right ankle. She peered to the head of the bed and could see the man's dark nostrils over his open mouth. She moved slowly, noiselessly, up the side of the bed, along the outside of Pastor's calf and thigh. His arms were under the blanket and Boxy had to side step to the very edge of the bed to avoid stepping in the crook of the man's elbow. Finally, she reached the head. The Pastor's snoring whooshed loud in her sensitive ears and even though she'd told herself she wouldn't, Boxy couldn't help but look into her enemy's sleeping face. All this fuss, she thought, because of one old man. His skin was gnarled like the bark on a tree, his nose long, thing and rounded. Boxy could see the edges of the man's long teeth, and she looked away so as not to spook herself.

The table next to the Pastor's bed was exactly as Cora had described it. The bible lay at the front and behind it, the keys. The keys, on their big iron ring, lay fanned out on the table, and all but two of them rested on a white handkerchief. What luck. Boxy dropped the bit of cloth she'd been carrying, reached, put one paw on the edge of the end table, reached some more, and positioned her other paw beside it. Her body stretched the length between the table and the Pastor's bed, where her back feet rested, and

Boxy imagined she was a bridge; a fallen tree over a lake of water. She eased her front paws up onto the surface of the table, and lowered her head. Closing her mouth around the stem of the outermost key, Boxy lifted it, and gently laid it on the handkerchief. She followed with the second key, but when she lifted that one, the keys on the handkerchief clanked together.

Boxy stopped. The Pastor's snoring stopped. She stood stone still, holding the key in her mouth, and felt a rocking in the bed next to her, felt her back feet shift up and down. Boxy's own breath huffed over the metal in her mouth, and her eyes widened until crescents of white showed above the globes of black. The Pastor's snoring began again, but softer. Boxy folded the four corners of the handkerchief over the keys, and picked up the cotton edges in her mouth. She eased her way back onto the bed and when she turned, she saw the Pastor had rolled over, and now faced the opposite wall. She exhaled over the white fabric.

The weight of the keys hung heavy in the trussed bundle as the little rabbit walked back down along the edge of the bed. When she got to the foot, she put her front paws over the edge first and allowed her body to slide down the incline of the draped blanket, to the floor. The keys hardly made a sound. Moving as fast as she could comfortably go without making a lot of noise, Boxy rushed out of the Pastor's bedroom with the big key ring, wrapped in cloth, swinging back and forth in her mouth.

In the hall she stopped, and smelled the air again. Twenty feet away she could see Basajaun's eye peeking around the corner, and she hopped the slow way down the hall, clicking every other step. She slid past Basajaun into the dead tree room, turned to face him, and laid the bundle of keys at his feet.

"Here they are. Take them. I'm going back in."

"What? Are you mad?" Basajaun hissed. "Wha—what for?"

"I just have to check something. I have to check."

"No. Absolutely not. I am running this mission, and I forbid it."

"No, Basajaun. This is my mission," Boxy said. She zipped around Basajaun, and shot back into the cottage.

"Boxy, no!" Basajaun ran after her. "Don't! It's dangerous!"

When Basajaun caught up to Boxy, she was spinning in circles atop the seat of the hard-backed chair in the living room, smelling the burgundy cushion.

"Come down," Basajaun whispered.

"He was here," Boxy had tears in her eyes. "What has happened to him?"

"Rabbits!" the burgeoning growl of the voice down the hall hit Boxy and Basajaun like a wave. Open-mouthed, eyes wide, they turned to face the footsteps sprinting in their direction. And the walls, so confining and unfamiliar, seemed to be closing in all around them.

Boxy's back legs launched her body like a shot, toppling the hard-backed chair over backwards. Basajaun scrambled, trying to bolt, but his claws clattered and slipped on the hardwood floor. Finally he caught his footing and tore toward the wall, running alongside it, but it was too late—the Pastor, crouched and running, swiped

185

toward him. He grabbed Basajaun's ears.

Basajaun watched the floor rush away from him. His hindquarters flew out in front on him, his feet flailed. He could feel his body plummeting, but up into the air; like falling, but backwards. The whole room rotated and flipped around for Basajaun's body was swinging wildly, like a pendulum, his own weight pulling against his ears. The Pastor's face flashed in front on him. When Basajaun's body stopped swinging, the face came into focus. The face of his enemy, just inches from his own, whose hand held Basajaun six feet above the floor, dangling by his ears.

The man and the rabbit looked at each other. Basajaun hadn't even known what the Pastor looked like—thin, white haired, and terrifying. The rabbit had never looked so deeply into a human's eyes, other than Cora's. But unlike Cora's, Basajaun could see no depth or questions or shadows or memories in the Pastor's eyes. There was only blackness.

The Pastor sneered at Basajaun. He swung the rabbit's body back and pinned it under his left arm, against his ribs. He wrapped his right hand around the base of Basajaun's skull. Basajaun opened his mouth to scream, but nothing came out.

Boxy charged at the Pastor's heels and sunk her teeth into the ropey tendon behind the man's ankle. The Pastor let out a growling bark and kicked backward, sending Boxy flying into the hall. But when the man stumbled, Basajaun laid his own teeth into the Pastor's wrist. The Pastor's taut, sinewy hands clutched the sides of Basajaun's body and squeezed, but Basajaun thrashed his legs, kicking, biting and scratching in a frenzy. Streaks and dotted lines of blood rose up out of the Pastor's arms.

"Ah!" the Pastor opened his arms and Basajaun dropped to the floor. All four of the rabbit's feet hit and he bounced forward, running so fast he wove from side to side along the hall.

"Boxy!" Basajaun yelled. Then he spotted the female rabbit darting into the doorway ahead of him. He followed, resolve rising in his chest as he felt his own feet hit the floor of the dead tree room. The opening to the marmot's hole was so close, but Basajaun stopped. "Wait!" he said. Boxy turned and Basajaun bolted back the way he had come.

"Basajaun, no! What are you doing?"

Just inside the doorway between the cottage and the dead tree room, laid the cotton-wrapped keys. Basajaun caught a glimpse of the Pastor's bare feet coming his way as he grabbed the handkerchief bundle with his teeth and ran for his life to the freedom of the outside.

Boxy and Basajaun burst out of the marmot's hole, kicking out a halo of dirt, and didn't stop.

"Run!" Basajaun yelled through the muffle of cloth in his mouth. Cora's expression dropped and all the color drained from her face. Boxy and Basajaun bent left and Cora sprinted in their direction, but a fading voice called after her.

"No, this way! This way!" the voice said.

Cora turned and saw Rutai the marmot running after them, his short legs blurring under his big, round, galloping form. "Wait!" Cora yelled to the rabbits. She didn't know if they'd stop. She didn't even know if she should, but in an instant all three of them were looking at one another as Rutai slid to a stop in front of them.

"This way!" he tossed his head to the right. "If you're trying to escape the man, you must come this way!"

"I think we should follow him," Boxy whispered. "Marmots may be fierce to protect their dwellings, but they don't lead other animals into danger. He knows this area because he lives here. I think we should follow."

Cora looked at Basajaun who froze, blinking and big-eyed. He looked to Cora like he'd seen his own death, but he managed to nod.

"If you lead us wrong, you will suffer greatly," Cora said to the marmot. Rutai didn't flinch.

"Come on!" he said.

The four of them ran through the trees. Cora swatted at the branches in her path and tried to keep an eye on the animals. She could see Boxy's tail and Basajaun's, and up ahead Rutai who, when running, looked like a small, fat dog from the back. He was much less graceful than the rabbits and not quite as fast, but he was a force to be reckoned with as he banged through the trees, moving with complete confidence at the head of their party. After running for a few minutes when the immediate danger, whatever that might be, seemed a ways behind them, Cora's mind flooded with questions about what had just happened, and what would happen next. She wondered when she would get a chance to talk to Basajaun.

The trees opened up on the top of a small hill. Rutai threw his body outward, tucking his legs up during the brief moment he was airborne, fell on his side almost bouncing, and rolled down the hill with surprising speed. Basajaun and Boxy jumped down the hill with great strides, clearing a few feet with each leap. Cora ran after them all, feeling awkward when the momentum of her upright weight made her stumble and trip on her own feet. At the bottom of the hill, she tumbled into a heap.

"Only a little further," Rutai said, more to Cora than the rabbits. His running slowed to a trot as he moved along the left side of the hill, around the back, to a smaller hill. The two hills almost met, or would have, long ago, but the earth had been dug and hollowed out between them. Cora thought it looked like the inside of a halved, hollow eggshell standing on its end. It made her remember how her father always laid the broken eggshells on the kitchen counter next to him while he cooked. When she was very young, Cora used to imagine that if she somehow shrunk down to the size of an ant, she could live inside one of the broken shells. It would be her little home. Cora was just tall enough to see over the counter then, and her father would smile as he watched his daughter slide her open hands against the eggshells, guiding them into a row.

Cora, Basajaun, Boxy and Rutai sat facing one another inside the concave, earth overhang. Basajaun laid the handkerchief bundle in the center of the circle, and stretched out his small jaw since it had been clamped shut so long. Using his teeth, he gently pulled open the edges of the handkerchief, and exposed the rings of keys. They had fought so hard to obtain it, but now it sat before them, forebodingly still and man-made, and so ill-fitting to their visceral, organic world. Even Cora, who had seen and used keys most every day of her short life, pulled her knees up away from them.

Basajaun used his nose to separate the keys, fanning them out on the square of cloth. He bumped one. "It's this one."

Cora leaned down into Basajaun's view. "Basajaun, what happened in there?"

"The Pastor saw us," Basajaun mumbled.

"It was my fault," Boxy said.

"But what happened?" Cora said.

"Bad things. Bad," Basajaun looked down.

"But what?" Cora said. Neither of the rabbits answered. "Are you okay?"

"We have to decide what to do," Basajaun tapped the key with his paw.

"Well, I think you should rest here a bit," Rutai said. "It's safe."

"What is this place?" Cora said.

"It's for courting," Rutai replied. "For marmots. When it's in season. But it's past time, now. It'll be empty 'til next year."

"I think we need to move the plan forward," Basajaun said. "I think we should go to the shed."

"But what if the Pastor follows us? What if he finds us? I think we should go back to the warren," Cora said.

"And lead him back there? No, we can't," Basajaun said. "Because of what happened, we can't. We can't risk leading him back to the warren, under any circumstances. To bring the enemy into the heart of all we hold dear? I can't risk it," Basajaun shook his head and looked at Cora. "But you could go home. To your home."

Cora paused. She hadn't even considered it. She thought of her father and the self that she used to be, the self that she'd left behind. It seemed like someone else. She looked at the rabbits, at the keys, at what they'd gotten themselves so deeply into, because of her. And she looked at Basajaun, her Basajaun. "I can't go home, not yet," she said. "I won't."

The girl and the rabbits sat, thinking. Rutai pointed at Boxy. "The lady hasn't spoken yet," he said. All eyes turned to Boxy. And when she opened her mouth, she had no idea what would come out.

"Basajaun is right, we can't go home to the warren. We are in limbo. We are almost done, but we are afraid of what will follow. As long as we prolong the mission, are in the thick of it, there is a chance. We are afraid to come to the end, because then the outcome will be finite. We are afraid of the outcome, in case it isn't what we hope."

"But the sooner we reach the ending, the sooner it will all be over," Basajaun said, and all of them, even Rutai, stared at the keys. "So be it."

Cora put her finger on the old, silver skeleton key, flat and thin like board. The same one Basajaun had selected. "That is the one," she said.

"Take care, my friends," Rutai said. "Take great care."

Cora held the key up next to the lock. The same pink and orange rust, the same lack of embellishment. It matched exactly. Cora looked up at the shed one more time. The key only had one notch.

Boxy and Basajaun held their breath as Cora put the key inside. She rattled it a moment, jiggling it left and right, and then felt the key catch. When she turned it, a shimmery, gray light came out of the keyhole. Boxy gasped. Cora kept turning the key and when it clicked all the way upside down, the light turned bright blue. The door shifted on its hinges and made a soft 'clunk' as it moved a millimeter down and forward. Cora and Basajaun's eyes met before she wrapped her fingers around the side of the door and pulled it open.

Blue light filled the whole shed. It fell out into the woods, and was followed by a wash of gray smoke. Cora took a step inside and Basajaun and Boxy flanked her feet, almost touching her ankles. The smoke floated over them and out of the shed, but Cora had to fan the air in front of her with her arm. She couldn't see.

A golden light along the floor illuminated the money. It was there—more than Cora had ever imagined—lying in piles, all around the edges of the room, it formed a ring. Cora stepped forward. A residual blue haze hung in the middle of the shed, and at first Cora thought it was empty air. But then she saw the outline of something, something big, hidden in the smoke. She waved her arm in front of her face again.

A man, sitting in a chair. But something was coming out of his head, two—Cora gasped. She cupped her hands over her mouth. The blue smoke was gone and two eyes stared at Cora—huge and round, and black as Basajaun's. A nose twitched. The form began to shift back and forth, struggling against the chains Cora could now see; they bound the figure all around, digging into his body. Into his fur.

A rabbit, the size of a man.

"Please help me," the rabbit said.

Cora felt a bash on her head, and everything went black.

CHAPTER ELEVEN

MAJU

When Cora woke, her head lay slumped into her chest. It throbbed. She tried to reach up to brush her hair out of her face, but her arms wouldn't move. She pulled them again, and heard the sound of metal clanking. She jerked. She managed to open her eyes, and saw thick chains around her chest and waist. Letting out a little yelp, she thrashed against the hard-backed chair she was chained to.

"It won't do any good. I've tried," a voice said.

Cora turned. The six-foot tall rabbit sat only a few feet from her; chained just as she was. She blinked at him and realized she was staring, so she turned away. The interior of the shed looked big, larger than the three poison sheds Cora had seen the insides of. But soon she realized that the actual building size was the same, it just looked larger because the wooden shelving, carpentry tables and counters, and all the tool racks were gone; torn out. Light outlines on the walls showed where the furnishings used to be. Now the room was a bare, hollow husk of weathered gray wood and dirt floor. And the ring of money that surrounded the rabbit, which now surrounded Cora as well.

"It will be okay," the rabbit said. "I'm sorry you are captured."

Cora peeked at the rabbit through her hair. "Who are you?"

"I'm Maju. I came here looking for Mari," the rabbit's eyes suddenly lit up. "Do you know her?"

"No, I'm sorry," Cora said.

"She's here, I just hope she's all right. I sent her a message the night I arrived. I sent it on the wind. But the captor found me first. I don't know how he did it. He brought me here, to this cell. He took Mari away from me," the rabbit's face crinkled with sadness. "And he keeps bringing all this money, piling and piling it," the rabbit looked over the winding money ring with sick disgust. "He says it's for me, if I give her up, but I won't! I won't ever. I tell him so over and over, but still he brings more. He says soon I will change my mind but he doesn't understand. I only want Mari." The rabbit closed his eyes. "He is keeping her a prisoner. If only she and I could at least be prisoners together. I miss her so, so much."

"Is she," Cora paused. "Is she like you?"

"No, she is like you, a human. But bigger. Well," the rabbit looked at Cora, "a little bigger."

Cora looked the rabbit up and down. She still couldn't believe her eyes. He was proportioned like a rabbit in every way, but on a massive scale. His big, powerful legs, his huge ears. Then she noticed a cord, a black cord, nestled in the fur on the rabbit's chest. She took a deep breath. "That cord—that cord you're wearing—what is it?"

"It is a gift from my beloved. It links me to her," the rabbit scrunched his head down and gingerly picked up the cord between his teeth. Lifting his head he pulled, sliding the cord out form under the chains, and out popped a gold-brown stone, dangling from the end of the string.

Cora instinctively reached for her own stone, but her hands lurched against the chains again. Her breathing quickened. "Someone gave me one of those."

"They did?" Maju exclaimed. "Perhaps they know my Mari! Who was it? What did they look like?"

"She has light brown hair, and blue eyes. She's older than me, a bit. She's very, very pretty. And she's pregnant."

"But that's—" Maju's shiny eyes widened into big, black marbles. "There's a name, another name," the rabbit rocked against his chains. His head bobbed. "The name that Mari had before I knew her. A human name. What was it? It was short, plain. It's," he looked at Cora, "Nellie."

Basajaun and Boxy hopped around the back of the old grain cellars. They were worn and sore, and very, very tired. Basajaun tried to keep his breathing shallow, for when his ribs expanded fully, a raw, tender ache fanned out across his side.

Boxy hopped up next to him. "Stop a minute," she said, "here, let me feel it," and she eased her paws against

Basajaun's ribs.

"Ah!" Basajaun jumped.

"They're not broken," Boxy said, "thank God. You'll just be very sore."

Basajaun had a flash in his mind of the Pastor's foot kicking him, sending him flying through the air. He'd landed, sprawled and flailing, on the dirt outside. Boxy had followed, the Pastor had got hold of her back leg, and flung her as though she were a rag doll. Basajaun noticed how Boxy was favoring her right foot. "Leave it," Basajaun moved away from Boxy's touch. "We have to get help for Cora, that's all that matters."

Basajaun surveyed the grain cellars. He hoped that he and Boxy would be able to lift the lids, but which one was it? He noticed a hole in one of the wooden covers, and stuck his head inside.

"Hello?" he said.

"Henry?" a voice replied.

Basajaun flipped his head to Boxy. "This is the one." She followed him inside.

Basajaun hopped over the tightly-packed earth to a form lying under a gray sheet. "We are here to ask for your help."

Two blue eyes peeked out from under the stiff sheet. "What?"

"Cora is in trouble," Basajaun said, "and I have nowhere else to go."

"What can I do?" Nellie sat up suddenly to face the rabbits, and Basajaun took in the girl's desperate expression. He hadn't expected to be met with such open

197

willingness, or to see his own newfound lack of reserve mirrored so effortlessly.

Basajaun's mind's eye hurdled through the past night. He saw the Pastor bringing a wood plank down on Cora's head, and Cora falling to the floor. And, almost worse, the shed door slamming closed between him and his human, separating them, and trapping her in a place he could not reach. Basajaun slapped his ears from side to side, hitting at the memory. "She's been taken prisoner by the enemy. The one you came here with."

"We don't know if she's alive," Boxy said. Basajaun scowled at her.

"He took her into the shed. Please. We can't get in," Basajaun said.

Nellie stood. "This is all my fault. I am what the Pastor wants. If he has me, he'll leave your friend alone."

"There's something else," Basajaun said. "It sounds—I don't know. I only saw it a moment. Perhaps my mind was going mad. The enemy has a rabbit. Chained." Nellie was grabbing her bonnet off the floor. "But it's a rabbit, as big as a man."

Nellie stopped cold. Her face dropped. She didn't breathe. "Is he alive?"

"Yes. I think so. He spoke," Basajaun said.

"What did he say?" Nellie reached down and grabbed Basajaun's small shoulders.

"I don't remember," Basajaun trembled at the intensity of the girl. "He said it to Cora. I don't know."

"He said, 'please help me'," Boxy said.

Nellie turned to Boxy, wild-eyed. "We must go. We

must go now."

"Nellie is your love?" Cora said.

"Yes," the big rabbit replied.

"Oh my," Cora said. "What happened? Did the Pastor do this to you? I mean, I know he locked you up, but is he the one who made you—like this?"

"No. It was a spell. It went wrong," the rabbit winced. He took a deep breath and tried to steady his voice. "But, we're going to put it right. We're going to fix it, we have to."

"So, you used to be a man?"

"No, I used to be a rabbit."

"But how?" Cora said. "I thought—" she shook her head a little. All the things she thought to ask sounded rude, so instead she said, "but, you *are* a rabbit."

"I used to be a regular rabbit. A small rabbit. Like those two that came in here with you. In Australia. Where Mari lived. Where I was born."

"How?" was all Cora could say.

"You think there are a lot of rabbits here? In Australia, there are droves. So many. There is never enough food for us all. Everyone hates us, and I understand why. We ruin crops—all the food people work so hard to raise—to feed themselves. There are too many of us, but we continue to increase our numbers with no regard. We're timid, but aggressive. Cowardly, but proud. Who respects us? No one. No one but our own."

"That's not true," Cora said. "That's not true at all."

"Since I was a pup, I watched and admired the human

199

men from afar. They worked so hard. They ate good meals that they deserved after their toil. They laughed. I wanted to be like them, big and strong. They helped each other, they didn't just vie for power and propagation."

"But they do!" Cora said. "They do that, really. All the time. More! You haven't seen it from the inside. It's not perfect, it's flawed, like everything else! Why do you—"

"We were overpopulated and dying. I wanted out!" the rabbit yelled.

Cora flinched a little. "I'm sorry."

"If I had one wish," Maju said, "it was to be a man. I wished it secretly, for to express such a want to any other rabbit would ensure me an outcast—even more of one than I was already—or worse. But the wish was lark. An impossible fantasy. Or so I thought.

"Mari came to us like a dream. She was little. Not quite as little as you are, but littler than she is now. I was little too. She would come in secret to bring us food. She never had enough for all of us, of course, just for a couple families, but she would trade locations each visit; bring the food to a different spot. And she talked to us, like we were worth something. She didn't just chase and kick and scorn and kill us. She treated us like equals. All the rabbits loved her. They all wanted to be close to her.

"But none of them wanted to be close to her in the way that I did. I saw how the human boys in the town looked at her and I could read their thoughts, because their thoughts were my own. I felt ashamed, and I didn't know what was wrong with me. I knew she deserved better than—than a *rabbit*," he spit the word. "And I knew loving her would

200

only bring me the heartache of desire unfulfilled. I did it anyway.

"She began to single me out and pay more and more attention to me, more than she did to anyone else, and even though it made everything worse, I welcomed it, ran to it. I figured I would be dead soon anyway, and I wanted to take whatever joy this mortal world would allow me in my short life. But then one day, she said it," the rabbit looked off into the dismal room, as though he were seeing his memories again, right before his eyes. "She said, 'I love you'. Not like she was saying it to an animal, or a pet, but like she was saying it to a person. A man."

A 'click' sounded in the keyhole of the shed door. Cora gasped. She tossed her head from side to side again, looking for the escape that had eluded her the moment she awoke in chains. Her heart began to beat fast. Breathless, she looked at Maju. He frowned.

"With luck, little girl," he said, "you will not feel pain."

The Pastor threw the door open and slammed it shut behind him. "Well, getting acquainted, I see?" he strode over to Cora. "You're enjoying the company, I expect. Since you've grown accustomed to animals, you *trollop*," he snarled.

"Are you going to kill me now?" Cora said.

"I wouldn't dream of it," the Pastor said. "Not yet, anyway. You're my bait."

Cora glared up at him from under her dark brows. "Bait for what?"

"For your father. You think I give a toss about what happens to you? It's him I want."

"Why?" Cora said. "What has my father done?"

The Pastor slapped Cora across the face. "Everything!" he yelled. "Every step of the way he has been a thorn in my side. It wasn't enough that he *questioned* me—the wretch—he tried to play Boston Tea Party out at the termination site!" The Pastor leaned close to her. "Play. Like a child. He thinks just because he is a runty, boy of a man he's immune to a man's punishment? Well, I will make a man of him yet."

Cora's eyes were wide. "But my father didn't have anything to do with that!" She pulled against the chains. "It was me—all me!"

"Yes," the Pastor pointed to Cora's chest with his bony finger. It almost touched her. "I suppose *you* masterminded the plans for building a wall, encasing the entire farmland?"

Cora swallowed. "Well, *no*—that part was him. But at the start, only at the start! He bowed out after that, I swear he did. He's a coward!" Cora gasped at her own accusation. She hadn't meant to say it. It just slipped out.

The Pastor laughed. "Now on that part, we are in full agreement. But you're not a coward, are you?" He leaned close to her. "I dare say you're not afraid of anything. How his seed brought you forth, I can't imagine. Your mother was undoubtedly more of a man than he ever was." The man stood. "But you are just a little girl. And a little girl couldn't single-handedly transpose and dump six hundred pounds of strychnine. No, that's man's work. And he was man enough for that, wasn't he?"

"No!" Cora thrashed wildly and the chair legs bumped

against the dirt.

"Name who did it, then," the man reached forward and pinched Cora's bicep between his thumb and index finger. He shook the small muscle. "Or did your bravery give you the strength of several fully-grown men?"

Cora scowled and the Pastor slapped her again, harder. His voice rose. "Name who did it! If not your father, who?"

Cora pressed her lips together and looked away, frowning, and the Pastor raised a hand to hit her again. But then he stopped. His hand dropped to his side, and his voice became calm. "Then within the day, your father will be dead."

"No!" Cora yelled. She clenched her teeth together and growled so she wouldn't cry, and tried to keep her breathing as even as possible as she narrowed her eyes at the man. "Well, you're out of luck. My father doesn't know where I am."

"You naïve, idiot girl," the Pastor said. "You think a father would care so little about his child, not to find out?"

"This is it," Henry said. He and Wayne stood before the low, square cottage.

Wayne put his hands in his pockets, and rocked back and forth on the balls of his feet. "You wait here," he said. "No reason to get you on the wrong side of the Pastor."

Henry was about to protest, but his eye drifted back to the living-room window he'd wished he'd been able to spy through the night before he freed Nellie. "I'll go around the side," Henry said. "You knock, and I'll look in the window."

Wayne nodded. He walked up the stoop, rapped on the door, and put his hands back in his pockets. He waited. No one came. Wayne slid his thumbs along his neck, turning up his shirt collar, and knocked again.

"I don't see him," Henry popped his head around the corner. "I don't think he's here."

Wayne looked up and down the door. "I want to get in. Inside."

"Okay," Henry stood beside the man.

"You should go home. I know I brought you out here, but things are going to start unraveling soon, and fast. Once it all starts, I can't stop or even delay it. I don't know what will happen."

"I know," Henry said.

"And I know you would stay. But I don't expect your help anymore, nor do I want it."

"I know."

"Once I break in this door, I can't protect either of us. You will be part of it, and be in danger."

"And you think that breaking into the Pastor's cottage is somehow more perilous than kidnapping his niece?"

Wayne huffed a little. "Fair 'nough."

"But there's no need to break the door in, I have a better way," Henry curled his hand in front of his face. "Follow me."

Dangling on his elbows off the edge of the sill in front of Nellie's window, Henry fingered the strange gouges in the wood along the windowpane. He leaned back. "Someone's already tried to get in here," he said to Wayne, who stood in the flowerbed. "I don't think they succeeded," Henry murmured back into the glass. He tried the window himself and it didn't budge. He jumped down.

"Is there anyone up the road at all, anyone around?" Henry said.

Wayne stepped back and surveyed the area. "No. Why? What is it?"

Henry picked up a rock, and chucked it through the window. The shattering glass crackled the quiet countryside, and Wayne jumped. "Someone else had already tried to get in before us," Henry said. "If we're lucky, they'll get blamed for that." Henry climbed back up to Nellie's window, carefully reached through the broken glass, and unhooked the latch.

"Maybe they did get in," Wayne said as he noticed the overturned chair in the Pastor's living room. "There's not much else disturbed," he tiptoed through the hall, "not that there's much to disturb, of course." At the door to the Pastor's bedroom, Wayne stopped. He laid a hand on the doorframe, and looked toward the empty bed. From where he stood in the hall he could see inside, but he was hesitant to let even the tip of his nose cross the threshold into the man's room.

Henry came up behind him. "Go on. Go inside."

Wayne looked at the floor as he stepped in, watching his feet cross into the sleeping place of the enemy.

"Everything in here looks the same," Henry said.

"You've been in here before?"

Henry bit the inside of his cheek. "The night I busted

Nellie out."

Wayne crouched over the bed. The room was immaculate and spartan, with not a thing out of place for there were so few things to be out of place to begin with. Henry curled and uncurled his toes inside his boots.

"Hey," Henry said.

"Hmm?" Wayne studied the Pastor's bedside table.

"Sir," Henry said. "I gotta ask you something. Please."

Wayne looked over, and wondered how he could've missed the fretted tone in the boy's voice. It showed now, all over Henry's face. Henry took a deep breath and held it in, letting the air move his cheeks. Finally, he exhaled.

"I don't get it. You're Cora's father."

"Yes, I am."

"Well then, isn't it your job to—*you know*—" Henry put out his hands and waited, but the man started at him blankly. "Isn't it your job to take care of her? If she's out runnin' all over creation, isn't it your job to know where she is? Make sure she's safe?" Henry paused again but still Wayne was silent. "You're her Dad. Why didn't you protect her?"

Wayne turned away, and his reply floated up from around the back of his head, over his hunched shoulders. His voice was so small, like a little boy. Like a child. "I couldn't," it whispered. And then it began to rasp. "I know. I know I should have. I know I was supposed to. But I just couldn't. How could I face her as a father after what I'd done, what I'd failed to do? The Pastor took my manhood away, made me a fool. And she knew it. How could I instruct her as a father would, when she knew I was a joke?"

"Cora—" Henry struggled, "she doesn't think bad of you. She doesn't. And what do you care what that Pastor says anyway? He's a wretch. What manhood means to him, that's not manhood. It's just bullying."

"I just couldn't," Wayne said again. "I couldn't ask her for respect when I had none for myself. I could see it in her eyes, her face—she would never answer to me again. And to ask her to, and be denied, that would be too shaming. So I avoided asking her to at all."

Wayne turned back to Henry, his big eyes looking more like Cora's than Henry had ever noticed. "I know it was wrong. I know I did wrong. And failed as a father. But it's just *so hard*. You don't know what it's like to have another man emasculate you and take away your self-respect."

Henry wanted to say yes, that he did. That he knew exactly what that was like. And that he still carried out what he had to do, anyway. But the grown man's remorseful face made him too sad.

"She's your daughter," Henry said. "You love her. Isn't that enough? Enough to make you go after her? To care?"

Wayne crouched so he and Henry were eye-to-eye, and leaned closer until he almost touched the boy. "They don't give you a book on how to raise a child, you know. Father her alone. You just have to try. And sometimes you fail. You think I don't care? I—" Wayne put his hand over his eyes and curled his head toward his lap. He choked. "I know, I am weak. And she is strong. It just happened one day. She became stronger than me. How do you parent someone who is stronger than you?"

"But it was you who raised her up strong," Henry said quietly. "That's something, anyway."

"Sometimes I think I had very little to do with that," Wayne sighed, and uncovered his eyes. He listened to the sound of his own breathing filling the sterile room. Henry didn't say anymore. Wayne didn't know what he was looking for, but he was both drawn to scrutinize Pastor Harding's bedroom, and repelled at the thought of being in there at all. The bed blanket touched his arm and Wayne shrunk away from it, brushing off the offending spot with his other hand. Then he noticed something white lying on the floor, between the bed and the end table. A scrap of cloth. Wayne squatted on the floor and picked it up.

His heart felt sick. For a moment everything around him went ghostly gray, and he struggled to focus even though it felt like all his insides were falling backwards out of his spine. His whole neck and throat tightened as he looked at the little piece of cotton in his shaking hands.

"Are you okay?" Henry said. "What's that?" he leaned down to look over Wayne's shoulder.

Wayne turned up toward him, and held out his two hands. The fabric was pulled taut between Wayne's thumbs and Wayne raised it higher, closer to Henry's face. The man's closed lips trembled, his eyebrows pleading.

"Oh," Henry breathed.

Wayne moved the cloth scrap back in front of face, and looked at it as though it were a living thing. Or a dead thing.

"It's gonna be ok," Henry put his small hand on the grown man's shoulder. Wayne didn't reply. Henry moved closer to Wayne's face. "She might still be all right," he murmured, but the man didn't turn, didn't speak. Henry looked toward the living room door and window, and back at Cora's father. "Mister, say something."

Wayne stared into the piece of cotton, as though it were what he was addressing. "Long ago, before the rabbits were a problem, I was standing in the back yard, about to chop some wood. Cora was a baby. Her Mother had just died; consumption. I hadn't talked to anyone for weeks, not one word. Not even Cora, although she didn't know because she was too little. I was so, so broken. And my self, everything about my life, was just sadness; just this terrible loss. When I knocked open the first log, I saw something dart out from behind the woodpile and toward the fence. It was a rabbit. He must have been hiding behind the woodpile, and the noise had scared him out into the open. He raced across the yard. He must've thought his life was in danger, otherwise he wouldn't have hurled himself between the slats in the fence trusting, or hoping, that he would make it through. He got stuck. His body was suspended between the panels of wood, with all four legs dangling off the ground. He thrashed for a few moments, then stopped, either accepting his fate or thinking on what to do next.

"I was so cautious when I approached him, because I didn't want to scare him into struggling more and doing himself harm. His eyes were big, shiny black but I could see he was watching me because the whites showed at the front of his head. I didn't touch him. He was breathing heavy, but holding perfectly still. I pressed the point of my ax between one of the slats and the support of the fence, and pried the panel loose. I pulled it to one side, and that was just enough for the rabbit to escape.

"He was free. I was ready to watch him the bolt across the pasture, but he ran a few feet, stopped, and turned around. He just sat there, facing me, watching me, looking into me, as though he were thanking me. As though he had some sense of—gratitude. Half a minute he sat there and I didn't move an inch. It did something to me. Everything I'd done in my life—the good and the bad—faded away because, to the rabbit, this one deed represented who I was. This one act of humanity was all he knew of me. I couldn't save my wife, but I could save that rabbit. And it was so easy, no effort at all. But to the rabbit, it was everything.

"The purity of his gratitude touched me in a way that was overwhelming. It is hard to explain and my description of it sounds small compared to what happened that day. The rabbit hopped away. I wept."

Wayne still didn't look up. Henry stood, and put his hands in his pockets. "Why are you telling me this?"

"Because it's why it happened. It's why all of it happened. Because I could never eat, kill, or massacre any creature that shows gratitude."

Henry's eyes fell on the Pastor's night table. He stopped. "The keys," Henry said. "Cora wanted the keys."

"What?" Wayne stood and wheeled around to face the boy. Henry stepped back. "What keys?"

"She noticed them, there," Henry pointed at the bare spot on the table, next to the bible. He swallowed hard. "The night she and I came for Nellie."

Wayne grabbed the boy's arms and squeezed. "She was with you? She was here?"

Henry took a deep breath. "She was with me. I'm sorry. She was here then, and now she came back for the keys."

CHAPTER TWELVE

TENURE

Nellie ran through the woods. She was formulating a plan in her mind, tweaking it and adding to it, laboring over it more and more as she considered all the variables and possibilities that lay before her. Boxy's directions to the shed were exact down to the last shrub, and as Nellie passed through the thin birches, she wondered how much further she had to go.

"Ah!" a pain twisted in the girl's abdomen. She grabbed the underside of her large belly and lurched forward. The pain came again. Nellie dropped to her knees and panted with care, allowing herself to catch her breath. She peered ahead through the trees, tensed, gulped and tried to acclimate herself to the feelings in her body. She hoped that if she made the sensations familiar, examined them and acknowledged their nuances fully, she could ignore them for just a little while longer. She tried to imagine that there was calmness all around her, though that was hard. She stood, rubbed her hands along her belly, and began to run again. Faster, this time.

Cora didn't see the door to the shed squeak open. Nor did she see Maju's hopeful eyes widen at the sight of the pregnant teenager's head, peeking through the crack. What Cora did see, over the Pastor's shoulder, was Nellie shuffling silently toward the man's back, smiling, with a finger over her lips.

Nellie laid a pale, slender hand on the shoulder of the Pastor's dark coat. The man reached across his chest and grabbed the girl's wrist, wheeling around. He yanked the offending hand, pulling it upward in triumph, and Nellie stumbled. She had to stand on her toes to reach the height the Pastor held her at. But when the man saw the teenager's face, he stopped.

"You?" he said. Nellie's heels slowly came down against the ground as the man's arm began to slack. "But— I thought—" he said.

Nellie closed her free hand around the Pastor's wrist. She lowered both their arms down to his side, and smiled, leaning her face toward his. She laid the same hand gingerly against his cheek, smoothing her thumb over his papery skin. "I've come back," she whispered.

"Uh—" the man choked and little tears began along the rims of his eyes. He blinked and grimaced, staring at Nellie, then fell to his knees and buried his face in her skirt. "You came back," he sobbed.

Cora gaped at the scene before her. She turned to Maju, who was watching the Pastor wrap his arms around the waist of the girl he had called his beloved. Maju was smiling, too. Ever so slightly.

"Yes," Nellie said.

"I'm so sorry," the Pastor cried.

"I know," Nellie replied, and stroked man's wiry hair. "And I want a trade. Me, for the little dark-haired girl. Let her go." Cora could see Nellie's shiny eyelids, for the girl was looking down, still smiling, at the crying man at her feet. She ran her hand over and over the top of his head. Then suddenly, Nellie's fingers shot out straight. She let out a little grunt, and her body began to crumple until she was squatting on the floor and wailing.

"Don't!" Maju yelled. "Don't hurt her!"

"It's not me!" the Pastor looked panicked. "I'm not doing anything!"

"No," Nellie squinted and grit her teeth, "it's the baby."

"Oh my Lord, the baby!" the Pastor exclaimed.

"The baby," Maju whispered.

Nellie fell back into the Pastor's arms, and he eased her down until she was lying on the dirt floor of the shed. He pulled off his frock coat, rolled it up, and wedged it under the girl's head and shoulders. "I don't know what to do!" he said to Nellie. She didn't reply, just grunted and strained and squeezed her fists until her knuckles went white. Cora had never seen the Pastor without a jacket. His form was small and lank under his white button shirt, and his bare forearms next to his rolled sleeves were thin but round and hard, like steel. Cora had also never seen the pleading expression that pained the man's face when he turned to she and Maju.

The expression faded in a moment. The Pastor scowled

at the giant rabbit, and instead turned his attention to Cora. In a moment he was kneeling next to her chair, unlocking and yanking off the chains that held her. "You must help me!" he said.

"I—" Cora said, "I don't know how to deliver a baby."

The Pastor grabbed Cora's arms and shook her. "You must help me!" he yelled.

"Okay!" Cora trembled. "I'll help. I'll help!"

The Pastor bent Nellie's knees and spread them open. "The baby comes out here," he said.

"Yes," Cora said. The Pastor just stared at her, as though he were awaiting instruction. Cora looked to Nellie, but her eyes were squeezed shut as she panted. "Go hold her hands," Cora said to the Pastor. "Let her squeeze your hands. It might help her feel better." The Pastor nodded and went to sit by Nellie's side. Cora watched the girl's delicate, porcelain hands wrap around the Pastor's long, rough, sinewy ones. The Pastor watched Nellie's hands as they squeezed. Cora lifted Nellie's skirt and looked at Maju. He nodded.

Basajaun and Boxy walked up the aisle of rabbits. Basajaun had watched Cora do this once, and had done it with her once himself, but never was the aisle so long. Every rabbit from miles and miles was there—the south, west and east fields. Thousands of brown bodies dotted back over the hill. Years prior, the rabbits had roamed the wide open grasses and dared to cross such spacious lands, but most of the young rabbits now didn't know what it was like to be on such a flat plain, with so few places to hide.

The older rabbits remembered, and memories of this different life flooded back to them as the looked at the fields and sky. Some of them looked at the youngsters, and the realization that what was a distant memory for them was completely alien to their children, brought tears to their eyes.

Basajaun stood tall and rigid before the rabbit populous, the light of the sun skipping down the bristled fur on his back. He was squinting and serious as he moved his gaze slowly over the crowd and, from where they stood, he was even more arresting than Artulyn had been the first time Cora met him. With his neck pulled down into his shoulders, Basajaun raised his nose and pointed it toward the horizon. He was one of many, but learned and different. This was his role now, and one he was more than ready to fulfill. The rabbit Chief looked at his son and hoped he made the right choice. He wanted to cover his own face with his paws, but he was in public, and couldn't dare let anyone see.

"My people," Basajaun said to the crowd. "No one is forcing you to be here. Each of you has come of your own free will. What does this tell you? When the message is spread that one of our own is in trouble, and that we are amassing an army, you could assume that your neighbor will go, that your friend will go, that your father or mother or sister or brother will go. It is easy to assume that there will be enough without you. It is easy to assume that your one presence will not make a difference when undoubtedly there will be hundreds of others. It is easy to bow out, so you can be safe. So when it is announced that one of our own is in trouble, and we all know how easy it would be for any or all of you to just stay safe in your burrow, but you come anyway, that tells us something. When we send out a help signal and every able-bodied rabbit in the entire miles and miles vicinity comes and sits here waiting, ready to do whatever it takes, ready for action, that tells us that what we are about to do, is *right*.

"Not everyone has a chance in their lifetime to do something that's right, to make that choice. So even though the choice is frightening, and even though the unknown is strange, I want you to realize that you've actually been given a gift: the opportunity to know that you did something that mattered. The fact that the decision is hard only proves this, for the hard decisions are the ones that count. So even if you're in danger, and even if you die, you'll always know that you did something that mattered.

"Some of you know Cora," Basajaun looked at Boxy, "some of you don't even know if she's real. I assure you, she is very real. She made the choice to do what's right, to go up against a seemingly impossible task. That task was to help us. No one else dared, very few cared, but she put herself in danger. And now, she is in danger, because of us. It is our duty to help her, because we are her only hope. Are you with me? Are you with me?"

The multitude of rabbits erupted into a mass of cheers. Basajaun held his paws out and gestured, explaining the plan, and the rabbits cheered louder. Boxy blushed as she watched him speak, and felt proud to be by his side. As that warm glow began to fill her from her ears to her feet, Basajaun grabbed her paw and held it up.

"And my great, brave comrade Boxy will lead the way!"

"What?" Boxy whispered to Basajaun.

"Don't go too fast," Basajaun whispered back, "keep it slow and steady. I don't want you to arrive there before I do."

"Why? What are you doing?"

Basajaun grinned at her. "Why, I'm going to get our secret weapon."

The rabbits cheered and chanted as Basajaun walked away from the crowd. Hearing the loud rabbit voices fade against his back, he felt a wave of pride. But a closer voice at his back stopped him. He turned around.

Basajaun's father blinked at him. "What you said back there," he gestured at the crowd, "it's all lies. All of it. None of it is true."

Basajaun frowned at the rabbit Chief. "Saving Cora is all that matters," he said, and turned and hopped away.

Basajaun found the two hills easily, though not as quickly as he'd hoped. He rounded the side, to the concave valley between them. He couldn't see into the dark hollow of earth.

"Hello?" Basajaun said.

"Who's there?" a voice growled.

"It's me. The rabbit from last night."

Rutai the marmot peeked out of the shadows. He stretched his neck out and looked past Basajaun, left and right.

"I didn't know if you'd still be here," Basajaun said. "I

must admit, I hoped."

Rutai came all the way out of the hollow. "Can't go back to the dead tree room now," he said evenly, "not ever."

"That is my fault," Basajaun said. "And I'm sorry. But I'm here to repay you, if you grant me one more favor."

"A favor?" Rutai said.

"It's not for me exactly," Basajaun said. "I mean, you'd be helping me, but it's for the girl. The human girl who ran with me."

"Cora?"

"How do you know her name?"

"She told me," Rutai said. "I'd never talked to a human before. She was—not what I expected."

"It's her that's needs help. She's in trouble. Terrible trouble."

Rutai paused and stared ahead. Basajaun had little experience with marmots and, while he could sense or read unspoken feelings of agreement or displeasure in another rabbit, he found that he couldn't decipher Rutai's silence at all. Basajaun's eyes drifted to the freshly scabbed gashes on the marmot's head.

"Name your price," Basajaun blurted out again. "Anything. As long as it's in my power, it's yours."

"Don't worry," Rutai said, "I will help. It was the trade I was thinking about. Normally I'm not one to work that way—bartering my action for the sake of opportunity always leaves a bad taste in my mouth. Especially since it is for that girl. But you have caught me in a bind. I do need something." Rutai exhaled a big puff of air into the dirt,

219

and tipped his ear behind him. "I can't stay here forever. It is the marmot courting place. Once spring comes, I have to leave. And I can't go back to the dead tree room. So I want a new home. A place to live. A good one, one that I know I can rely on permanent-like, and where I'll be safe. I want to live with the rabbits."

"You want to *live* with us?" Basajaun said.

Rutai narrowed an eye at him. "Is that a problem?"

"No," Basajaun shook his head quickly. "But don't you have anywhere else to go? I mean, most marmots want to be near each other. Most wouldn't want to be seen in the company of rabbits."

"I am not most marmots."

Basajaun opened his mouth to ask a question, but then flapped his ears a little instead. "Of course," he nodded. "You're very welcome. Join us, and follow me. Hurry!"

"Wait, I want to ask you one more thing."

"Yes?"

"What you're doing, it's important, isn't it? Not just to the girl, but to something bigger."

"Yes. It is."

"I can see the baby's head!" Cora exclaimed. Maju craned his neck toward them, but could see no more than he could before. Nellie screamed.

"Maybe if you try to—push it out," Cora said.

"How?" Nellie panted.

"I don't know," Cora said. "Just—push."

Nellie grunted and it grew to a scream again. The Pastor hadn't said a word since Cora had sent him to sit at

Nellie's side.

"Maybe I should get some help," Cora said, to whomever would listen.

The Pastor's eyes pierced Cora. He growled. "Don't you dare leave me, or I'll kill you!"

"I won't leave," Cora stammered. "I didn't mean—"

Cora was interrupted by another of Nellie's screams. But she looked down, and saw the baby's shoulder. "Oh my gosh—Nellie!" Cora reached down, and eased the baby into her arms. "Oh Nellie," Cora cried, "it's a boy." Cora cradled the baby, and held him close.

"My God," Maju said.

The baby began to howl, and Cora almost smiled. She saw a rope or root of some sort coming out of the baby's navel, and suddenly knife darted forward and sliced it. A few drops of blood fell on the dirt, and the Pastor put the knife back in his pocket.

"Give me the baby," he said.

"What?" Cora said.

"No!" Maju yelled.

"Give me the baby."

Cora looked at Nellie. "Nellie, don't you want to hold your baby?"

"Give me the baby," the Pastor had let go of Nellie's hands, and he gave Cora an icy glare.

"Don't do it!" the rabbit struggled against his chains. They shook.

"No," Cora hugged the baby closer to her chest. "This is Nellie's baby. You can't have him."

"You daft child," the Pastor put his hands on Nellie's

221

stomach. "It *is* my baby. Hers and mine."

"Bu—but—" Cora stammered.

The Pastor looked at Cora's blank, bewildered face, and laughed. He laughed harder and louder until his laugh built to a cackling roar. "Little girl," he said, "you don't know the first thing about the world."

"You're a monster," Cora gasped.

Now the man was wild-eyed. He slid his hand under the back of Nellie's head and eased it up. The girl opened her eyes woozily. "This is the monster, right here. Pretty, isn't she? Who could refuse her? No man, not even a holy man."

Cora buried the baby against her neck. She began to cry. "You're a very bad man."

The Pastor sneered. "Yes, of course. Ask the girl here. Ask her what a 'bad man' I am. Such a bad man, that she snuck, uninvited and unseen, into my parochial house. She came into my bed." The man pointed at his chest, "I loved her. *She* seduced *me*."

Cora scowled and looked at Nellie, but Nellie's face made her pause. The girl's icy blue eyes shimmered. "Cora—" she said.

"What?" Cora looked back and forth at Nellie and the Pastor. "What's going on?"

The Pastor looked intense, and more serious than Cora had ever seen him. "Give me the baby," he said.

Cora stood, and began to back up. She looked down at the baby's pink, shiny face. In it she saw Nellie's blue eyes, and the tip of the Pastor's nose. And Cora's voice was so small, she hardly heard it. "No."

"What?" the Pastor growled.

Cora backed up more. "No."

The Pastor stood. "That's my child, give it to me!"

"But, why do you want it?" Cora said.

"Because it's *mine*!" the Pastor advanced on Cora. "So help me, girl, give me that baby, or you'll be sorry," the man's hands reached for her.

"No," Nellie stood up. Her knees buckled and she fell, catching herself against the ground on her palms. She looked up at the man, and her wet hair hung in her face. "The girl goes free. It's me you want. It's a trade. You said."

"I said no such thing," the Pastor hissed at Nellie. "And if you want her to go, you better instruct her to do as I say."

"Cora, give him the baby."

"No," Cora shook her head again.

The Pastor grabbed Cora's arm. His fingers dug in. "Do you know what she wants the baby for?" he pointed to Nellie. "Has she told you?" Cora held the baby in her free arm and pulled against the Pastor's grip. "Give me the baby *now*!"

"Cora!" a voice yelled behind her.

Cora recognized the voice. It couldn't be? She turned to the figure in the doorway. The man who made everything ok, or used to. "Daddy?" she breathed.

"Cora, give him the baby," Cora's father ran toward her.

Cora looked at her father, in his white cotton shirt and jeans. His arms reached for her. When Cora looked into his eyes, she remembered how much he loved her, how much she loved him. She could give up the baby now, go home. Be safe. Her eyes pleaded. "I can't."

A thin, red stream spurted out of Wayne's forehead as he fell backward, arms outstretched, hands clawing at the air. The thud of his body as it landed on the dirt was almost as loud as the gunshot that preceded it.

"Daddy!" Cora ran to her father. She laid the baby in the crook of his arm and grabbed his shirt. "Daddy!" she tugged at the collar. The man's shoulders rose only millimeters off the ground and his head tipped back, still leaning against the earth. Cora shook him. Or tried to. "Daddy," she sobbed.

Footsteps came up behind Cora. The Pastor looked down at her, he towered over her, and slid the small pistol into his coat. He reached down, and picked up the baby. Cora sputtered and stared at him before turning back to her father's body, and laying her head on his chest. She grabbed fistfuls of the cotton shirt, and cried into it.

Suddenly, a clattering ran past Cora, around the side of the shed. A galloping, brown streak—it ran through the money, scattering the paper notes and kicking the coins. Money flew everywhere.

"Wha—what's that?" the Pastor yelled. He shifted the baby to one arm and fumbled in his coat for his gun. The brown streak ran circles around his feet and the Pastor spun around, trying to get a look at it. The animal ran and jumped into Nellie's arms. The Pastor's eyes grew fierce. "You—" he growled, "you have cheated on me again!"

"No!" Nellie opened her hands and looked at the

224

animal in her lap. "I don't even know who this is! I don't even know what it is!" the marmot turned in Nellie's lap to face her. The Pastor stomped toward them.

"You have split your love between man and beast, and this is one beast too many. I will not compete with two!" the Pastor's voice rose to a shrill pitch and he pulled out the gun. He clutched the crying infant to his side, and the gun danced and shook on the end of his outstretched arm, in front of the girl. "I will kill you!" he screeched, "I will kill you where you stand!"

"Don't you touch her!" Maju screamed. "Don't hurt her!"

Nellie looked down at the marmot. She gently scooped him into her arms, and placed him on the ground. She stood. "I have never split my love between man and beast, for it was never split. I have only loved one, whether he man or beast or both or neither or nothing in between. I only ever loved Maju. Everything I did, I did for him." She closed her hand around the wrist that held the gun. "And you, were nothing more than a pollinator." Nellie aimed the gun at her head. "So go ahead, kill me. You were never anything to me."

"Mari, no!"

"Ah!" the Pastor screamed and bashed Nellie in the side of the head with the butt of the gun. Nellie fell and the man screamed again. He turned the gun on Cora. But before he could take a step toward her, his hand dropped. His shoulders rolled, his mouth hung open, and he almost dropped the baby. The man's eyes moved from left to right, across the shed. Five hundred rabbits sat, still as stone, watching him.

The rabbits swarmed. They ran at the Pastor, jumped at him; one after the other pelted into his chest and legs. Some grabbed onto his coat and held on, and the man swatted and punched at them, but for every one he knocked away, two more came in its place. Cora saw the arm holding the baby begin to straighten and she ran, catching the child before it hit the dirt. The Pastor looked at Cora, and reached his empty hand toward her.

"Help me," he said.

But Cora turned, and walked away.

The Pastor screeched. He fell down and more and more rabbits poured into the shed—over a thousand. The Pastor tried to scoot backward, but the rabbits covered him, pinned him. The man strained against the animals, but the mass immobilized his limbs.

"Stop!" a voice yelled. One rabbit, who looked no different from the rest, climbed up and over the animal pile, to the Pastor's face. The rabbit stood nose to nose with him, and smiled. "I want to lay the death blow," Basajaun said, and raked his front claws down the man's face. Deep grooves of blood streaked the Pastor's forehead, eyes and cheeks.

"I can't see!" the man screamed.

"Now!" Basajaun yelled, and the rest of the rabbits swarmed over the Pastor's head and body, until he disappeared. Cora laid the baby on her father's chest, hiding her face between the life that had just entered the world, and the one that had just passed away. She didn't look up until there was silence.

Cora sat in the crook of her dead father's arm, cradling the sleeping baby, who lay bundled in the black frock coat. The silence in the shed was sharp and all encompassing, and Cora's wan, stony face was fixed and rigid. Outside, the rabbits who waited for her rustled, circling closer to the door. Inside, neither Basajaun, who sat at Cora's side, nor the giant rabbit, who still sat chained, said a word. Finally, Nellie stirred. The girl put a hand to her head, wincing, and looked around the shed.

"Are you okay?" Cora said.

"Yes, I think so," Nellie shook out her head, her light brown hair hitting her shoulders and cheeks. "Maju?" she said. Cora nodded toward the girl's side. "Oh, you're okay!" Nellie ran to the giant rabbit and threw her arms around him. She cried. "I can't believe that we made it."

"Fate forgive me for ever putting you in such danger," Maju tried to sound stern, but he laid his head on Nellie's shoulder, and wept. "But fate has made you mine at last."

Nellie wiped her tears, and ran to the Pastor's body. She pushed against his hip, rolling the corpse to one side, and pulled the big ring of keys out his pocket. She let go of the dead body, and it thumped as it fell back on its back.

"You're free," Nellie turned the key in the padlock at Maju's waist. "You'll never be chained again. Not by anything." The rabbit stood and the thick, heavy chains fell off his body. He was formidable. Six feet of fur and pure muscle, and soft, kind eyes, which showed the depth of dual awareness—man and animal, and the limbo between. Nellie hugged and squeezed him and he wrapped his short front legs around her back. "Everything's going to be okay," she cried. "We'll never be apart again." The teenage girl and the giant rabbit leaned on each other, and embraced as though they'd never let go. Cora rose as quietly as she could. Basajaun slipped outside and Cora was almost to the door when Nellie heard her feet on the ground.

"Cora," Nellie said, her face perplexed, "my baby."

Cora turned the baby toward her chest, and ran out of the shed.

CHAPTER THIRTEEN

EQUILIBRIUM

A small, wiry rabbit led Nellie and Maju through the heavy grass. Maju could move like a catapulted streak without realizing it, so he concentrated on slowing his lopping leaps in time with his beloved's footsteps. The grass grew higher and higher, up Nellie's ankles and calves, up to her knees, and finally covered the small rabbit guide altogether. Nellie trotted after the shifting grass in front of her.

"Where are you?" she said.

"Here. We're almost there," the wiry rabbit said. Maju nearly stepped on him when he stopped at the cleared path on the ground. The little rabbit paid no notice, but looked left, looked right, and continued into the low dirt valley between the tall grass. He hopped slow now, concentrated, with his nose up and his neck stiff. Nellie touched Maju's paw before she followed.

The path opened up into a tiny clearing, where eight of

the largest rabbits in the warren sat, staggered, in a ring. Straight and tall, with their shoulders pressed into neck ruffs, the rabbits' faces were tight, sober and piercing. They barely glanced at the human girl and her enormous rabbit companion. One curled his lip as he sniffed the air.

The wiry rabbit nodded at the guards, and turned back to Nellie and Maju. "I must check with her majesty," he said, "you wait." The two center guards hopped away from each other, revealing a large hole in the ground. It was a hole big enough even for Maju to pass through, and the grass surrounding it was freshly grazed to a carpet of stubs. Encircling the hole was a wreath of tiny blue violets and pinecones, intertwined and woven together. In front of that, a handful of smooth, pale stones formed a smaller circle on the dirt. The wiry rabbit disappeared through the flower wreath, into the earth.

He returned quickly. "Her majesty is not ready to see you," the rabbit said. "She said to come back tomorrow."

Nellie's face dropped. Maju grabbed her hand and wavered on his big feet. "Please," Nellie said, "she must see us."

"She mustn't *do* anything," the wiry rabbit said flatly.

Nellie crouched down, and whispered, "She has my baby."

The guard rabbits frowned at one another, grunting softly. Nellie wrapped her fingers into her skirt and gripped the fabric.

The wiry rabbit sighed. "Just a moment, I will ask again."

Nellie and Maju waited. Nellie looked hopefully at the

guards, but they didn't meet her gaze. "I'm sorry," she said to them. They didn't even blink.

The wiry rabbit's head popped out of the hole again. "All right. She will see you. You're very lucky."

"Oh, thank you," Nellie said.

"Follow me."

Nellie put her feet into the hole and eased her way into a sitting position inside the tunnel. Pushing her way down with the heels of her hands, little showers of dirt fell on her hair and dress. When her legs emerged outside the tunnel, Nellie stretched her feet out and all around in the air, but she couldn't feel a floor or any surface to stand on. Eventually, she turned over on her hands and knees and lowered herself into the burrow. Maju came after, gliding through the tunnel in seconds, and landing gracefully on the ground as though the burrow were made just for him.

Cora sat in the center of the immense, underground burrow, surrounded by ten more rabbit soldiers. Beside her, tall and serious like a soldier himself, sat Basajaun. In Cora's arms, laid the sleeping baby.

"Oh, he's all right," Nellie said, reaching her shaking fingers toward the infant.

"Yes," Cora said.

"May we," Nellie stammered, "may we take him?"

"Sit down," Cora replied. The baby shifted in her arms and made a sleepy, cooing sound. Nellie and Maju sat and Nellie tipped her head to one side, looking at the baby. Cora's lips barely parted when she spoke. "Now you have to answer to me. I want to know everything. I want you to tell me—everything."

Nellie put her hand on Maju's leg, and took a deep breath. "Maju and I, fell in love—"

"No," Cora shook her head suddenly. "I know that bit. It's the rest I need explained. He said he used to be a regular rabbit, like these," Cora nodded from side to side at the soldiers. "How did he get like that?" Nellie scrunched her face, and frowned.

"It was a spell," Maju blurted out. "Mari did it for me. I begged her. I wanted to be a human man, like I told you," he lowered his eyes, "so I could be with her. She said she didn't care, that she would love me if I were a raven or a ladybug or a big tree in the open air. But I could never be happy as I was. Maybe it was selfish, for her love should've been enough, but I wanted to be a man so much. And wanting her made me want it even more.

"Mari collected herbs, plants and roots. Bits of earth. Stones. Mostly she used the herbs and leaves for medicine. When she had a cut once, she discovered that if she put some clean comfrey in the wound, it healed twice as fast. She used to look for these things when she came out to feed us rabbits, so in thanks, we would collect whatever we could find for her. Moss, funny-shaped chunks of wood. To most humans these things are trash, but to Mari, they were treasures." Maju smiled at Nellie and she beamed into her lap, blushing.

"One day, when one of the does was digging a new tunnel, she found two very strange, very beautiful brown stones, buried in the earth. She brought them to Mari right away. Mari said they weren't stones, but very, very old wood. They felt just like stones, but when Mari dipped them in the lake and washed off the dirt, we saw they had a strange, wood-like pattern. Brown, tan and shiny, with looping swirls like the inside of the tree. Mari said that through years and years, the wood had become compressed and hard like stone. It was very beautiful.

"She said she had never seen anything like it, and asked us rabbits to bring her to where the stone-wood was found. When Mari put her hand into the hole, a great gust of wind came out around her. We were stunned. Mari said there was magic in the stones, or the hole, or both. She came every day to sit there. Just sit. She would hold the wood-stones, one in each hand, and close her eyes." Cora looked at Nellie, who stared at a lock of her own hair that she was rubbing and smoothing between her fingers. "Finally, one week later, she said the wood-stones had told her how to make me a man. She wound a small spike into one of them, and strung it to hang around my neck. Then she grabbed a fistful of earth out of the hole, and asked me to lie on my back, over the hole. She threw the dirt at my chest. Then she sliced a line all the way up her arm, and bled it onto the stone. At first, nothing happened.

"Then I began to grow; I couldn't believe it! I could feel my legs getting bigger, feel myself getting stronger. I could feel it happening! I felt new, and renewed, and I stood to show my man self to the woman I loved. But she looked away. She looked so, so sad.

"It was all wrong. And worse than ever before, for now I was neither man nor rabbit; well, rabbit, yes, but a monster. I could go nowhere, belong nowhere. I thought the stones were punishing me for wanting more than I deserved. I went away." Maju's voice drifted and he turned from Cora, rubbing his big hind legs. Cora waited, but Maju laid his ears down, and looked at the wall of the burrow.

"I hadn't heard the stones right," Nellie said. "Or rather, I hadn't wanted to. I thought what they said made sense and was in my power, but I was the one who had presumed too much. I went back to sit again, like before. I sat for two days; I didn't move this time. I wasn't going to make another mistake. Once I understood, it seemed so simple. You see," Nellie leaned in toward Cora, her blue eyes icy and flickering, "what I tried to do, it was not allowed. The stones were two, and would not allow me to tip the scales. Our forms are not designated, they are random. You might be a girl as much as you'd be a fish. But a balance comes out of this assignment, no matter how accidental it may be. Mostly it is what it is, only because no one wants for more than what is familiar and, in their mind, destined. The hole, the stones, allowed me a window to change but only in exchange." Nellie moved her hand between herself and Maju. "We could not take without giving back. If one rabbit was to go to human, than one human had to go to rabbit."

Basajaun blinked. Cora stared ahead. "Go on," she said.

Nellie smoothed her skirt over her lap. "The men, the boys, all of them—they all looked at me. They have since, well, since before I was your age," she looked at Cora, who didn't respond. Nellie sighed. "Looked, and other things, too," she nodded matter-of-factly. "It would seem then that the choice was easy, no choice at all. But really, that made it harder. I had to find one who wouldn't miss me after, and who wouldn't miss anything else that might come after. Someone who would let me disappear, and never think of me again. I had to pick the one man in town who'd never looked at me at all. Once I'd realized that, the choice was easy. I went into the chapel house in the middle of the night. And really, it was so easy. It took no prompting, and hardly any time at all. You wouldn't believe it, but he was quiet, vulnerable. He never spoke. I never spoke. But I think—he cried. I should've known, that should have told me, that he would not let me go away.

"He followed me to the hole where the stone wood was found and tore it apart, ripped up the earth. It was there he found the third stone. None of us knew there was a third, identical to the other two. He used it to learn the magic. He became much more proficient at it than I. He sought out other artifacts too—ancient things I didn't even understand. He was obsessed. He was unhinged.

"You see, it is because of me that Pastor Harding went mad on the rabbits. When he came to town, he only *wanted* to kill them. After me, he needed to. He blamed the rabbits for driving him to sin, he said their presence in the ether and their fornicating ways had wormed their way into his head. And mine. He said I was a temptress, and told me he hated me over and over, but then he'd lock me in his house, and wouldn't let me leave. Sometimes, he hit himself on his legs, on his face. He said that if he killed all the rabbits he could kill all the sin that was taking us over. But really, he thought that if he killed them all, he could kill my love for Maju, and I would finally be his."

235

Cora looked at the baby. Nellie's fingers twitched on her knees, and she put a hand on Cora's leg. "I'm so, so sorry that I brought this all to your town. I know it's all my fault. I didn't know the governor was going to send Pastor Harding away. Or that they would give me to him as a going away present. But Maju and I have worked so hard just to be together. Is that so terrible? Why can't we finally be happy?" Cora began to rock the baby back and forth. She felt Nellie's hand squeeze her leg. "Cora, it's my baby. And I had it so that Maju could be whole."

Cora didn't look up. "Just let me think," she whispered. "Come back later. I need to think."

Nellie's face trembled. She opened her mouth, and closed it again. Her eyes glinted like marbles and, releasing her fingers from where they held Cora's leg, Nellie slid her hand up and rested it on the baby's arm.

One of the guard rabbits grunted and butted Nellie's hand away. "Later, miss," he said. Another rabbit put his face close to the girl's, and growled, "You heard her majesty, get out." Four of the rabbits advanced on Nellie and Maju, nudging at their legs until they stood. Maju's head hung low, but Nellie looked at Cora one last time.

"Wait," Cora said. She looked to Maju, and pointed at Nellie. "Why do you call her 'Mari'?"

"Because it means 'Goddess', my greater half," the giant rabbit said. "When my mother named me Maju, she told me it meant 'God'."

"Oh," Cora said.

"You know what 'Basajaun' means, don't you?" Maju climbed into the tunnel.

Cora shook her head.

"No," Basajaun said.

The rabbit's voice drifted out of the tunnel. "It means, 'wild man of the woods'."

"Cora, you all right?" Basajaun said. He'd wanted to let her speak first, but for a full half hour she'd done nothing but stare into the face of the sleeping baby.

"It's not fair," Cora said. "They're sacrificing him."

"Sacrificing?" Basajaun said. "Is that what you think?"

"No," Cora said. "That's not what I meant. But they can't ask him what he wants. What if he doesn't want to be a rabbit?"

"They don't care," Basajaun said. "But is it really so bad, to be a rabbit?" Basajaun looked at the baby, at that strange, pink little face.

"The stone," Cora said, "the second wood-stone. That's the one she gave me."

"Yes, I know."

"But there were only two, only two that she had. And they were magical. Really magical."

"I thought we knew that," Basajaun said.

"I guess," Cora reached under her shirt, under the baby, and pulled out the shiny, brown-tan necklace. She held it up to her face. The baby stirred. "But, why did she give it to me? She hardly knew me."

"She knew you were special."

Cora looked at the baby, who yawned and bumped his own cheek with his tiny hand. "I always wanted a little brother or sister," she whispered. Basajaun could see

237

Cora's forehead, nose and chin peeking out of her hair. He watched her, studied her, thinking.

Basajaun hopped around the trees that dotted the grass in front of his father's burrow. He paused. He hadn't seen his father since the address he'd given as Cora's champion. He hoped his father wasn't sleeping. Or angry.

"Father?" he whispered into the opening of the burrow. "Father?"

"Yes?"

"May I talk to you?" There was no reply to this, but Basajaun slipped into the hole anyway. The rabbit Chief lay with his back to the burrow door. "Didn't you hear me?" Basajaun said.

"Is it important?" the rabbit Chief said.

"Yes, very."

"It always is." Basajaun's father breathed laboriously as he rose to his feet and turned to face his son. "You manipulated your subjects, to serve your own purpose."

"Manipulated what?" Basajaun said. "Their devotion to someone who has helped them beyond measure? Believe me, Father, if it was manipulation, it didn't have far to go from actual care." Basajaun waited for his father's retort to this, and was surprised when it didn't come. Finally, Basajaun took a deep breath. "Father, I need to ask your advice on something."

"No," the Chief rabbit said quickly.

"It will only take a moment, I just—"

"No—that is my answer to the question. I know what you're going to ask. I knew what the question was the moment I heard you rustling outside my burrow. I knew it the moment you returned from slaughtering the enemy. You've asked, and I've given my answer. You're only dragging it out because it's not the reply you wanted. Well, you cannot request advice then choose the response you receive. My answer is still 'no'."

"You *don't* know what I'm going to ask!" Basajaun stomped his back foot against the ground, hard.

"No," the Chief rabbit said. "Don't let her do it."

Basajaun startled. He stammered, "But—I just—I—let me explain—"

"How do you feel about her?"

"What?"

"About *Cora*. How do you feel about Cora?"

Basajaun's eyes darted all over the burrow. "I don't—I don't have to tell you!"

The rabbit Chief sighed. "Do you love her?"

"I—" Basajaun said.

"Do you *love* her?"

Basajaun frowned.

The Chief gestured a paw in the air. "Oh good gracious boy, if you can't even answer, just—"

"Quiet!" Basajaun yelled. "Just *listen* to me. Just wait. Just wait a moment." Basajaun huffed then not in anger, but in deep concentration. The rabbit Chief sat, and waited. He watched Basajaun rock back and forth and curl his front claws in and out of the dirt. Finally, Basajaun whispered. "When I look into her eyes, I can see her soul."

The rabbit Chief put his paw on his son's. "If you love her—really love her—you won't let her do it."

Basajaun took a deep breath. He yanked his paw away, and ran out into the clearing. The rabbit Chief hopped slowly after him, but stopped on the open grass. He didn't follow his son, just watched Basajaun's white tail grow smaller and smaller, over the plain. The old rabbit turned, and eased his way off in the other direction.

The Chief rabbit had traveled further in the past days than he had in months. His joints ached. All manner of things ebbed through his mind as he hopped. Mostly he thought about the girl, and about all the sacrifices she'd made for one so young. He hadn't liked to consider her at all, for thinking of her made his neck itch, like it always did when he couldn't sleep at night.

He found the wreathed burrow hole easily. As he hopped around the hole, his back foot bumped one of the light stones arranged on the ground in front of it. Using his nose, the rabbit Chief rolled the stone back into the open spot it had left. Then he walked past the big burrow opening, and pushed his way into some nettles that grew several yards away. The hole in the ground there was small and the tunnel was long, but it opened up only a few inches from the deep burrow floor. The rabbit Chief plopped several feet behind Cora's back, gently.

Cora glanced back at the noise. "Oh, pardon me, sir," she said.

"No, that's all right. Don't stand," the rabbit Chief hopped over next to Cora, noticing Maju's great footprints going up the other end of the burrow.

Cora rocked the baby, who gurgled and squirmed in her arms. "I thought you were Basajaun."

"No, I sent him on an errand," the rabbit Chief said. His eyes passed over the ten guards. "Do you mind? I'd like to talk to the lady alone." The big rabbits looked at one another.

"It's all right," Cora said. "If we need anything, we'll call."

The rabbit Chief watched the soldiers file out. "They do anything you say, don't they?"

"I feel funny about it," Cora said. "All that attention. It makes me embarrassed."

"You get used to it," the rabbit Chief sat slowly, grunting a little.

"Are you all right?"

"Yes. Just old."

"I'm sorry."

"I wanted to give my condolences," the Chief said, "about your father. He was a great man."

"Yes, that's what Basajaun says." Cora smoothed aside the blonde wisps on the baby's forehead.

"He says it because I told him so. You know, some people thought of your father as a savior."

"Who?" Cora said.

"Me."

Cora looked at the rabbit Chief. He could see her eyes moving all over his face, searching for something. "What do you mean?"

"He saved my life."

"Really?" Cora's eyes lit up. "How? When?"

"I was very young," the old rabbit closed his eyes a little, "and reckless. I was looking for mushrooms in the dead tree pile behind your house. I wanted to bring them to a young lady rabbit, to impress her." He smiled. "The lady who would be Basajaun's mother. I didn't hear your father come out. When I bolted, I got stuck in a wood wall—trapped. My own mother had warned me about the traps that men laid, how they used such things to catch us so they could eat us like monsters. I was cursing myself for being so careless, but mostly I was terrified. I couldn't believe I was to meet such an end. I begged—inside my mind I begged—for mercy. For some sort of compassion, despite my folly. When I saw your father coming with a big weapon, I knew it was all over.

"Then suddenly, I was free. At first I was thankful that my end was short and painless, I thought that was the sympathy allotted me. But I wasn't dead—I was alive! The man, your father, had let me go. I couldn't imagine why. But I turned, and looked into his face. And I saw the compassion I had been begging for. Your father had been given all the power in the world, and he used it to do good."

Cora thought about the loose board on the backyard fence at her old farmhouse, and how she used to sandwich her rag doll under it when she needed a free hand to look for frogs in the grass. She had asked her father once why he didn't fix it, and he had said he left it for a friend, which hadn't made sense to Cora at the time. As she thought this, she sighed. But it was more than a sigh; it was an exhale of something she'd been holding in for days and days. And it was as though in her breath, some part of herself was drifting away.

"Oh," she said. "That's all?"

"That's all?" the rabbit Chief said. "That's not enough?"

"But, it's so simple," Cora said. "I was expecting something—bigger."

"He saved my life. What could be bigger than that?" the Chief rabbit said. Cora huddled the baby closer to her, and the old rabbit sighed now himself. He felt that itching in his neck again, and he tried to smile. "Well, I'm sure you are very happy for Basajaun."

"Yes," Cora said, "I think he will be a wonderful Chief."

"Not just that. He won't have to do it alone."

Cora looked up.

"Hasn't he told you?"

"Told me what?" Cora said.

"Why, Boxy has agreed to be his mate."

CHAPTER FOURTEEN

PERMANENCE

Cora watched her feet move over the familiar, cobbled court. Years she had walked this road, and indeed it felt like years since she'd seen it, even though it had only been a handful of days. And even though she couldn't possibly have grown any taller since she'd last passed through the town where she grew up, the stone road seemed smaller, somehow, or further away. Cora could smell distinctly an odor she remembered from those not-long-ago days when she was unfettered and free, one she hadn't smelled since before the Pastor came: the smell of rabbit meat cooking.

Very few people were out of their ramshackle homes that morning, but those who were looked shocked by the sight of the dirty, ragged, twelve-year-old girl carrying the newborn baby. Cora took her time. She didn't meet any of their gazes, and none of them approached her either. Until Cora heard footsteps running fast up toward her. And shouting.

"Cora! Oh, Cora!" Without warning, Henry grabbed Cora around the shoulders and hugged her. He took care not to squish the baby between them, and Cora stood for a moment, stunned, before she put her hand on his back. "I thought you were dead. I'm sorry," Henry let go of her to rub his wet cheeks with his palms. "I'm just so happy to see you!" he hugged her again. "You're filthy! Are you ok?"

"Yes," Cora said.

"Your father, he made me go for the Constable. Cora, we were too late. My God, I'm so, so sorry."

"There's nothing you could've done," Cora said.

"He just kept looking for you. He just wanted to find you, so much," Henry touched Cora's arm.

"He did that," Cora said.

"He got to see you again. That would've made him happy."

Cora tried to smile, but it made tears well up in her eyes too, so she stopped.

"The baby," Henry pulled aside the cloth around the baby's face. "Is Nellie ok?"

"She's fine. I'm just watching the baby for her."

With his hand on the baby's cheek, Henry looked up at Cora. "Can I see her?"

"Not just yet. She's resting now, but she's ok."

"Cora!" another voice yelled from a quarter mile back. "You found her!"

"I didn't tell him you were there that night," Henry whispered.

"Oh, honey," the town Constable ran and kneeled at

Cora's feet. He put a hand on her cheek and smiled, his mouth closed and pursed, the rims of his eyes shining, "I don't think I could've forgiven myself if anything happened to you. It was terrible what happened to your father. Just terrible." He hugged her. "For your father to go up against Pastor Harding like that, after all the Pastor said and threatened to him? Well, I wish I'd had the courage. I curse myself for not having it," he squeezed Cora's shoulders. "Your father loved you, girl, more than anything. He was a very good man. Always stood up for what he thought was right. You should be proud of him."

"I am," Cora said.

The Constable turned to Henry. "I'm sorry boy, do you mind? I'd like to talk to the little lady."

"Oh, no sir. I don't mind," Henry half-nodded to the man, and smiled at Cora. "Pardon me," he squeezed her arm.

"I wish I'd had the courage," the Constable said as he watched the boy trot across the courtyard. "The Pastor never let anyone in that fourth shed. I tried to break in when I began to suspect, and here that's where the money was all along. I'm sorry. I don't know how your father did it and fact is, we can't find out. Pastor Harding's body was taken apart by—must've been wild dogs, wolves, or something."

Cora stared at the man.

"Did your father have any family?" the Constable said. Cora shook her head. The man put his hands on her shoulders again and looked at her. "Cora, Mabel and I would love to have you stay with us, if you'll have us. You know we never had any kids of our own, and your father was a good friend to me. Mabel and I have watched you grow all these years now, and we want to make things nice for you, so you keep growing. We'll find someone to take over the farm. You can even keep a hand in, if you'd like. If that would make you feel more at home. But you can make a new home, with us. Come live with us. Will you, please?"

"I'd like that," Cora said.

"Oh—" the Constable hugged her again, "Thank goodness."

"I'm just watching this baby right now," Cora said, "The Pastor's niece's baby."

The Constable ruffled Cora's hair. "Well, we'll figure that out in good time. No rush. Why don't we get the both of you back to my house now? You can rest, get something to eat. I suspect you need it."

"That'd be nice," Cora said. The Constable put an arm over her shoulder, and began to guide her up the road. "Wait," Cora said. "Could we stop at my house first? I want to get some of my things."

"Of course," the Constable smiled. "Grab whatever you want today. Anything we can't carry, we'll come back for."

The Constable stooped as he walked into the farmhouse kitchen. Not because he had to—he was shorter than Cora's father—but almost out of a sort of reverence. Cora pulled out one of the heavy wooden chairs, the one facing toward the door and away from her bedroom. The one where her father usually sat.

247

"Here," she said, "sit down." Cora walked around the table, to face the man. "I'd like to have some time alone, to pack. Is that okay?"

"Of course dear. Take as long as you need." The Constable smiled, elbows on the table, and folded his hands. "I'll wait here." The man stared off in front of himself, beaming, and Cora went into her bedroom, and shut the door.

She laid the baby on her bed, and he squirmed. The Pastor's frock coat began to slide off and Cora could see the baby's little feet weaving in the air. She took a look around her room at all her things, and all her memories. And a pressure like swollen lead filled her chest as she kneeled down and looked under her bed at Basajaun's chicken-wire cage. The cage her father had made. Cora reached inside the cage and brushed her hand over the hay that lined its bottom. She stood, and put her fists against her forehead. In the midday of the silent room, so many voices screamed at each other inside her head. They were all her own.

Cora ran to her bureau and yanked open the bottom drawer. She grabbed fistfuls of crisp linens and heaped them at her sides until she saw it, nestled against the wood back: her yellow, cotton-eyelet dress. She snatched up the dress, shook out the tidy folds with one toss, and threw it on the bed. Leaving the clothes she'd been wearing in a pile on her floor, Cora pulled the dress over her head. Then she picked up the baby, looked over her shoulder one last time, and climbed out the window.

Cora ran down the back hill as fast as she could. The

baby bounced and gerbled in her arms, and she held him close to her face so she could watch her feet dart over and between the bumps and rocks on the ground. She ran through the woods, over the patchy clearing, and through the shrubs and grasses. She gulped big breaths of air as she ran, but didn't stop or rest. Carrying the baby as she crawled along the bush tunnel proved more difficult, and he giggled and cried intermittently. By the time Cora burst through the crackly foliage into the green-blonde clearing, her knees were scratched and dirty, and her cheeks were red. Cora stumbled and panted for breath, but the baby, unscathed, cooed as his hand brushed one of her dark curls. Every rabbit in the clearing gaped at her. Most of all, the rabbit Chief and Basajaun.

"Hi," Cora wheezed. "I—need to talk to you all." She paused to catch her breath, and walked into the center of the clearing. Turning slow circles, Cora looked at all the rabbits—all her subjects—who had put so must trust in her before they even knew if she was capable of anything. She grimaced, thinking, and finally opened her mouth.

"I know that I don't really belong here. And I know that it may seem strange for me to come back to you now. But we've been through a lot together, all of us. So even if you may think me better suited to my world," she looked at Basajaun, "I hope you will be happy to have me here."

"Cora," the rabbit Chief grumbled, looking from side to side, "what do you mean?"

"I'm sorry, sir. I know Basajaun will be happy with Boxy, but I still—"

"What?" Boxy stepped out of the crowd. "What did

you say?"

"What's going on?" Basajaun said to his father. The Chief rabbit hunched his shoulders.

"Basajaun," Boxy walked toward the Chief's son, "is it true?"

"I don't know what she means," Basajaun said. "I never said that."

"Oh," Boxy said, and blinked her large, dark eyes. She bowed her head. "I'm sorry. I feel very embarrassed now." She turned back toward the crowd.

"Oh Boxy," Basajaun gasped, "no. I'm so sorry."

"No," Boxy replied. "Don't be. Artulyn was right about me. I wanted you. I did. And I'm sorry. I just always had this secret wish that, someday, I could turn the head of someone like you."

"Boxy," Basajaun said. "You're wonderful. Amazing. You will. You will turn the head of someone better. Much, much better."

"No," Boxy shook her head slowly. "It was a pup fantasy, one I should've given up long ago. Because rabbits like you don't exist. Not really. Not for rabbits like me, anyway."

"I'm sorry."

"I knew I wouldn't be your first choice, I just never thought it possible that—" Boxy looked at Cora. "Well, I guess I'm not the only one whose head you turned." The female rabbit hopped slowly back into the throng of rabbits, and disappeared. Basajaun turned to his father.

"Father, what have you done?" he growled.

"Leave it," the Chief rabbit replied. "It didn't work."

"But how could you let her think that? How could you spread—"

"It wasn't supposed to get back to her," the Chief rabbit grumbled. "I just," he paused, and looked at Cora. She stared at him, even though she couldn't make out what he was saying. The Chief leaned close to his son, and whispered, "First things first—you need to take care of this," he pointed a paw at Cora. "You need to fix it."

Basajaun scowled at his father. He hopped over to Cora, his dark eyes searching hers.

"Cora, you can't do this."

But it wasn't Basajaun who spoke, it was another voice, coming out of the brush. Cora and Basajaun turned. Maju was hopping toward them, moving like liquid as his great strides covered the grassy expanse in moments. He was followed by Nellie. And Henry.

Cora looked at Henry. "What are you doing here?"

"I wanted to help," Henry said.

"Why did you bring him here?" Cora said to Nellie.

"He wanted to help," Nellie replied.

Maju towered over Cora, and he stood close. "You can't do it."

"But I want to do it," Cora said.

"You'll never get to grow up. You—"

"I'll grow," Cora said. "I'll grow as a rabbit."

"You'll never get to be a woman. A human woman."

"My whole life, this town has showed me what it means to be a woman," Cora frowned. "Believe me, I won't miss it."

"How can you say that?" Maju said. "And, don't you

know how much shorter a rabbit's life is than a human's? Cora, it is so much shorter."

Cora hiked the baby up in her arms, and looked the giant rabbit straight in the eye. "If I were to grow into a person who wouldn't want a rabbit's life, or who would choose a human life simply because it is longer, then I wouldn't want to be that person anyway."

"But, it's so much better to be a human," Maju's eyes pleaded. "So much better in every way."

Cora raised her chin at him. "How do you know?"

The giant rabbit sighed. He stepped aside, and moved close to Nellie. Henry came forward, with his freckled face downcast and his hands in his pockets.

"Nellie has found her—'beloved'," he glanced sideways at Maju. "You know," he shrugged, "you could stay."

"No," Cora said. "My mother died before I could even remember, and now my father is gone too. There is nothing left for me here. Besides, I've seen all I want to of this world. I've had enough."

Henry swallowed. "Nothing left for you here—at all?"

Cora put her hand on Henry's shoulder, and kissed him on the cheek. "Don't worry, you're a nice boy. You'll do fine."

The clearing of rabbits watched as Cora walked over to Nellie, and placed the baby in her arms. "I've named him Wayne," Cora said. "Take good care of him."

Nellie gasped. She held her baby for the first time, feeling his weight and movement against her. She beamed, and blinked away her tears. "Oh, I surely will. Thank you

Cora, thank you so much."

"Cora."

Cora recognized this voice behind her. She turned, and kneeled on the ground. She put out her dirty hands, and Basajaun placed his two front paws on her palms.

"Will you do me the honor of being Chief—with me?"

"What?"

"We'll lead the whole warren, but we'll do it together. As equals, side by side."

Cora smiled, and she felt the rabbit's little paws dent the skin on her hands.

Basajaun's black eyes shone. "Cora, I don't want to be away from you, ever, ever again. I love you."

Cora closed her hands around Basajaun's paws. "I love you, Basajaun. All I ever wanted was for us to be together."

Rutai's squat, furry body lopped down the hill. He edged around the side of the flat back valley, slowing when he reached the opening of the oblong, oval cavern.

"Hello?" he called into the hollow. No one answered. Rutai stepped inside. A tawny brown, rounded back sat in the middle of the marmot's familiar old hiding place. It didn't turn. "Hello Boxy," he said.

"Hey," the rabbit said.

"Everyone's looking for you," Rutai stepped closer.

Boxy's ears rested flat against her shoulders. She still didn't move her gaze from the back wall. "How did you know where I was?"

"There's a difference between hiding when you really

want to be found, and hiding when you want to be left alone," Rutai said as he walked to the rabbit's side. He could see her profile, and her twitching nose. "I took you for the latter. This was the only place I could think of that was known to you, but unknown to your clan."

Boxy didn't reply.

"I'm to stay in your warren now. Live among you, forever. Isn't that nice?" Rutai said.

"Yes," Boxy nodded, her head down.

"Are you going to the ceremony?" Rutai said.

"I don't know," Boxy said. "I just feel so stupid."

Rutai looked around at the marmot courting place. "When I was young," he said, "I had a friend. Our mothers were very close, and took to foraging together, so he and I were left alone to play—Bandel and I. He was my best friend. He understood me in a way that was very special. I did the same for him. He told me all the secrets of his family, and we talked about things—important things— things that no one else seemed to care about. Like why the sun moved in the way that it did or what happens to a marmot after he dies. He was so kind—gentle. And handsome too. He told me we would always be together, no matter what.

"I don't know how it is for rabbits, but a marmot is very young when he is to begin selection for a mate. The selection is done in isolation. It is a private thing, I mean. Parents and elders don't push pups toward a mate like some animals do; you are supposed to connect on your own accord. There were these rules," Rutai looked at his paws, "these rules a marmot was just to know. But nobody told me. The winter end that I was of age—the age to begin my mate selection—I was excited. I knew there was only one I wanted. I asked Bandel if he'd like to mate with me.

"He reported me to the council. I thought you were just supposed to mate with someone you liked. I didn't know it had to be a female. I tried to explain to the elders and I even offered to mate with a female but my world, my whole world, came crashing down on me. I was ostracized. I was ordered to leave the clan, under penalty of death. They didn't even let me see my mother before I went. I never knew what she thought."

"That is terrible," Boxy said. "Just terribly unjust. I'm so, so sorry." She was quiet a moment, staring at the dirt. She squinted. "I'm sorry, but—why are you telling me?"

"Because," Rutai said, "I thought you might like a friend."

For the first time, Boxy looked at him. She smiled. "Yes, I would like that. I would."

"Come on," Rutai stood. "We'll walk back to the warren together. Embarrassment is always less embarrassing when you have someone by your side."

Cora, Nellie and Maju stood atop the highest hill on the country plains. They'd had to walk four miles to find it, and another half-mile up the steep incline to reach the top. Around them was a ring of several thousand rabbits, and also Henry, who stood next to Boxy and Rutai the marmot. The rabbits could see the treetops that guarded their warren, all the way over to the south end of the town, and beyond. Basajaun watched Cora stretch out her arms nervously, as the wind fluttered the skirt of her yellow, cotton dress. Nellie, who carried baby Wayne, pointed for Cora and Maju to walk to the apex of the hill. The young girl and the giant rabbit faced each other.

"Are you sure?" Maju whispered.

"Yes," Cora said.

Nellie passed the baby to Henry, and kneeled at Cora's feet. Moving furiously, she crawled in a circle all around Cora and Maju, pulling up handfuls of grass—which she kept gripped in her fist—until a bare, dirt ring formed around them. She separated the loose grass into two bunches.

"Here," Nellie put one bunch in Cora's hand, and the other between Maju's paws. "Hold it," she said to both of them. She reached out to her sides, and edged her slim fingers under the two wood-stones that hung around the girl and the rabbit's necks. Nellie closed her eyes, and closed her hands around the shiny, brown rocks.

She swooped the necklaces up and off over Cora and Maju's heads. Cora gasped, and her own free hand instinctively grabbed at the bare spot on her chest, which hadn't been bare in so long. With her eyes still closed, Nellie laid the necklaces on the ground, between Cora and Maju's feet. She took a sharp rock out of her apron pocket, and pulled up her left sleeve. A pink scar ran all the way up the inside of Nellie's pale arm, and she laid the rock against it, tracing the line until red blood beaded up on it again. She swiped the open wound with her fingers, and touched Maju's necklace. Swiped it again, and touched Cora's necklace. The bloody smears turned dark on the shiny wood stone.

Nellie fingered the two stones in the grass. At first Cora thought the girl was just smoothing the blood over the necklaces, because she could see red smears spreading over the patterned brown rock. But Nellie's pointed fingertips kept feeling the bloody stones' outlines, moving deft and quick, like a spider wrapping its prey. The blood was blushing the girl's nimble fingers with a rosy wash, but soon it painted them over with deep red, as though they'd just been dipped into a rouge pot. And Cora noticed Nellie was muttering something, whispering, somewhere halfway between chanting and hushed singing. Nellie's voice was even and monotone, but sweet, and the words moved easily in and out with the girl's breath. Nellie picked up the stones in her fists and squeezed. Her knuckles went white and her closed fists began to shudder as the girl bore down, but still her low singing moved in level, melodic breaths.

When Nellie stopped chanting, the hill seemed unearthly quiet. He eyelids flipped up and she crossed her arms in front of her body, laying Maju's necklace in front of Cora and Cora's necklace in front of Maju. She pushed all four fingers, and her thumb, into the pale flesh surrounding the still-healing gash on her arm. When she squeezed hard, fresh blood began to feather around the edges of the darkening line. Nellie squeezed some more, stopping and starting, and milking the cut until it was bloody again. Then she ran her fingers over it, and wiped a new smear of blood on each of the stones. She looked back and forth at Cora and Maju.

"Put them on," she gestured at the necklaces.

Cora picked up the black cord. The new stone dangled before her and she studied it, noticing all the ways that it was different, and also similar, to the one she had worn. Her hands quivered. She saw Maju holding her necklace too, suspended, swinging in front of his face. He looked afraid. Cora smiled at him, to let him know that it was okay. To let him know that she was secure, and he should be, too. 'Goodbye,' she thought to the world she was born into, and she and Maju pulled the necklaces over their heads.

At first, Cora didn't feel anything. But she saw Maju getting taller, bigger, which didn't make sense to her, since Maju was already the size of a man. Then she noticed that the sky seemed to be rising higher into space. Everything around her escalated and moved further from her view, growing larger as it climbed. Cora's big world was getting bigger and she could see all the details around her amplified—the yellow sunlight catching in the blue and lavender creases of the clouds, and the raised veins on the undersides of the leaves as defined as the veins in her own arms. Cora was so stricken with the wonder of it all that she didn't look down until her new wood-stone, still around her neck, was resting in the grass.

A young man crouched over Cora, with dark hair and brows, and light brown eyes. His face came into focus. "You ok?" he said.

"Who are you?" Cora said. Then she saw Basajaun's face—her Basajaun's face—coming close as though she were lying on the ground. "You're big," she said to

Basajaun.

"No," Basajaun smiled, "you're little."

"Basandere," the young man said. "It means, 'wild woman of the woods'."

Nellie came up behind the young man, and put her hand on his shoulder. The man stood, grabbed Nellie up in his arms, and held her tight. Laughing, and crying, he cradled Nellie's face in his hands, and kissed her.

Cora reached for Basajaun, and saw her own little front paw. Basajaun buried his face in Cora's neck, and pressed his cheek against hers. "Are you ok?" he said. Cora leaned into him, and squeezed her eyes shut tight. She intertwined her front legs around his and felt his heartbeat on her paw, heard his breath in her ear. He seemed close to her, finally, really.

"Yes," she said, "my beloved."

EPILOGUE

Wayne crouched down, and rested his knees in the dirt. He leaned on the heels of his hands, and almost fell forward when his cheek brushed the grass. He wiped the dirt off his nose with the back of his hand, and flattened his arms on the ground, peering under the low bush.

"What are you doing, sweetie?" Wayne's mother squatted beside him.

"I saw a rabbit, Ma!" the boy grinned, squinting. "It ran under here!"

"Oh," the woman said. She tipped her head to the side and smiled, running her fingers through the boy's sandy brown hair. "You know, a rabbit saved your life once."

"Really? How did he do that?"

"She," the woman said. "And she did it by being very brave, and very true." The boy looked under the bush again. "You know, I wouldn't be surprised if she came to check on you from time to time."

"Really?" Wayne said into the shrub roots. "Can I talk

to her?"

"Oh, she and her husband are very busy. They are the leaders of all the rabbits for miles and miles around. It is a great honor."

"Wow."

"But maybe she will come visit you again," the woman reached a hand down to her son, and watched his tiny digits disappear in hers. "Come on now, your father will be back with the wood. I think he's building your rocking horse tonight."

"Oh boy! Can I help?"

"Of course," the woman said. "He couldn't do it without you."

Basandere peeked her head out of the shrub, and twitched her nose. She could hear faintly the little boy's excited voice as he jumped up and down, holding his mother's hand. She watched the mother and son until they reached the back door of the farmhouse, where the woman picked up the child and walked inside. Basandere slipped out of the bushes, glanced left, glanced right, and gave a final look to the closed door. Then she ran like a streak over the hills and grasses, all the while thinking of her pups, her subjects, and her dearest Basajaun, who waited for her on the horizon.

Rosemary Van Deuren has worked previously
as a freelance illustrator, sculptor and painter.
She currently lives in Michigan with
her fiancé, Guy, two ferrets—

and one rabbit.

Basajaun is her first novel.

You can visit her online at
www.rosemaryvandeuren.com